KU-523-719

ROBERT WILSON

Robert Wilson was born in 1957. A graduate of Oxford University, he has worked in shipping, advertising and trading in Africa. He has travelled in Asia and Africa and has lived in Greece and West Africa. He is married and writes from an isolated farmhouse in Portugal.

He was awarded the CWA Gold Dagger Award for Fiction for his fifth novel, *A Small Death in Lisbon*.

Praise for Robert Wilson

A DARKENING STAIN

'Unmissable . . . Unflinchingly imagined and executed. No hint of competition. First in a field of one'   *Literary Review*

BLOOD IS DIRT

'For once a novelist influenced by Raymond Chandler is not shown up by the comparison, matching his mentor's descriptive flourishes and screwball dialogue . . . A class act'
Sunday Times

THE BIG KILLING

'Something special in the line of original crime fiction . . . If I come across as original and blackly funny a thriller again this year, I'll feel myself doubly blest'   *Irish Times*

INSTRUMENTS OF DARKNESS

'An atmospheric and absorbing debut, *Instruments of Darkness* vividly paints a credible picture of a world I know almost nothing about. Now I feel I've been there. Robert Wilson writes like a man who's been doing this half his life'
VAL MCDERMID

ROBERT WILSON

A Darkening Stain

HARPER

HarperCollins*Publishers*
77–85 Fulham Palace Road,
Hammersmith, London W6 8JB

The HarperCollins website address is:
www.harpercollins.co.uk

This special paperback edition 2007

1

First published in Great Britain
in 1997 by HarperCollins

A catalogue record for this book is
available from the British Library

ISBN 978 0 00 779115 6

Set in Meridien by
Rowland Phototypesetting Ltd,
Bury St Edmunds, Suffolk

Printed in Great Britain by
Clays Ltd, St Ives plc

For Jane
and
my sister, Anita

My thanks to
the Commonwealth Forestry Association
for their help.

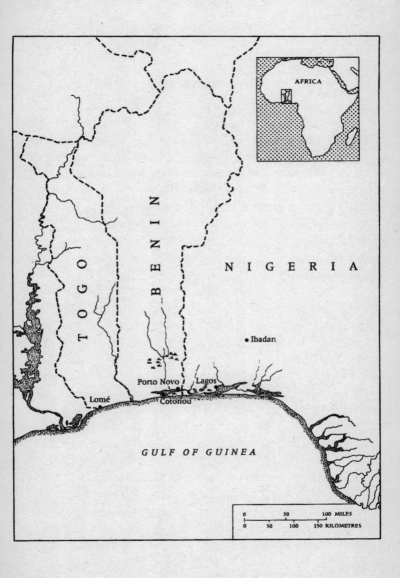

The sky is darkening like a stain;
Something is going to fall like rain,
And it won't be flowers.

'The Witnesses' (W. H. Auden)

Chapter 1

Friday 19th July, Cotonou Port.

The thirty-five-ton Titan truck hissed and rocked on its suspension as it came to a halt. Shoulders hunched, it gave a dead-eyed stare over the line of scrimmage which was the chain across the opening of the port gates. On the wood panelling behind the cab were two hand-painted film posters of big men holding guns – Chuck Norris, Sly Stallone – the bandana boys. He handed down his papers to the customs officer who took them into the gatehouse and checked them off. Excitement rippled through the rollicking crowd of whippet-thin men and boys who'd gathered outside the gates in the afternoon's trampling heat, which stank of the sea and diesel and rank sweat.

The Titan was loaded with bales of second-hand clothes tied down on to the flat-bed of the truck by inch-thick hemp rope. The driver, faceless behind his visor, kicked up the engine which blatted black fumes from a four-inch-wide pipe, ballooning a passing police-man's shirt. A squeal of anticipation shimmered through the crowd.

Six men, armed with wooden batons the thickness of pickaxe handles, climbed on to the edges of the flat-bed, three a side. Each of them twisted a wrist around a rope

1

and hung off, twitching their cudgels through the thick air. The crowd positioned themselves along the thirty metres of road from the gates to the junction with Boulevard de la Marina. The officer came out with the papers and handed them back up to the driver. He nodded to the man on chain duty who looked at the crowd outside and grinned.

The huge truck farted up some more and lurched as the driver thumped it into gear. He taunted the crowd with his air brakes. They giggled, high-pitched, nearly mad. The chain dropped and the battered, grinning face of the Titan dipped and surged across the line. The men hanging off the back roared and slashed with their batons. The truck picked up some momentum, the cab through the gates now, and the crowd threw themselves at the wall of bales, clawing at the clothes packed tight as scrap metal. The batons connected. Men and boys fell stunned as insects, one was dragged along by the leg of a pair of jeans he'd torn from a bale until a sharp crack on the wrist dropped him. The Titan snarled into second gear.

I saw the boy coming from some way off. He was dressed in a white shirt, a pair of long white shorts and flip-flops. He turned the corner off Boulevard de la Marina up to the port gates and was swallowed up by the mêlée who were now running at a sprint. A baton arced down into the pack and caught the boy on the back of the head. He fell forward, bounced off the hip of some muscled brute who held the reins of a nylon pink nightie stretched to nine feet, and disappeared under the wheels of the Titan.

The crowd roared, and the section around where the

boy had fallen collapsed to the ground. The truck pulled away, crashing through the gears. It didn't stop for the Boulevard de la Marina. The driver stood on his horn. Cars and mopeds squirmed across the tarmac. The men riding shotgun stopped swinging their batons and hung on with both hands. The Titan let out a final triumphant blat of exhaust and headed into town.

I got out of my Peugeot and ran across to where the boy had gone down. People came from all angles. Closer, I could see his arm, the white bone of his arm and the blood soaking into the sleeve and up the chest of his shirt. Some of the hoodlums around him were smeared with his blood, four of them upped and ran. The rest were staring down at the mash of flesh and bone and the thick red ooze on the road. Then the boy was picked up and borne away, his crushed arm hanging like a rag, his head thrown back, eyes rolled to white. Three men ran him down to the main road and threw him into a car which took off in the direction of the hospital. Then they stood and looked at his blood on their shirts.

I was called back to my car which was waiting to get into the port. Horns blared. Arms whirled.

'M. Medway, M. Medway. Entrez, entrez! Main-te-nant. Main-te-nant.'

I drove in, threading through the line of trucks waiting to get out, past a pile of spaghetti steel wire just beginning to brown with rust. It was five o'clock in the afternoon. I took a small towel from the passenger seat and wiped away the tears of sweat streaming down my face.

I was heading for a ship called the *Kluezbork II*, Polish

flag, 15,000 tons deadweight. Bagado, my ex-partner in M & B 'Investigations and Debt Collection' and now back in the Cotonou force in his old job as a detective, was waiting for me on board. He had a problem, a five-men-dead problem. But it wasn't as big as the captain's problem which was five men dead on *his* ship, all stowaways, his vessel and cargo impounded indefinitely and he passing the time of day right now in a hell cell with twenty odd scumbags down at the Sûreté in town.

Bagado had told me to get down to the port as fast as possible because the stink was getting bad and they wanted the bodies on ice pronto, but it was important for me to see the situation down there. Why me? He'd blethered on about my shipping experience, but what he really wanted to do was to talk and since his boss, Commandant Bondougou, had split us up and taken him back into the force he didn't like being seen down at my office too much.

The ship's holds were all open and I caught the smell of the five men beginning to putrefy from the quay. The engineer pointed me to number three hold's hatch where some sick-looking young policemen were hanging around for further instructions. Bagado was waiting on a platform halfway down into the hold. He stood, hands jammed into the pockets of his blue mac, which had more creases than an old man's scrotum. He nodded over the platform's rail at the five dead men. Three of them were propped against the metal wall of the hold looking as if they'd just dozed off while staring at the wall of timber which was the cargo in hold number three. The other two lay on their fronts, in the metre

4

or so in between, like tired children who'd dropped to the floor mid-play. It was a peaceful scene uncreased by violence.

'What are you doing up here?' I asked.

'I don't know what killed them yet,' said Bagado, coming out of his trance, flat, depressed. 'I don't want to go down there and end up like that.'

'How long's the hold been open?'

'Three or four hours.'

'That should have got the air circulating. Let's take a look.'

We climbed down the ladder on to the floor of the hold.

'Looks as if they suffocated to me,' said Bagado. 'No violence, anyway.'

'We're a long way from the engine room,' I said. 'Who found them?'

'The first mate was doing a routine stowaway check and didn't like the smell in here . . . brought the master to the platform . . . that was it.'

'The only time I've heard of people suffocating in holds is on tankers, especially after palm oil. Gives off a lot of carbon dioxide. They send in the cleaners and they get halfway down the ladder before they realize they can't breathe. I heard of eight people dying like that in one hold up on Humberside.'

'But this hold isn't enclosed like a tanker's,' said Bagado, leaning against the timber wall.

'Wouldn't matter if the oxygen's displaced from the bottom,' I said, and walked between the bodies to the other side of the hold. Bagado pushed himself off the timber to follow me.

'Damn,' he said, looking at the shoulder of his mac, a big stain on it.

I touched the logs. They were still wet with sap.

'This timber's fresh,' I said.

'Loaded out of Ghana three nights ago.'

'I've heard about some of these hardwoods. They give off fumes, some of them toxic. They're pretty volatile in the heat. You put that in an enclosed hold, the oxygen levels drop . . .'

'Cause of death – fresh timber,' said Bagado. 'Could be.'

'Who are these guys?' I asked. 'They got any ID?'

'They're all Beninois.'

'How'd they get on board?'

'With the stevedores. They were loading cotton seed in holds one and two over the last couple of days. Four teams of them.'

'You know that?'

'A guess. We're picking up the *chef d'équipe* now,' he said.

'What am I doing here, Bagado?' I asked. 'You didn't get me down here to talk botany.'

Bagado shouted up to his juniors. A head appeared over the platform's rail. He rattled instructions out using Fon rather than French. The head disappeared. Feet rang on the rungs of the ladder. Bagado turned back to me, a faint sneer on his face from the stink of the bodies and something else.

'Let's go up on to the platform,' he said.

'Was that guy listening in on you?'

'As you can see,' he said. 'I do have a problem.'

We climbed back up on to the platform.

'But not with these five,' I said to the soles of his feet.

'Bondougou,' he said, the name mingling naturally with the rotten air. A name that brought tears of gratitude to the eyes of corrupt businessmen, politicians and civil servants. The name of the man who'd targeted Bagado's life and set about dismantling it piece by piece. The first time Bagado and I met he'd just been sacked by Bondougou for issuing an unauthorized press release about a dead girl's tortured body. He'd come to work with me after that, until our recent split, and those circumstances weren't exactly lavender-scented either. Since then Bondougou had given Bagado investigations and pulled him on almost every one as soon as he started getting anywhere. The only people he got to put in the slammer were the ones who'd reined in on last year's Christmas gift to the Commandant. Bondougou and Bagado were polar opposites. They needed each other only for metaphysical reference.

'So, tell me,' I said, once we were up on the platform.

'He has to be . . .' Bagado's voice faded, as he leant over the rail.

'Come again.'

'He has to go.'

'And you think I'm the man for the job or I'm the man who can find you the man to do the job?'

'Be serious, Bruce.'

'So, what does ''he has to go'' mean? I assume you're talking about into the ground six foot under or stuffed head first down a storm drain after heavy rain. He's not the kind to take early retirement just because he's upset a few of his detectives.'

'That would be a very satisfactory outcome. The storm

drain I think is the more likely . . . but you know me, Bruce. It's just not possible for me to even think like that.'

'Whereas I . . .'

'Quite.'

'. . . go grasping the wrong end of the stick,' I said. 'We used to be partners, didn't we, Bagado?'

'And very complementary ones too, I thought.'

'I don't remember getting any compliments.'

'I can't think why,' said Bagado, his neck disappearing into the collar of his mac.

'So what's Bondougou's game? What's he done to . . . ?'

'He's gone too far,' he said, to the dense knot of his dark tie.

'Well, I thought he must have done more than scribble over your prep,' I said, wiping a finger across my forehead and dropping a hank of sweat through the metal grating of the platform floor.

'Five girls have gone missing . . .'

'In Cotonou?'

'Schoolgirls,' he nodded. 'The youngest is six, the eldest, ten.'

'And he won't let you near it?'

'He's put one of his resident idiots on it.'

'Any bodies turned up?'

'No.'

'You think all five are connected?'

'Things like that are always connected.'

'Why do you think this is Bondougou's business?' I asked. 'Just because he won't let you near it, or what?'

'He's on it. He reads everything that comes in. Takes all the reports verbally first. He's very interested.'

8

Bagado started to snick his thumbnail against his front teeth, a tic that meant he was thinking – thinking and worrying.

'How am I supposed to fit myself in on this?' I asked. 'If Bondougou finds me sniffing around he'll hit home runs with my kneecaps. And the usual usual – I've got a living to earn somehow.'

'I know, I know,' he said, and stared down into the hold at the five dead men. 'How are we going to get these men out of here?'

'Put them in a cargo net and lift them out.'

'Let's go,' he said. 'Before I get morbid.'

'You mean you *aren't* morbid yet?'

We climbed back up on to the hot metal deck and leant over the ship's rail, gulping in air cut with bunker fuel and some muck they had boiling in the ship's galley – whatever, it was fresh after all that. The full weight of the afternoon heat was backing off now, the sun tinting some colour back into things.

'I want you to help me, Bruce.'

'Any way I can, Bagado,' I said. 'As usual I'm running this way and that, feet not touching the ground.'

'Who's that for?'

'Irony, Bagado. Don't go losing your sense of irony.'

'I'm losing my sense of everything these days . . . because there *is* no sense in anything. It's all *non*-sense. How did I get to this pretty pass, Bruce?'

'This pretty what?'

'Pass.'

'Is that one of your pre-independence colonial expressions?'

'Concentrate for me, will you?'

9

'OK. You've been manoeuvred into a position by Bondougou and now you've decided to manoeuvre your way out and I'm going to help you.'

'How?'

'You've only just saddled me with the problem. Let me run around a bit, break myself in on it.'

'No hit men.'

'I don't *know* any hit men. How would I know any, Bagado? Just because I mix in that . . .'

'Irony, Bruce. I was being ironical.'

Chapter 2

I drove out of the port, the sky already turning in the bleak late afternoon. People were still standing over where the boy's arm had been crushed, the stain darkening into the tarmac. I turned right on to the Boulevard de la Marina, heading downtown. Bagado had told me to keep my mouth shut about the stowaways and the fresh timber theory. If he wanted to land the marlin instead of the minnows he needed some tension to build up on the outside and the best way was to let the rumour machine run amok.

The traffic was heavy in the centre of town, with the going home crowd heading east over the Ancien Pont across the lagoon. The long rains had been going on too long and the newly laid tarmac for last year's Francophonie conference was getting properly torn up. Cars eased themselves into crater-like potholes. Bald truck tyres chewed off more edges as they ground up out of the two-foot trenches that had only been a foot deep the week before.

Night fell at the traffic lights in central Cotonou. Beggars and hawkers worked the cars. Mothballs, televisions, dusters, microwaves. I didn't do too much thinking about Bagado's problem. Disappearing schoolgirls was not my business and the only way Bondougou was leaving was if he overplayed a hand against somebody a lot nastier than I and they gave him the big cure. That might happen . . . eventually. But me? I'd rather steer clear of that stuff. Make some money. Keep my head down. Things were going better than usual. I had money in my pocket and Heike, my English/German girlfriend, and I were getting along with just the odd verbal, no fisticuffs. I got a surge just thinking about her and not only from my loins.

A cailloused hand, grey with road dust, appeared on my windowsill. It belonged to one of the polio beggars I supported at what they called 'my traffic lights'.

'*Bonjour, ça va bien?*' he asked, arranging his buckled and withered limbs underneath him.

'*Ça marche un peu,*' I said, wiping my face off. I gave him a couple of hundred CFA.

'*Tu vas réussir. Tu vas voir. Tu vas gagner un climatiseur pour ta voiture.*'

Yes, well, that would be nice. These boys understand suffering. I could do with some cool. I could do with an ice-cold La Beninoise beer. I parked up at the office, walked back to the Leader Price supermarket and bought a can of cold beer. I crossed the street to the kebab man, standing in front of his charcoal-filled rusted oil drum, and had him make me up a sandwich of spice-hammered meat, which he wrapped in newspaper.

The *gardien* at the office said I had visitors. White men. I asked him where he'd put them and he said he'd let them in. He said that they'd said it would be all right.

Did they?

I went up, thinking there was nothing to steal, no files to rifle, no photos to finger through, only back copies of *Container Week* and such, so maybe I'd find a couple of guys eager to see someone to brighten the place up and keen to part with money just to get out of the place.

Sitting on my side of the desk, just outside the cone of light shed from a battered Anglepoise, was a man I recognized as Carlo, and on the client side a guy I only knew by sight. Suddenly my lamb kebab didn't taste so good. These two were Franconelli's men. Roberto Franconelli was a mafia capo who operated out of Lagos picking up construction projects and Christ knows what else besides. We'd started our relationship by hitting it off and then I'd made a mistake, told a little fib about a girl called Selina Aguia, said she was interested in him when she wasn't (not for that reason, anyway). Now Mr Franconelli had a healthy, burgeoning dislike for my person and I knew that this little visit was not social.

'Bruce,' said Carlo, holding out his hand. I juggled the beer and kebab and he slapped his dark-haired paw into mine. 'This is Gio.'

Gio didn't take the heel of his hand away from his face and gave me one of those minimalist greetings I associate with coconuts.

Carlo sat back out of the light and put his feet up on my desk, telling me something I didn't need to be told.

'I'd offer you a beer . . .' I said.

'Thanks,' he said. 'Gio?'

Gio didn't move an eyelid.

'He'll have a Coke. He don't drink.'

I slammed my can of beer down and slid it across to Carlo. I shouted for the *gardien* and gave him some

13

money for another beer and a Coke. I took the third chair in the room and drew it up to the desk. Carlo nestled the beer in his lap and pinged the ring-pull, not breaking the seal. I continued with the lamb kebab and gave Gio a quick once-over. Brutal. Trog-brutal.

'You eat that shit off the street?' asked Carlo.

'Keeps up my stomach flora, Carlo,' I said. 'I don't want you to think I actually *like* it.'

Carlo said something in Italian. Gio wrinkled his nose. Animated, heady stuff.

'You don't mind if I smoke?' asked Carlo. 'While you do your stomach flora thing.'

'I'm touched you asked.'

He lit up. The *gardien* came back with the drinks. Gio and I opened our cans.

'Chin-chin,' I said.

Carlo kept on pinging.

'This a social?' I asked, wiping my fingers off on the newspaper.

'Mr Franconelli's got a job for you.'

'I didn't think Mr Franconelli liked me any more.'

'He don't.'

'Does that mean he won't be paying?'

'He'll pay. You're small change.'

'What's the job?'

'Find someone,' said Carlo, stretching himself to a shivering yawn.

'You can tell me it all at once, you know, Carlo. I can take in more than one thing at a time – beer, kebab, your friend here, who you want me to find – all in one big rush.'

'The guy's name is Jean-Luc Marnier.'

14

'Would that be a full-blooded Frenchman, a *métis*, or an African?'

Carlo flipped a photo across to me. Jean-Luc Marnier was white, in his fifties, with thick, swept-back grey hair that was longish at the collar and tonic-ed. It had gone yellow over one eye, stained by smoke from an unfiltered cigarette he had in his mouth. Attractive was just about an applicable adjective. He might have been movie-hunk material when he was younger and smoother, but some hardness in his life had cragged him up. He had prominent facial bones – cheeks, jaw, forehead all rugged with wear – a full-lipped mouth, surprisingly long ears with fleshy lobes and a blade-sharp nose – a seductive mixture of soft and hard. His dark eyes were shrewd and looked as if they could find weaknesses even when there weren't any. I thought he probably had bad teeth, but he looked like a ladies' man, which meant he'd have had them fixed. The man had some presence, even in a photo, but it was a rogue presence.

'Is he a big guy?' I asked.

'A metre seventy-five. Eighty-five kilos. Not fat, just a little heavy.'

'What's he do?'

'Import/export.'

'For a change,' I said. 'He have an office?'

'And a home,' said Carlo, sliding over a piece of paper.

'Why can't you find him yourself?'

Carlo pinged the ring-pull some more, getting on my nerves.

'We've looked. He's not around. Nobody talks to us.'

15

'Does that mean he's been a bad boy?'

'Take a look at the guy,' said Carlo.

'What do I do when I find him?'

Gio looked at Carlo out of the corner of his hand as if he might be interested in something for the first time.

'You just tell us where he is.'

'Then what?'

'Finish,' he said, and crushed his cigarette out in the tuna can supplied.

'You going to kill him? Is that it?'

Carlo and Gio stilled to a religious quiet.

'Forget it, Carlo,' I said. '*That* is not my kind of work.'

Carlo's feet crashed to the floor. He slammed the beer can down on the desk top and leaned over at me so that our faces were close enough for beer and tobacco fumes to be exchanged.

'I thought you were the one who liked me, Carlo.'

'I do, Bruce. I like you fine. But not when you're dumb.'

'Then I don't know how you ever *got* to like me.'

Carlo grunted about one sixteenth of a laugh. He put his hand on my shoulder and gave me a little massage, brutally thumbing the muscle over the bone.

'I know a lot of smart people who tell me they're dumb.'

'It's a trick we learn,' I said.

'Now, Gio, you might be surprised to learn, is a very remarkable teacher 'cos he can make dumb people think smart and smart people think dumb. Not bad for a guy who's never been to school, still has trouble readin' a book with no pictures.'

I took another look at Gio, at the slab-of-concrete

16

forehead, the short neck with black hair sprouting up it from his deep chest, forearms like animals' thighs, rower's wrists and agricultural hands, the odd knuckle missing from thumping the mule straight whilst ploughing.

'He's got intelligent hands,' I said. 'I can see that.'

'Careful, Bruce. His English is not so good but he has a good ear for tone and if he thinks you don't take him seriously he has a number of very short lessons he can give.'

'Look, Carlo, I'm not being difficult. You've just asked me to find a guy and in not so many words you've told me that when I find him you're going to . . .'

Carlo tapped me on the forehead with an envelope. I shut up. He laid the envelope on the desk.

'There's some money in there and I put a little item in with it that I think you'll find very interesting. I don't think it's something you'll want to talk to Mr Franconelli about, but it should help you make your mind up. Now, you've got forty-eight hours to find Marnier. We'll be staying in the Hotel de la Plage – walking distance, but don't come and see us. Leave a message at the desk for us to call by or meet up some-place. OK?'

Carlo let go of my shoulder and stood up. He opened up his can, sprayed me down with the spurting beer and emptied the foam over my head.

'Thanks for the beer.'

'Don't mention it, Carlo,' I said.

They left the office.

Fifteen minutes to trash my life, that was all it took. I turned the envelope over. It was stuck down. I felt the

17

thickness of the money and couldn't find the strength to open it just yet.

Now Bagado and I both had our millstones and Bagado was going to have to tread water with his while I got out from under my own.

Chapter 3

Heike wasn't home. She'd taken to working late, getting all virtuous since she'd started on her health kick. She'd stopped smoking, which meant I didn't have to listen to the tar bubbling in the stem of those plastic holders she used to use. She'd hung up her drinking waders too, except for the odd glass of wine at dinner. I'd always thought her beautiful even with her vices, maybe because of her vices, now, without them she was the same but just more so. The health aura seemed to bring out her intelligence too, or maybe she just remembered things when all the parking spaces weren't taken up by hangovers. I confess, it was making me nervous having her out there in this condition.

I waved at Helen, our cook, who was out on the balcony grilling chicken. I stripped and showered off Carlo's beer shampoo. I tried not to think about Jean-Luc Marnier or Roberto Franconelli by thinking about my first night with Heike instead. How we'd met in the desert, she with her girlfriend in a live Hanomag truck, me on my own in a dead car being towed behind.

We'd stopped and eaten dinner around a fire, it being brisk in the desert at night. She hadn't said a word to me, the girlfriend did all the talking. Afterwards I went for a walk by myself to look at the stars, breathe in

19

the emptiness and feel the African continent pulsating under my feet, thumping in my chest as if I had a bull's heart.

I thought I was on my own but then Heike was next to me. We exchanged looks but still no words and in a matter of moments we'd struggled and wrenched ourselves out of our disobedient clothes and were lying naked on the desert floor in a mad, frantic embrace. Our limbs and genitals locked together, the live ground pumping something so exotic through us we shouted when we came. The girlfriend had heard the ruckus and was forced to ask shyly and from some way off whether Heike was all right. Heike had croaked something back at her which she must have heard before from cheap hotel rooms, backs of cars, dark garden ends, because the clear desert air carried her gooseberry weariness back to us.

Having dispatched some of the nastiness, I wedged myself in amongst the floor cushions, stiffened myself with a gulp of Red Label and opened the envelope Carlo had given me. There was 250,000 CFA in it, $300, enough for 48 hours' work plus expenses. There was also the other item. A newspaper cutting from the *Guardian* in Lagos. This is what it said:

Yesterday a police autopsy revealed that Gale Strudwick, who was discovered dead in the swimming pool at her home on Victoria Island three days ago, had died of drowning. A police spokesman said: 'There was a large quantity of alcohol in her system and she had recently eaten a heavy meal. We do not suspect any foul play.' Friends had described her as 'severely depressed' after her husband, Graydon Strudwick, died of renal failure in Akimbola Awoliyi Memorial Hospital in March.

I sank the whisky in my glass and poured another good two inches and socked it back. Then I poured another inch and in the spirit calm thought that must have been one hell of a meal to sink her to the bottom of the pool, and Gale was not a big eater. She wasn't a depressive either, not about Graydon, anyway.

Gale Strudwick had been a friend, someone I'd known from my London days who, before she'd confused herself with money, sex and power, I'd liked as well. We'd got ourselves knotted up together in some bad business with Roberto Franconelli and her husband three or four months back. We'd both witnessed some example-setting from the Italian one night which had left me feeling like never talking again in my life, especially about football. Gale was a drinker and more lippy, more provocative, more aggressive about the money she needed to maintain the five-mile-high lifestyle she craved and which she wasn't going to get from her dead husband's estate. The cutting was a warning: Be sweet and you shall continue, be sour and you shall be sucking the mud from the bottom of the lagoon.

I rammed the money and clipping into my pocket and stared into my glass thinking about Gale – tough, sexy Gale – who'd talked herself a yard too far over the edge.

Heike breezed in trailing health and efficiency, and I had that feeling of looking up from the complexities of my life to see an aeroplane leaving a chalk mark on a clear blue sky and wanting to be there and out of this.

'You look whipped,' she said, dumping her bag on her way into the kitchen. How do women know your mental state just by walking into a room? She came back sipping a beading bottle of Possotomé mineral water, holding a glass of ice cubes.

'I *was* feeling bullish,' I said.

'I like bullish,' she said, kneeling down, straddling my lap and giving me a big, cool kiss. 'What happened?'

'You first. Yours looks better.'

'I pulled in six hundred thousand marks from that company Wasserklammer today and they only attached strings to half of it so our little Nongovernmental Organization can expand the AIDS project in Porto Novo.'

'You must be the boss's blue-eyed girl.'

'I've always been Gerhard's blue-eyed girl,' she said, exuding stuff from glands to make stallions whinny.

'True,' I said, damping my bitterness.

'Now he thinks I'm a star.'

'You don't want him thinking you're going to take over. I don't think his ego could handle it.'

'The agency's not *so* far advanced that they think a woman could cut it as a boss in Africa.'

'But we know they're wrong.'

'Are you trying to get round me?'

'Why would I want to do that?'

She kissed me again and let me know through some uncrackable eye semaphore that the long empty African evening was going to be full. I asked after Moses, my driver, who was being treated for HIV by Heike's agency. It was one of our evening rituals, and not a bad one because he was always improving, getting stronger. This time she said I might even have him back behind the wheel in a week's time.

I put my hands up underneath her skirt and stroked her thighs. She ran a cool, wet hand through my hair and I nuzzled her breasts.

'Not yet,' she said. 'You haven't told me yours.'

'You don't want to know.'

'You've been doing well recently. All that work in the port.'

'Something's just caught up with me and I have to jump.'

'Try saying no.'

'I did. It was rephrased in a way that begged the answer yes.'

'Couldn't have been that bad if they were begging.'

'Sorry. Wrong word. These guys do *not* go around begging. They ask, then they lean and then . . .'

'I don't know how you get involved.'

'They come into my office and involve themselves, Heike, for Christ's sake. I don't even have to be in.'

'So you knew them?'

'Yeah, well, something left over from that Selina Aguia business back in March.'

'Oh God, not her.'

'Not exactly, but someone we both got to know around that time.'

'We were going through one of our bad patches at the time, I seem to remember,' she said.

'One of those momentary dark clouds that used to flit across the sunshine of our lives.'

'Flit? I don't remember it being as quick as a flit.'

23

'Forget about all that,' I said. 'I want to think about something else. I want to think about going away.'

'Back to Europe?'

'I was just thinking about that first night in the desert. Our first time.'

'Oh, you mean the ground,' she said.

'Yeah, the ground. You remember that ground.'

'Let's do it,' she said. 'Let's go up to Niger and lie on the ground.'

'We can do a bit more than just lie.'

But she was off and thinking about it, planning it all in her head. I took my hands out from under her skirt and eased them up her T-shirt and cupped her breasts and she pressed her sex down on to my lap so I hardened. We kissed some more and I was all keen on doing some re-enactment, but Helen came in from the balcony, slapping her thigh with a wooden spoon, and asked us whether we wanted our yam boiled or fried.

'We could go up there when my mother comes out.'

'When your *mother* comes out?' I asked. 'Your mother's coming out here to Cotonou?'

'Why not?'

'*The* holiday destination on the mosquito coast apart from maybe Lagos,' I said. 'I noticed you didn't say your father was coming.'

'No. He's been before. Spent a couple of years in Ghana in the fifties. He says he doesn't need to come again.'

'Well, that means he's told her it's not lion and hippo country out here.'

'She knows that already.'

24

'And she knows about the malaria, the heat, the sweat, the pollution . . .'

'Why *do* you live here, Bruce Medway?'

'I'm just saying it's not Mombasa beach around here. It's not jambo country.'

'I know. I just want you to tell me why *you* live here.'

'It's not the climate. It's not the cuisine.'

'Just tell me why.'

'I'm just saying that those two things are important holiday . . .'

'I don't want to know about what's important for holidays. I want you to tell me why you live here.'

'The people.'

'The people?'

'If I thought I wasn't going to see Bagado or Moses or Helen again for the rest of my life, I'd feel . . .'

'Yes? What *would* you feel?' she asked, teasing me a little, big Bruce Medway talking about his feelings.

'I'd feel impoverished.'

She kissed me.

'You're all right, really,' she said, patting my face, running her hand through my hair again, stroking the old dog.

'Am I?'

'And anyway, Mum's not coming for the climate or the cuisine or the people. She's coming to see us.'

'Us?'

'That's you and me, Bruce. The loving couple.'

'She doesn't know me.'

'I know this may sound strange, but she wants to. She wants to *get* to know you.'

'Why would she want to do a thing like that?' I asked,

suddenly feeling myself on the brink of something, not the yawning black ravine but something bigger than me, like a view that goes on for ever to some distant mountains.

'I'm pregnant.'

Chapter 4

Saturday 20th July, Cotonou.

It rained in the night, louder and longer than Buddy Rich could have ever coaxed out of his snare. I stared at the slice of window reflected on the wall, at the water rippling shadows down the pane. I listened to Heike sleeping, felt the warmth of her hip on my thigh, her ribs feathering my flank. Happiness crept into my chest and curled up there tight as a ball of kitten. But no sooner was it there than I felt this terrible despair at ever being able to hang on to it. Happiness was a moment rather than a state.

I fainted into sleep without realizing it. I thought I was still staring at the rain running, running down the wall to nowhere, but somehow I'd got up and was looking down at myself. My shadow blocked the slice of window. A terrible darkness fell so that I no longer knew whether I was the one standing or lying, no longer knew if I'd been happy even for a moment.

I left for work in the morning – disturbed. Part of me was flinging myself around like a ballerina born to it but the rest, the bigger part, was weighed down, burdened by some unknown foresight. I drove and let yesterday crash over me, haul me down to its root, and roll me around in the airless, noisome turbulence.

27

Five men dead, schoolgirls disappearing off the streets of Cotonou, Le Commandant Bondougou, Carlo, Gio and Franconelli. What Bagado didn't know, something that had come my way by accident in that ugly business at the beginning of March when Franconelli set his terrible example, was that Bondougou, the Cotonou Chief of Police, was a Franconelli man. Bondougou covered up all the murders, and there were a number, from that horrific night and not a peep was heard in any of the media. That knowledge sat on my chest like a 300 lb bench press that I'd been foolish enough to think I could lift.

For me to find Carlo and Gio waiting in my office after Bagado had implied that he wouldn't mind seeing Bondougou end up as the main dish in a shark fest was a cruel irony. Me help Bagado sideline Bondougou? If miracles came my way and I found myself well placed to nudge him into the feeding frenzy I could only see myself going straight in after him.

I parked up at the office, tweaked the *gardien* awake and sent him across to the Caravelle café for coffee and croissants. The tailor's shack opposite my office was coming alive into the grey, sodden morning with the aid of the usual North Korean folk music from the radio. I wasn't talking to those guys. I'd asked them to make me a pair of trousers out of the last two metres of super-lightweight cotton I could find in Cotonou and they'd ballsed it up and left themselves no extra to adjust. Still, there were always spare boys around to run errands for me, do a bit of following and such, so I didn't dress the boss down too much for botching my trews.

The office stank of beer. I opened the windows and went out on to the balcony with my phone book and flicked through to the number of the biggest shipping agents in Cotonou. I put a call in to my friend Appollinaire Agossa, a young dude type who listened out for me.

'Polly? It's me, Bruce.'

'No need to introduce yourself, M. Bru, you're the only man I know who calls me Polly.'

'Am I? My privilege. Do you know a guy called Jean-Luc Marnier?'

'No.'

'Can you find out for me? He runs an import/export company called La Côte Oueste. Looks like a crook, too.'

'They're all crooks. How long have I got?'

'Ages. Ten minutes?'

I hung up. The *gardien* came in with the best thing of the morning and I gave him a tip to go and buy his *bouille*, the wet sugary bird food they like to eat for breakfast. I gave him some extra to go and find a girl to clean the office up properly too. I drank coffee and fluffed eating the croissant badly so it was all over me when Polly called back.

'That was quick,' I said.

'Only because we've been working the ship for Marnier's company, loading cotton seed.'

'The *Kluezbork II*?'

'You've heard?'

'I was on it yesterday afternoon.'

'They think the crew did it and they were going to throw them to the sharks when they got out to sea.'

29

'That's not logical, Polly.'

'That's the rumour.'

Bagado's machine working already.

'You got anything sensible or interesting on Marnier?'

'He imports veg oil in drums and bottles it here in Cotonou to sell locally. He exports cotton seed and fibre. Somebody said he's done cashew but I don't remember the name La Côte Oueste. I've heard he does business out of Lomé and Abidjan too. That's it.'

'Well, that all sounds very legal to me.'

'He doesn't *have* to be a crook.'

'The people I know he's dealing with say he does,' I said. 'Anyway, thanks. When's your birthday?'

'You missed it.'

'I'll make it up to you, Polly.'

'Don't call me Polly, that'll do.'

'You're lucky you're not pretty.'

'That's not what the girls say in the New York, New York club.'

'It's dark in the New York, New York, and you're black.'

'*Au revoir*, M. Bru.'

I got in the car in a sweat from the coffee and headed east to cross the lagoon to Akpakpa and the industrial zone where Marnier's company had their offices, about four kilometres out on the Porto Novo road. Bagado's car was sitting beside a large puddle near the Ancien Pont, and there was a big crowd streaming down the bank to one side of the bridge. I parked up and went with the flow. I knew it was bad because some wailing had started up towards the front and people were crowding on the bridge looking down at the water's edge, the Catholics among them crossing themselves.

An ambulance arrived and reversed down the bank. I followed it in and broke through the police cordon to find Bagado standing alone by a small skiff with sails made out of polypropylene sacks. His hands were jammed down into his mac pockets, stretching it tight across his back. His body language was grim. I drew alongside. His jaw muscle, working over some high-density anxiety, popped out of the side of his cheek.

His head turned five degrees to me and then went back to the skiff. In the belly of the boat, blown up to the point where the brown school pinafore was stretched taut, was the decomposing, fish-ravaged body of what I assumed was one of the missing schoolgirls. On the ground by the skiff, with his head between his knees, was the boat's owner. His skin was grey and there was a patch of vomit between his heels.

'He found her up on the sand bar. She was on her way out to the Gulf and the sharks and we wouldn't have known anything more about her,' said Bagado.

'Where's Bondougou?'

'He's coming. You'd better get out of here. This crowd could go off any minute.'

'You'd better get going too, Bagado.'

'I just want to look at this a moment. Hone my wrath.'

I worked my way back through the jostling crowd. Younger men at the back were beginning to get excited. They had sticks and rocks and their fists were jabbing the air. Some of them were hawkers from the traffic lights, looking to break up the boredom of their day with a bit of blood-letting. I got into my car and crawled across the bridge, pedestrians pounded on the roof.

La Côte Oueste Sarl wasn't difficult to find. The *gardien* let me in through a gate that could handle plenty of trouble should it come along. He pointed me up to some offices flanking the warehouse where I could see a bottling plant not in use. Most of the offices had their blinds down, but I found one with a glass door and beyond it a white woman in a short, tight red skirt, black vest and red high heels with little leather bows on the back. She had her back to the door and was spraying a huge umbrella plant. She was stretching up with one leg bent at the knee as if she was hoping that there was somebody else in the office to take notice. The air was freeze-dried inside and I didn't disturb the woman's work by coming in. She persisted with the disapproving atomizer – tsk, tsk – tsk, tsk.

'*Bonjour*,' I said.

She span round faster than if she'd been caught with her hands in the till and went over on one of her high heels. She fell back into a plump black leather chair which swallowed her with a gasp. The atomizer, which I could now see was a water pistol, was pointing at me.

'You don't frighten me with that,' I said to her in French.

She laughed badly, as if there was plenty needed tightening up in the nerves department.

'You scared me,' she said, putting the pistol down. 'I didn't hear you come in.'

'You don't look as if you've got a weak heart.'

'I don't,' she said, and went behind the desk.

To keep herself in that trim she must have had the heart of a steeplechaser. Her body had a fat percentage in the single figures and it looked as if it was monitored that way. She must have had a set of scales with the grams marked off and a red line for anything over fifty kilos.

Her face was as taut as a jockey's, the muscles evident under the stretched skin. She had a small mouth, very small. It couldn't have used up more than an inch. It looked as if it was going to be very economical. She put a set of long red talons through her short bleach-blonde hair and kicked herself away from the desk on a castered chair. She crossed her legs, keeping her eyes on mine, seeing where they went, and leaned back, showing me the workings of her abdominals under the spray-on vest.

'I've come to see Jean-Luc. Is he here?'

'You should have called,' she said.

'Does that mean he isn't?'

She blinked once, slowly, and breathed in through her nose as if that was some kind of a reply.

'Does that mean I need an appointment?' I asked.

A little tongue came out of the little mouth and nipped back in again.

'I'm doing all the work here,' I said, 'and you're the one behind the desk.'

'What do you want to see him about?'

'Veg oil.'

'You don't need to see him to buy veg oil. I can sell you that.'

'I'm not buying, I'm selling.'

'He's not buying,' she said. 'I know.'

'I wouldn't mind hearing that from him.'

'I speak with his voice.'

'Since the operation,' I said.

She frowned.

'*Une petite blague*,' I said.

'*Très petite*,' she confirmed.

'Are you his managing director, then?' I asked. 'You didn't give me your card or tell me your name.'

'Carole,' she said, and as an afterthought, 'Marnier.'

'You must be his wife.'

'I could be his sister, his half sister or his sister-in-law.'

'If he had a brother . . . which he doesn't,' I guessed.

The knot of muscle at the back of her neck keeping her shoulders braced loosened about a millimetre.

'You didn't say your name.'

'Bruce Medway.'

'No card?'

'No,' I said, getting some of my own economy going.

She uncrossed her muscly legs, pulled herself back up to the desk and tucked herself in tight underneath it.

'Is Jean-Luc in trouble?' I asked.

'Trouble?' she said, hitting the wrong note, making it sound like an understatement for his current situation.

'Everybody gets trouble in Africa,' I said. 'Sooner or later. I heard there was some on board the *Kluezbork II* yesterday, not that . . .'

'What?'

'Not that it would have anything to do with Jean-Luc . . . necessarily. But you know how Africans like to make trouble because . . . well, trouble is money.'

34

'What trouble?'

'Five dead men.'

She didn't blink for some time, her eyes glazing and pinking at the rims in the cold air. Her mouth formed a perfect 'o', lower case.

'Five?' she said, interrogatively.

'Should there have been more?'

'I don't know what you're saying . . . what you're asking. Are you asking anything?'

'I'm saying he needs some help with that . . . and I can give it to him.'

'Help with what?'

'Help with the five dead men and his cotton seed on the same ship.'

'How do you know . . . ?'

'Of course, I'd have to see him personally on the subject.'

'But . . .'

'And you seem to be the only one who can . . . facilitate that.'

All the talk about the *Kluezbork II* had confused her. She didn't seem to know about the dead stowaways, but she was aware of the cotton seed and that the repercussions could be expensive. I walked across to the window and parted the Venetian blinds with two fingers. The warehouse was very quiet, nobody in there at all.

'And I'd still like to talk to him about veg oil, if that's possible?' I said, moving back round to her side of the desk.

She picked up the phone and dialled a Benin mobile phone number, one of the new ones which had come in since the Francophonie conference last year. I memorized the number.

She spoke in rapid French, with her little mouth kissing the mouthpiece. I heard nothing. Then she shut up and listened. After a minute she put the phone down and tapped the polished desk top with her red fingernails. She kicked off her shoe and I heard her foot rasping up and down a calf that hadn't been razored recently.

'You and Jean-Luc been married long?' I asked.

She looked up into her head.

'Four years,' she said.

'You like it in Africa?'

'Very much.'

'Where do you come from in France?'

'Lille.'

'The weather's not so nice in Lille.'

'Ça c'est vrai.'

I lowered myself into one of the black leather chairs. Carole kicked off her other shoe and wriggled her feet back to life after they'd been crammed to the points of her five-inch highs with their prissy little bows. The phone went off louder than a ref's pea whistle. It jolted her. She snatched at it and listened and then held it out to me.

'What the fuck do you want?' asked a voice in English with barely a trace of French accent.

'Nice English, Jean-Luc. Where'd you pick that up?'

'I know who you are. Now what the hell do you want?'

'To meet,' I said. 'I don't want to talk on the phone.'

'Too bad,' he said. 'I *only* talk on the phone. Who're you working for?'

36

'Myself.'

'Bullshit. The kind of work you do, you don't get off your ass unless somebody's paying. So who's paying?'

'A man's got to live even if he doesn't have any clients.'

'So what's all this stuff about veg oil?'

'OK, you're right. I'm not interested in veg oil. I had to get started somewhere. Your wife wasn't blowing your trumpet for you.'

'With a mouth that size she doesn't blow anything,' he said crudely, and laughed with congested lungs, which set him off coughing.

'Maybe you'd like to talk about the *Kluezbork II*.'

'What's that about?'

'You know, Jean-Luc.'

'Yeah, I know. What can you do about it?'

'Those stowaways came in on one of your cotton seed stevedore shifts.'

'And?'

'You know how it works, Jean-Luc. You're responsible. You're the white man, for Christ's sake. You're as good as a monarch.'

'OK. So you can get the ship out. How much?'

'My fee is two hundred and fifty thousand CFA ... upfront. Plus some grease to get things rolling. And if you're going to be as shy as this you're going to have to make provision for expenses.'

'I have to be shy.'

'If we meet, Jean-Luc, maybe you can tell me about *that* problem as well and perhaps you can start living a life again.'

'I'll call you,' he said, and hung up.

Carole stood by the door with a little bag under her arm and some gold-rimmed sunglasses with red lenses on. She'd made a bad mistake. The lipstick she'd applied was dark purple. Her mouth looked like a split plum and didn't go with anything else.

'I've got to leave now,' she said.

Chapter 5

I sat in my Peugeot 504 saloon, picking at the piping on the seat cover. After a few minutes, Carole tottered around the puddles to an electric-blue Renault 5 Turbo. She smoothed her hands over her microskirt-encased bottom which showed no trace of visible panty line, got into the car, shucked her heels and took off at a fair lick. She had a grinning furry monkey hanging off four yellowing sucker pads in the rear window.

I let her get ahead and put four cars between her and myself on the Porto Novo/Cotonou road going back into town. She cut away from the line of traffic heading across the Ancien Pont, which she could see was backed up, probably because of the dead schoolgirl. The Renault 5 dodged through the muddy backstreets of Akpakpa and humped on to the metalled road going across the Nouveau Pont.

In front of the huge sprawl of rust-roofed stalls around the Dan Tokpa market she slowed and rocked up on to the central reservation and stopped next to a petrol hawker. She messed around in the car for a few minutes and came out wearing trainers. She crossed the road and went into the market, past the squatting money changers who must have said something other than Deutschmark, Dollar, Franc Français because she lashed a young guy with a caning look that had all the old hands laughing.

The market was heaving with people and filth from after the rain. The corrugated-iron roofs were set at decapitation height for my 6' 4''. Carole's trim, fatless, five-foot-nothing figure was more suited to this terrain, and I lost her in amongst the electrical goods no more than fifty yards in. I took time to extricate myself. A white man gets a lot of attention in a market like this and I was sold to every inch of the way. I arrived at the exit in time to see Carole's Renault 5 hop off the central reservation and heard the whistle of her turbo as she nipped through the traffic lights and headed up Boulevard Saint Michel.

I'd just passed my first stupidity test with an alpha. I wasn't a great one for punching the roof of my car and damning my eyes under these circumstances. It had happened many times before and I'd always been surprised at how many of my clients didn't mind hiring someone more stupid than themselves. People like me served a purpose. The trick was to find out the purpose before my usefulness ran out. Jean-Luc Marnier was doing some planning around me and I realized I was going to need more dirt on him before we met.

I went back down Sekou Touré to the centre of town and parked outside the Gerbe d'Or patisserie. There was a guy called Al Hadji Bélijébi who came from Niger and had some offices above a pharmacy near here. I knew him because he was a rice importer and his rice had been occupying my warehouse space in the port. He was impressed by the politeness of my pressure. He didn't move his rice but we did become friends of a sort and he'd help me out if he could.

The secretary in the cold dark hallway up to his office

buzzed me through. Al Hadji was sitting in magnificent blue robes behind the usual businessman's ninety-cubic-foot desk, which he must have lowered through the roof, or built his office around. We shook hands. He chucked his new mobile lovingly under the chin and offered coffee.

'Is this business?' he asked.

'Do you know a guy called Jean-Luc Marnier?'

Bélijébi's face stilled at the name. He nodded.

'I know him,' he said. 'But if you don't, it might be better for you to keep it that way.'

'Does that mean he *is* a crook?'

Bélijébi didn't answer.

'When did you last see him?' I asked.

'Not for months.'

'What's his game?'

'This is only talk, you understand. But the men I've heard this from are not idle gossipers.'

'As long as you tell me more than he's in import/export, I'll listen.'

'It's what he imports and exports that's important.'

'Not just veg oil and cotton seed?'

'No,' he said, screwing a massive gold ring up and down a finger. 'He exports people.'

The round pin finds the round hole.

'There's a long tradition of that kind of thing along this coast,' I said. 'Didn't it all start from that place west of here, Ouidah? Some Brazilian supplying slavers with . . .'

'Not slaves. These are paying customers. People paying to get an EC passport and passage.'

'Full paperwork service supplied.'

41

'I don't know the details.'

'Does he *import* anything interesting?'

'I don't know,' he said, staring at the desk.

'Is this something else I shouldn't know about?'

'I really don't know,' he said, not looking up.

'Does Marnier have any friends, or just dissatisfied business associates?'

'There's a Frenchman who runs a bar down in the Jonquet zone. Michel Charbonnier. I think he's supposed to be a friend but if you go and see him don't use my name.'

'That sort of bar?'

'Are there any others down there?'

'Does it have a name?'

'L'Ouistiti.'

'What's a *ouistiti*?'

'A marmoset, I think you call it.'

'How cute.'

'You'll see,' he said, finishing his coffee, 'if you can stay up that late without getting into trouble.'

I went back home with a baguette from the Gerbe d'Or in the passenger seat and let Helen make me a salad. I was going to sleep out the afternoon, which was oppressive with more storm clouds building. I didn't manage it. I ended up lying in bed thinking in very tight circles about Marnier.

If Bélijébi was hearing right, the five dead men on the *Kluezbork II* were Marnier's stowaways – another good reason, alongside the Franconelli factor, for him to keep his face off the street and his wife on the hop. I was sure Marnier would want to hear my 'inside' on the *Kluezbork II* and I was equally certain that I *was* going to get to meet him, but that any face-to-face would be a big surprise, even bigger for me because I had no solution to his problem.

Bagado was also in this equation, which had the look of one of those differential jobs I never got the hang of in maths. He'd kiss me if I served up Marnier the marlin just as certainly as he would brickbat my balls if he found I'd slipped one past him, even if it was to save my own ass. And that, after all, was the nub as far as I was concerned – Marnier or me.

There was no question it was going to be Marnier, but I wanted a better feel for what Franconelli's men had in mind and why. Now that I knew we weren't dealing with a Simple Simon I had to get myself tutored up. At least I'd made contact with Marnier and had a mobile number for him, which could give me a quarter chance of squeezing more juice out of Carlo.

I left a message at the Hotel de la Plage for Carlo and Gio to meet me at the La Verdure restaurant/bar in downtown Cotonou. I certainly didn't want them coming to the office now that I knew Marnier was out there keeping himself informed.

I slept a brain-damaged sleep and woke up with an eye glued shut and the realization that I hadn't checked out Marnier's home address. I had to do that before I went to the La Verdure. Get rid of all the obvious stuff first.

The home address that Carlo had given me was up in Cadjehoun, an area next to the smart Cocotiers district, which had gone through a rebuilding project to house minions for the Francophonie. I found Marnier's house at the end of an afternoon darkening early with rain

43

clouds. It wasn't new and was built on the same principle as mine – servants' quarters and a garage on the ground floor, and an apartment on the first. There was a chain across the short drive and a *gardien*'s stool positioned by the open gate. The gardens out front were in superb condition, with a variety of palms and shrubs getting high on the long rains. I parked, stepped over the chain and shouted for the *gardien*. Two ribbons of fresh tyre marks went into the empty garage, taking mud with them.

A young guy stripped to the waist and sweating appeared out of the shrubbery with a hoe in one hand and a heavy chopping machete in the other.

'*Le patron il est ici?*' I asked.

'*Il est parti depuis longtemps.*'

'*Et la patronne?*'

'*Il n'y a pas une patronne.*'

Interesting.

'*Qu'est-ce que c'est la dernière fois que tu a vu le patron?*'

'*Cinq ou six mois.*'

'*Qui t'a payé?*'

'*Uhn?*'

'*Tu n'as été pas payé?*'

Floored by that question he looked off into the garden. It was nearly night by now, with the storm brewing. I slipped him 500 CFA which he kept in his hand and looked at. A trickle of sweat slipped down his chest.

'*Le patron n'est jamais ici,*' he said.

'*Il habite où maintenant?*'

'*Je ne sais pas, Monsieur. Vraiment.*'

He tried to give me back the money. I told him to keep it and asked if I could take a look around. He

44

didn't like it but the money had complicated things. I went up the outside stairs and looked into the living room. In the failing light a basically furnished place revealed itself. The only expensive item a big TV and stereo system. I looked up on the roof and sure enough there was a large and expensive satellite dish. The place wasn't abandoned and I was sure people had lived here until very recently. There were drinks and glasses out on a tray on a sideboard and a book with a bookmark in it on a pile of glossies on the coffee table. I should have come straight here once Carole had lost me. The alphas were coming up thick and fast on the stupidity tests.

I left. The *gardien* looked as if he was going to cry. I drove back into town. The evening fish market was up and people were buying steadily under the orange glow of the streetlights. Parking boys kept trying to usher me into vacant slots in front of the smartest shops in Cotonou. Girls with pyramids of oranges on trays on their heads begged me to buy. I parked up outside the railings of the La Verdure.

I was ten minutes late. Carlo and Gio were sitting on the back terrace in front of a beer and a Coke. The girls were hovering. The Italians talked without looking up at each other, as if there was some kind of confessional going on. A tall Nigerian girl I knew from playing pool in here with Heike of a Saturday night bumped a hip into Gio and risked running her hand through his hair. He braced a shoulder which was enough to tip her away and then he leaned across and slapped her hard on the long bare thigh she had on show below her miniskirt. There wasn't anything playful about the slap and she yelped. She retreated to the other girls in the bar, where I was ordering a *demi pression*, and showed off Gio's perfect paw mark purpling up into a soft welt she'd have for a week. I told the girl to get some ice on it and went out to join the funsters.

I gave them a good evening and pulled up a chair to the table for two. They said nothing. Carlo took the foam off his *demi*. Gio's peasant hands rested on the table top, taking a momentary break from violence.

'I've made contact with Marnier,' I said.

'Where is he?' asked Carlo, sucking in an inch of beer, glass held between two fingers.

'He's inside the cellphone footprint of Cotonou.'

'That's something,' said Carlo.

'He's got another reason to keep quiet.'

'What's the first reason?'

'You guys.'

'Does he know about us?'

'How much work did you do before you came to me?'

'I went to his office and his home.'

'You didn't take Gio with you, did you?'

'No,' he said, and nodded at Gio to keep him calm. Christ, the guy was on no fuse at all.

'Did you speak to anyone?'

'*Una ragazza.*'

'Bleach-blonde, miniskirt, nails?'

'Yeah.'

'So Marnier knew about you before I got to him.'

'What's the other reason he's hiding?'

'Five dead stowaways were found on a ship he was working yesterday.'

46

'So?'

'They're his. He put them there. It's a sideline.'

'You telling us you can't do the job?'

Gio's body odour was starting to get a little feral.

'I'm doing it, aren't I? I'm here telling you how it is,' I said. 'Now look, maybe there's a few things you can do for me. First of all, never come to my office for whatever reason. He's going to come and see me sometime . . .'

'Then we'll come and talk to him.'

'No. I'll fix up a meeting and you can turn up and talk to him then. If you sniff around my office he'll never show in the first place.'

'What're the other things?'

'Why do you want to find him and what're you going to do to him when you find him?'

'When *you* find him,' he said, and then started blabbing to Gio in some dialect which sounded like a couple of Portuguese talking about opera.

'You said he's on a cellphone,' said Carlo.

I wrote the number for him on a beer mat. They talked some more and Carlo nodded into the bar. Then he got up and said he'd speak to Franconelli, ask permission. Gio sucked on his Coke through the lemon and ice cubes.

'You speak any English, Gio?'

'No.'

Well, I tried.

We sat there for ten minutes. Two sailors were playing pinball in the bar and the girls were all over them. They shrugged off the flashier-looking but tougher Nigerian girls. They preferred the smaller, plumper

Beninois girls who had a sweeter act but were no less focused on the bottom line.

Gio ordered another Coke to slurp. The waiter didn't have to ask me. Carlo rejoined us.

'Mr Franconelli says you're to do what you're fucking told and find Jean-Luc Marnier and don't ask any questions about stuff that doesn't concern you.'

'Right.'

'You ask me you're better off not knowing dick. That way it's safer.'

'You mean if I was indiscreet . . .'

'Mr Franconelli will know and he will not be happy.'

'As unhappy as he is with Marnier?'

'Maybe more unhappy . . . I don't know. I don't know why you want to know this shit.'

'Only that it'll help me know where to walk and not to walk with Marnier. He sounds like a complicated man who's sensitive to trouble. If he's going to trust me enough to come out of hiding I'd like to know where he's sensitive, don't want to lean on his bad arm if he has one.'

Carlo and Gio exchanged a look.

'But now that you've put it the way you've put it maybe I don't want to know as much as I thought,' I said.

'Probably you don't,' said Carlo.

'Maybe what I'll do is ask you some questions and you give me "yes" and "no" answers. How about that?'

'We could try that.'

'Does Marnier import goods for Franconelli, here, in Benin?'

'Yeah. He has done.'

48

'Has he handled it the way Franconelli expected it to be handled?'

'Not quite.'

'Has he been cheating on you guys?'

Carlo ducked and weaved as if this was not the real issue but could be part of the problem.

'Is this a wrist-slap or is Marnier headed for the big elsewhere?'

Carlo rattled a couple of sentences out to Gio. Gio shrugged, said nothing, giving his usual expert opinion.

'That depends on what he says to us,' said Carlo.

'Why didn't you get Gio to talk to the *ragazza*? I'm sure she'd have sung to him if he'd asked her nicely.'

'That's not how Mr Franconelli wanted to work it.'

'Good family man?'

'If you like.'

I finished my beer. Gio looked into the bar at one of the Beninoise who had her hands down one of the sailor's trousers while he was playing the pinball machine. He wasn't fighting too hard and he was losing a lot of balls.

'Anything else?' asked Carlo.

'I don't think so,' I said, a little nervous at how things were coming to a close, worried that Franconelli had chosen me specifically for the job and that once it was done maybe I'd find myself taking a look down the barrel of a Beretta and getting an eyeful – visions of Gale Strudwick face down in a Lagos swimming pool, the rain coming down on her hardening flesh.

We stood. Gio's chair fell backwards and landed with a sharp crack that made me start. Gio smiled at me, which was not nice. Worn teeth with a discoloured crust up by the gums over a dark, hollow Palaeolithic mouth, maybe a stalactite coming down at the back there.

'Twenty-four hours,' said Carlo.

Gio patted my cheek with a surprisingly soft and dry palm.

Chapter 6

The usual evening train pushed through the traffic, horn honking, heading out across the bridge to the industrial zone with a line of empty cars that screeched and grated on the rails embedded in the tarmac. I stopped off at the Lebanese supermarket round the corner from the La Verdure and bought a half of Bell's and some black wrinkly olives imported directly from the Bekaa Valley. I went back to the office with my goodies. The *gardien* was off somewhere doing what *gardiens* do best, not looking after the place. The door of the office wasn't locked as it should have been. I opened it, stood on the threshold and looked in. It didn't stink of beer any more, which was good. I put a hand in to turn on the light.

'Leave it off,' said a voice in English with plenty of French sewn into it. 'Come in and shut the door behind you.'

Someone was sitting in my chair, backlit by the glow from the streetlights and supermarket hoardings on Sekou Touré. The people who come to my office these days just don't recognize their side of the desk. I got annoyed.

'Who the hell are you?' I asked.

'You've been looking for someone. Have you forgotten already?'

'Well, you're not Marnier, not with all that *ronronne-ment* in your voice.'

'Only cats *ronronnent*.'

'You know what I mean. So who are you?'

'I'm representing Marnier. Jean-Luc's not ready to come out into the open yet.'

'Well, that's tough because I'm only going to talk to Marnier, the man himself. And while we're talking about talking, you can do your talking from the client side of the desk and let me sit in my own chair.'

'I don't want to be involved in this business. I'm doing a favour for Jean-Luc. I'd rather you didn't see my face.'

'If you're worried about your ugliness, don't be. There's plenty of that in this business.'

'What do you know about ugliness?' he said, as if I was new on the playground.

'It's not skin deep like yours probably is.'

'You've got a very strong backhand, M. Medway.'

'That wasn't a compliment,' I said, and nodded at him. 'How'd you like my forehand?'

'*Vous êtes un peu fâché. M. Medway. Ça ne va pas en Afrique*,' he said, imitating a French West African accent.

'It's just been one of those days,' I said. 'The rainy season or my biorhythms, I don't know which.'

'I don't want to be here, you know.'

'Well, you are. So you're in it.'

'I *have* to be here.'

'You owe Marnier?'

He ducked his head as if weighed down by his dues.

'I've a feeling Marnier's debts could run very deep, the kind of man he is,' I said, and the man nodded. I sat down and put the whisky and the olives on the desk.

'There should be a couple of glasses in the top drawer, help us relax a little in each other's company.'

'*C'est mieux comme ça,*' he said, and took out the glasses.

I filled them.

'Olive?'

We sipped whisky and ate olives, made mounds of pits on the desk top.

'What's your task, Monsieur . . . ?'

'Jacques will do.'

'Tell me, Jacques.'

'The name of your company is M & B. Who is the "B"?'

'Bagado. He's a police detective. He lost his job a few years back and we worked together for a while. Now he's back on the force. Been back three or four months now. So he doesn't work with me any more.'

'What's your involvement with him?'

'We talk. We like each other. We're friends. My girl-friend likes him a lot too. They're friends. We don't talk about work. Not much, anyway.'

'Do you exchange information?'

'I don't tell him about all my bad-boy clients, if that's what you mean. If I did, I wouldn't get any work, might even get myself uglied-up a little, like you or worse. You know what business can be like out here, Jacques.'

'I know,' he said, sounding miserable about it.

'Does Marnier have something in mind for me? Something for me to do? I mean, I've already met his wife but maybe he doesn't trust her opinion, maybe the words come out too small from that little mouth of hers. Yeah, he certainly didn't seem to think much of her in one department.'

'I don't know what Jean-Luc is thinking. He asked me to come and talk to you so I do. Carole? I don't know what he thinks about Carole. I don't know where she is any more. Maybe you coming along was all they needed to know that things were getting . . . hot.'

'So now they've disappeared. They're not at the office. I dropped by their home and they're not there either. Do you know where they are?'

'Why were you in their office?'

'Ambulance-chasing. Looking for work. I had some privileged information.'

'From your police friend?'

'Maybe,' I said. 'I thought the information might make his life less problematic and fatten my pocket at the same time.'

'Tell me.'

'Only Marnier. Face to face.'

'He says he wants you to do something for him.'

'Then he'll have to tell me himself. And if he wants me to pick something up from somebody or drop something off to somebody, at night, on a lonely road in the rain . . . forget it. Not for any money. Go and tell him that, Jacques.'

'But . . .'

'I don't want to hear any more. Tell Marnier to make direct contact or what I know stays with me and what he wants me to do, I won't. Now buzz, busy bee, because I'm tired of this.'

The phone rang. Jacques jumped. I tore it off the handset.

'Bruce Medway.'

'Jean-Luc Marnier.'

'We were just getting bored with each other, me and Jacques.'

'I could tell,' he said, which made my neck bristle.

I stood and looked through the windows and out on the balcony.

'Are you watching this?'

'Tell him to leave.'

I buzzed Jacques off and he stalked out, keeping his face away from me.

'He's shy, your friend. Are you coming up?'

'*Doucement, doucement, nous sommes en Afrique.*'

I got round my side of the desk with my ear still connected and settled uncomfortably into the warmth left over by Jacques.

'Carole tells me you're "*beau*" . . . Is that right?' asked Marnier.

'I've just been talking to your friend about ugliness . . .'

'But are you "*beau*"?'

'That's a strange question, Jean-Luc.'

'Not for me, it isn't.'

Something about the slant of those words reined me in, so I didn't forget myself and crash in there and say that in the photo I'd seen of him he didn't look too leprous.

'Well?' he asked.

'I never made the May Queen but I've had my moments,' I said. 'I was just telling Jacques that ugliness doesn't bother me too much. There's a lot of it around in this world.'

'That's unusual for someone pretty. *Normalement les beaux aiment seulement les autres beaux.*'

'Who said that?'

55

'Me.'

'The truth is, Jean-Luc, I might have made the cut at the school dance when I was a youngster, but now I'm in that battle zone over forty, you know what it's like, wrinkle and sag, wrinkle and sag.'

'Stay out of the sun. Drink water, my friend.'

'We're not going to stay friends for long with that kind of advice.'

He laughed. A crackle of static shivved my right ear.

'Now, Africans, M. Medway, now they have skin. Beautiful skin. But maybe that's the nature of beauty . . . it's always flawed. We wrinkle and sag and they're . . . well, they're born black.'

'I'm sure they don't see it that way.'

'You'd be surprised.'

I could hear him coming up the stairs now. His feet sliding until they stubbed the next step, his breathing wheezing up badly even after five steps. The man out of condition on all those French filterless cigarettes he stained his hair with.

'Smoker's lungs, Jean-Luc, maybe it's time for you to give up before you belly up.'

'Look who's got the advice now,' he said, stopping on the stairs, the air roaring over the webs of phlegm in his lungs.

'I'll shut up, Jean-Luc, let you get to the top of the stairs . . .'

'Without annoying me. If I get angry I can't breathe.'

'I'll remember that.'

He got to the top of the stairs and coughed his heart up and spat it out on the floor in the hall.

'Sorry,' he said, creeping round the door, 'for the mess.'

Whatever crap I was going to come up with stopped in a lump under my voice box. I'd done my bit of bragging about how much ugliness I could take, but I wasn't prepared for what Jean-Luc Marnier sprang on me. His face was hardly a face any more. It wasn't even an anagram. Not even an anagram put back together by a surgeon speaking a different language. It was an onomatopoeia. It yelled horror.

A scar like a bear-driven stock market collapse travelled from his right eye socket, across his cheek whose bone was knocked flat, underneath his nose where it joined the rip of his mouth for a second before going down to his jawline and into his shirt. There was nothing neat about the stitching. The skin was puckered and bulged in torn peaks. The end of his nose was missing and there was a deep divot across the bridge, which meant he breathed exclusively through his mouth and his right eye was a glazed wall, its socket shattered. Where there should have been a left eyebrow there was a thick, livid welt which ran round to his left ear, which wasn't there. Below the ear a chunk of his neck was missing and the skin had been stretched over it. The other side of his neck looked like molten lino.

He straightened up at the doorway and walked to the chair like an old soldier pulling himself together, General Gordon, maybe. He sat down and reached into the pocket of his light-blue sleeveless shirt with only two fingers and a thumb on his right hand. Scars like a railway terminus ran up his arms and it wasn't difficult to see that he'd been cut to the bone. He jogged a cigarette out of the packet and drew it into his mouth. He lit it with a Bic and blew smoke out on the end of a residual cough. Something else different to his photo. He'd dyed his hair black. There was some desperation in that.

'Now you see why your looks are interesting to me,' he said, shyly, like a schoolboy with gravel-ripped knees.

I searched for vocabulary but found only first syllables. I reached for Jacques's whisky and slid it across to Marnier and took a half inch off my own.

'That's what I bring out in people,' he said. 'Is that Jacques's glass? Would you mind washing it out?'

'What happened to you, Jean-Luc?' I asked, taking another glass out of the drawer and filling it for him.

'Machete attack. Typical Africans . . . they didn't finish the job.'

'Not here, in Benin?'

'No, no, Liberia. I shouldn't have been there. Some tribal problem. The village I was in was attacked. Ten men moved through the village hacking at anything that moved. They sprayed the place with a little gasoline and whumph! They killed twenty-eight people in less than ten minutes. When they left, the locals, who had run, came back. They stitched me up, did what they could for me, got me transport back to Côte d'Ivoire. But, you know how it is, these refugee hospitals they don't have much call for cosmetic surgeons. So . . .' he finished, and revealed himself with what remained of his hands.

'How long ago was all that?'

'Must be three or four months now. I was lucky.

58

None of the wounds got infected. The local people covered them in mud. That's where all our best antibiotics come from.'

'You must have lost a lot of blood.'

'Not so much that I let them give me a transfusion. I couldn't have black man's blood run through my veins. Don't know what it would do to me. Make me late . . . unreliable, things like that.'

'You don't think much of Africans for a man whose life was saved by them.'

'No, no, I like them. I was just joking. I'm very fond of Africans. They are marvellous people. Those local people who helped me. So innocent. So charming. So caring. But I have my prejudices too and at my age they're difficult to get rid of.'

'I don't want you to think I'm being facetious, but for a man who's suffered what you have and only four months ago . . . you've made a good recovery.'

He grunted out a laugh or a dismissal, I didn't know which, and stuck his cigarette in his terrible mouth and loosened off the belt of his trousers.

'Some of my less obvious wounds,' he said, closing his eye to the smoke, 'are still open and very badly infected. I'm nervous in crowds. I don't like loud noises or sudden movements. I find people difficult . . . to trust.'

'But this isn't the only reason you're hiding, Jean-Luc, is it?'

'This?' he asked, pointing at his face and then laying a snub-nosed .380 revolver on my desk. 'I'm not hiding because of this. I'll say something for the Africans . . . it doesn't bother them. They look at me as if it is normal for a white man to have such a face. And they don't pity me either. I like that. My own people. Pah! That's something different. They look at me as if I'm an affront. They look at me as if I should have had the sensitivity to consider their feelings. I should have thought before offending their aesthetic senses. I should be in purdah. Our society is obsessed with beauty, don't you think, M. Medway?'

'And your wife?' I asked, the question in my head and out of my mouth before I could snatch it back.

'What about my wife?' he said, quick and vicious.

'How has she coped with a man who left her whole and came back . . . It can't have been easy.'

'A lot of people underestimate Carole. They spend too long looking at her ass. You know, even before this I was not leading-man material. She didn't marry me for my looks, M. Medway. And I was fifty-two years old. She was twenty-eight. What does that tell you?'

'That maybe you've got a good sense of humour.'

'Now you *are* being facetious.'

'A little. But that's what women like in a man, so they say. You look down their ads in the Lonely Hearts columns and they all ask for GSOH . . . but they never tell you what jokes they laugh at.'

'And the guys? What do the guys ask for?'

'Sex, fun, zero commitment. But they do offer something very important to women. FHOH.'

'What's that?'

'Full Head Of Hair.'

Marnier roared. He ran a hand through his thick black locks.

'I win,' he said, and laughed some more.

'So why did she marry you?'

'That's personal. I only mentioned it to illustrate a point.'

'She keeps herself in very good condition.'

'Perhaps you're one of these guys who looks at her ass too long,' he said, touchy.

'She didn't give me much opportunity.'

Marnier roared again, hard enough to split any stitches he might still have left in him.

'She lost you without even having to think about it,' he said. 'Ah, M. Medway, I think I'm going to like you.'

'That worries me.'

'I don't like many people.'

'If you're including Jacques in your list, I might as well tell you he didn't seem to like being your friend too much.'

'Jacques?'

'The guy who was in here just a minute ago.'

'Him?' he said, contemptuous. 'He's a fool.'

Suddenly, for a whole load of very good reasons, I had the desire to get out of there, get back home, get away from all this . . . all this manoeuvring, all this manly sizing up.

'Let's get back to why you're hiding, Jean-Luc.'

'Is there more whisky?' he asked, finishing his glass.

I refilled him but not myself. Discourage the man. Let him drink alone. I showed him the olives.

'Lebanese,' he said, chewing one.

'Time's wingèd chariot, Jean-Luc.'

'What?'

'It's hurrying near.'

61

'You have an education,' he said. 'Now look, I want you to do something for me.'

'Is it to do with why you're hiding?'

'I'll be honest with you . . .'

'Is that unusual?'

'You're very interesting, M. Medway,' he said, looking at me out of the corner of his head.

'Call me Bruce, for God's sake.'

'You're quicker than I thought, Bruce,' he said.

'I can be slow too. As Carole found out.'

'And my *gardien*,' he said. 'It means you have a good understanding of your strengths and weaknesses. Self-knowledge is a rare thing.'

'Pity I don't adhere to the little that's come my way.'

'Then you're unpredictable as well . . . not a bad thing.'

'Let's get back to what you want me to do for you. The *Kluezbork II*, for instance.'

'That will resolve itself.'

'You're not hiding from angry relatives.'

'I don't follow.'

'Of the five dead men. Your stowaways.'

'Mine? Where did you hear that from?'

'It's well known that you shift a little human cargo along with your cotton seed.'

'They won't be able to stick that on me.'

'They're talking to the *chef d'équipe* of that final shift . . .'

'They won't get anywhere.'

'You don't know the man who's running the investigation.'

'Your M. Bagado? He still won't get anywhere.'

'You're covered then?'

'You don't think I can work out of Cotonou without a lot of . . . support. Very expensive support, I might add. You must realize by now, Bruce, that's the beauty of Africa. Everything is possible *avec la graisse.*'

'This isn't port business. It's police business. And Bagado doesn't . . .'

'Let me ask you something,' he said, lighting another cigarette from the butt of the last. 'Have you heard of Bondougou? Le Commandant.'

The name disappeared into the smoke over Marnier's shoulder and then on into the darkness of the room.

'I see.'

Marnier gave me a huge Gallic shrug and stubbed out the butt in the tuna can available. He picked up the refilled glass of whisky.

'Your health.'

'Yours too,' I said, pouring myself one and joining him. 'You need it more than I do.'

'If I stopped smoking,' he said, 'I'd come apart. The tar glues me together.'

'I don't want to think about that for too long,' I said. 'Are you hiding or aren't you? You went through quite a performance to get to me.'

'You came to see me first. I don't know all your connections yet. Maybe someone has asked you to find me,' he said, shrewd eyes on mine.

'Is that why you're keeping my phone occupied?'

'Expensive but safe.'

'So somebody's after you?'

'Somebody's always after me.'

'You're that kind of businessman.'

63

'Sometimes people disagree with the way I make things work.'

'For them or for yourself.'

'Ha! Yes,' he said, and fingered the couple of inches of thick scar tissue he had between the corner of his mouth and jawline.

'Maybe you're not being so honest about how your face was cut up,' I said.

'It was a machete attack.'

'I can see that.'

'Let's talk about what you're going to do for me.'

'Good, I've got a home to go to.'

'How nice,' he said, irritable now, the breathing going suddenly. 'I want you to take me to Grand-Popo.'

'You've got a wife. She's got a car. Renault 5 Turbo. Fast, comfortable.'

'Carole's been under enough strain as it is.'

'What are we going to do in Grand-Popo?' I asked. 'The beach is nice.'

'I'm going to meet somebody.'

'For dinner. I've heard the Auberge isn't bad. Better for lunch, though.'

'Perhaps. I've taken a small house so we'll have some privacy.'

'Who are you meeting? If that's not too intrusive.'

'A man from Togo. That's all you need to know.'

'But we're going to meet in this house you've taken, not out on some open piece of wasteland in the dark. I don't like those kind of meeting places and I've been to a few in my time.'

'Now you're adhering to that little self-knowledge of yours.'

64

'And why not?'

'Don't worry, I'm in no condition to be stumbling around in the dark.'

'When do we go?'

'Tomorrow. You'll be told what time. Make the whole day available . . . and night,' he said, standing and taking a bent brown envelope from his back pocket. 'This is the first half. Two hundred and fifty thousand CFA. The rest when we get back to Cotonou. That is your rate? Two hundred and fifty thousand a day?'

He stubbed out the cigarette and picked up the revolver and mobile phone. He stuffed the revolver into his waistband and pocketed the phone.

'We're still connected,' he said, patting his phone. 'I'll let you have your line back in five minutes. It's been a pleasure, Bruce.'

'Jean-Luc,' I said, and we shook hands.

He left and I put the phone back on the hook. I went out on to the balcony and watched him appear underneath me. He glanced up and nodded. He hailed a *taxi moto* and just about managed to get his leg over the back of it. He waved without turning round and the moped wobbled off into the orange-lit pollution of the city. I waited five minutes and put my call through to Carlo in the Hotel de la Plage.

We met in the booze section of the supermarket. I told him what he wanted to know and that if he was going to follow he'd better be discreet but keep close because if it was going to happen it might be sudden and it might not be in Grand-Popo. Carlo fingered the bottles and nodded with his bottom lip between his teeth.

65

'You want to tell me how to do my job some more?' he asked.

I picked two bottles of white wine off the shelf.

'You didn't tell me he'd taken a beating since the photograph.'

'He has?'

'He's a mess,' I said.

Carlo tutted, shook his head.

'Machete attack in Liberia,' I said, as we walked past the fruit on the way to the checkout. 'Lucky to survive.'

'Mr Franconelli said he was a hard man.'

'They tell me the peaches are good.'

'Maybe I'll get a kilo,' said Carlo.

'You do that.'

Chapter 7

I got back home at 8 p.m. with the two bottles of Sancerre. Heike was in and on the iced water. I joined her and she served me with a raised eyebrow.

'I don't *mind* watching you get off your face, you know,' she said.

'Maybe *I* mind,' I said. 'Don't want you to see something you don't like.'

'Something I've never seen before?' she said, snaking an arm around my neck, crushing me into a kiss.

'I was going to say . . . something that could sneak out after I've had a few which you've never noticed before, being in the same condition, as you are most of the time you're with me.'

'You think I could stay young and beautiful drinking the way you do?' she said, stroking my face hard, trying to iron out those creases.

'I was also going to say that sobriety's a very unforgiving state.'

'Then you must be a very forgiving person,' she said. 'But with nothing to forgive. You're flying already. I could smell you from the door.'

'That Sancerre's going to go down as well,' I said. 'And when I've finished this glass of water I'm going to have a Grande Beninoise. I've been talking a lot and it's dehydrated me.'

'I'm glad you're not reforming just because you're going to be a father.'

'Maybe in the last few months before D-day I'll start trying to be good.'

'They've already got a brain after two months. They hear things.'

'But they don't know what they mean.'

'Babies are very tonal,' she said.

'It'll learn to sleep to the clinking of glass.'

'Because it's all crap after that.'

'Well, *I've* just been told I'm very interesting.'

'By your drinking pal?' she said. 'That's a very sad thing for you to be saying, Bruce Medway.'

I opened the beer and drank it like I said I would. We sat down to eat, a Spanish chicken dish called *chilindron*, which was good for the climate. The chilli kept the sweat up. I idled over the Sancerre while Helen cleared the plates and brought the Red Label out, which she put down with a thump and a sigh. I sent her back with it and she gave me one of her half-lidded, muddy-eyed looks that told me I wasn't fooling her.

'Don't hold back on my account,' said Heike.

'I've got to go out tonight,' I said.

'Oh yes?'

'Clubbing.'

'Anybody I should know?'

'It's work.'

'You shouldn't bring it home with you.'

'I wouldn't, but the guy I want to see runs a bar down the Jonquet and it doesn't get going until midnight.'

'Which bar?'

'A place called L'Ouistiti. I'm told it means "marmoset" – you know it?'

'I've had a drink in there before now.'

'Who with?'

'An American Peace Corps worker. It's their after-work joint. Grim, unless you like grunging it.'

'You know me, Heike,' I said. 'Who was the Peace Corps worker?'

'Robyn.'

I dead-eyed her.

'With a "y",' she added.

'Aha-a,' we said, tipping our glasses at each other. 'Just checking there.'

'I'm flattered,' she said, sounding the opposite.

'This *ouistiti* place . . . ?'

'It's run by a guy called Michel Charbonnier.'

'You know him?' I asked.

'He's a creep.'

'What sort of a creep?'

'A sex creep.'

'Touchy, feely?'

'Breathey, breathey.'

'I'll keep my distance.'

'I don't know how you do it, Bruce.'

'Bring myself to the marks for the Michel Charbonniers of this world?'

'He's probably the lighter end of it too.'

'You'd have liked the guy I was with this evening.'

'The one who thought you were interesting? I don't think so. That hotel-barroom mutual back-slapping bullshit isn't my kind of conversation.'

'I've got to go away tomorrow too . . . an all-nighter.'

'With Mr Interesting . . . on our day off?' she said, irritated. 'He must have made a big impression. Where're you going?'

'Maybe Grand-Popo.'

'What sort of an answer is that?'

'A tricky one.'

'This isn't going to be a row but . . .'

'I've noticed that when one of us isn't drinking we don't row.'

'When *I'm* not drinking. You're never not drinking.'

'If it's not going to be a row why's it already sounding like one?'

'I don't *want* it to be a row but . . .'

'No more "buts". You've softened me up. Ask your question.'

'What's the attraction?'

'Of the work?'

'It's not the money, is it?'

'Why do you think Bagado likes the work?'

'Note,' she said, pointing at the imaginary stenographer, 'he didn't answer the question. Bagado, well, Bagado has different motives. He has a *sincere* belief that he's acting for the force of good against evil. He's on a mission, a crusade.'

'And I just like rummaging in drawers.'

'Maybe that's it.'

'I'm not as cynical as you might think.'

'Most of the time you seem to be acting for the good.'

'That sounds like Bagado talking,' I said.

Silence.

'You never told me very much and nowadays even less,' she said.

'I don't tell Bagado either. He's a policeman. I can't. And anyway, you don't want to hear.'

'True.'

'So what does Bagado say about me?'

'You won't like it.'

'Maybe I'll withdraw the question then. I get enough unpalatable stuff rammed down my neck all day without having to hear what my friends say about me, behind my back, to my wife.'

'Not yet, Bruce.'

'Not yet what?'

'I'm not yet your wife.'

'I said *wife*?'

'Your slip's showing. The Freudian one.'

I reached over. She leaned back. I ran my hand up the back of her neck. She resisted. I forced her into a kiss until she broke away.

'I won't take that as a proposal. If it's subliminal it doesn't count,' she said. 'It's still in the head.'

'And you want it from the heart.'

'I didn't want it to sound *too* much like romantic trash.'

'Leave that to me, I'm good at the pulp end of things.'

I got an inadvertent look.

'What else has Bagado said to you?'

She shrugged and sipped her glass, which was empty. 'You two've been going through my school report again.'

'He doesn't think you're *bad* . . .'

'I know, I know . . . he thinks I'm "morally weak".'

'He thinks your only guiding principle is your own fascination.'

I called Helen in with the Red Label. She dragged it in kicking and screaming. I poured a finger and brimmed it with water.

'One thing you might want to remember is that if Bagado hadn't come along, I wouldn't be involved in *any* of this. I was doing fine until . . .'

'*He* embroiled you in *his* crusade?'

'Yes, I think that's fair. He's the one who involved me in bigger things. People killing and getting killed and sometimes for no other reason than a base human emotion like . . . jealousy.'

'Jealousy?' she said with mock outrage, not rising to the bait. 'Jealousy's a *very* strong emotion.'

'Especially sexual jealousy . . . so I've heard.'

'Maybe for men.'

'No, no, women too. How'd you like it if I told you I'd been sleeping with somebody else, you pregnant and all.'

Her face stilled in an instant and she started in on me, eyes jutting.

'See what I mean?'

She sat back, caught out.

'You and I are different,' she said.

'No, we're not.'

'Our relationship is based on sex.'

'Is it?' I asked.

'That's how it started, remember the desert?'

'The *ground*,' I teased.

'Piss off.'

'There *is* more than just sex . . . isn't there?' I said, reaching for her hand.

'Sometimes,' she said, allowing me a fingernail. 'And

if you did sleep with someone else, whether I was pregnant or not, I'd . . . I'd . . .'

'I believe you.'

'How did we get on to people killing each other . . . ?'

We laughed and I gulped some Johnnie Walker.

'I don't know,' I said. 'An example of my overfascination, how I get over . . . No, I know what I was going to say. Africa. What I've learned from Africa, from this work, is that I'm not indifferent any more. My life's not set in aspic like it was in London. I don't just work, play, sleep. I'm not protected from ugliness by my job. Reality isn't TV. I see the limbless poverty at every traffic light, the fat people in bars eating money sandwiches which, as you've probably gathered, means I don't totally and unequivocally love the place. It drives me crazy. I go mad when the Africans decide not to do things, when they tell you everything except the one thing you want to hear, when they disappear off to their village without a word, but then I'm charmed by their innocence, the way they join their lives to ours. That's Africa for me – not a whole lot between those two mood swings – wild anger and happy delirium.'

'Have I ever seen you on one of those deliriously happy days?'

'You were asleep last night so you didn't see it.'

She leaned over and kissed me and went for the watered down whisky while she was at it. I pulled it away.

'Just a smell,' she pleaded.

'Seven months to go,' I said, and let her have a sip.

'Longer than that. I don't think babies like milk cut with Red Label.'

'This one will,' I said, slipping a hand up her top. She pulled away.

'Don't,' she said, 'we're not finished yet.'

'We must be after all that crap.'

'Bagado,' she said, flatly, 'doesn't think you're much good at the work.'

'Don't let *him* speak at my funeral.'

'He says you're good at the business stuff – loading ships in the port, managing gangs and transport – but crime. Solving crime. Seeing what's going on around you, making deductions, cracking problems . . . no.'

'No?' I said, lightly.

'That's what he says . . . and you know why?'

'You're going to tell me. I can feel it in my water.'

'You get involved in events. You get carried away. No objectivity.'

'Very interesting. Is that it now? Can we . . . ?'

She came around my side of the table. I pushed my chair back and she sat astride me and put her arms around my neck and her lips up to mine.

'That's it,' she said.

'You know something,' I said, pushing her top up over her head, finding no bra. 'Talking about solving crimes. I solved one of Bagado's yesterday. Five men dead in a ship's hold. Suffocated, no sign of violence. How did they die? I came up with fresh timber. Then Bagado came within an inch of telling me he wouldn't mind somebody taking Bondougou out of the game. What does that sound like to you?'

'Role reversal,' she said, and pressed my head down on to her breasts.

'Thanks.'

74

'Now shut up.'

I lifted her up on to the table and stripped her panties off. She tore at the front of my trousers. I sucked on her nipples until they were nut hard. She grabbed me and steered me into her and my knees gave at the feel of her soft, wet warmth. I drove into her lifting her off the table, my hands and arms full of her creamy back. She held my face to hers with the back of her hand round my head and rucked up my shirt.

'Turn the lights off,' she said. 'I'm not entertaining the whole street.'

She wrapped her legs around me. I walked to the wall and lashed out at the lights. Half her face appeared in a corner of light from the street. Her head rose and fell against the wall. My trousers sank to the floor with the weight of keys and money and the jolt of each thrust.

'Just don't go indifferent on me,' she said, and dug her heels into my buttocks, urging me on.

Chapter 8

I left Heike sleeping and took a taxi into the Jonquet at midnight. I found the L'Ouistiti in front of the taxi rank to Parakou. The bar left you in no doubt as to its intentions. Even the name, to my ear, had a girlie mag, fluffy bra, stripper's pout to it.

The building's plasterwork was as flaking and pitted as an old doxy's make-up and, rather than redo it, they'd just slapped some blue paint on top – gloss, as if that would make it better. Now the paint had started coming off in dermatological skeins so that 'scabby' was not being unfair. The lighting, beyond the plastic strips of the fly curtain, was red and sore as if the room had been chafed raw. The girls standing in the rasping light, who weren't hitting on customers yet, had their smiles up on the shelf with the bottles of grog. They were neither drinking nor smoking. They were talking amongst themselves but not chit-chat. It looked more medicinal than that.

I'd hardly got my leg over the back of the moped when my arms were taken up by a girl on either side, so that trying to pay the driver left me in an Olympic wrestling hold requiring a knot expert. They bundled me towards the entrance. The bar was narrow and stretched a long way back and looked intestinal in the light, the few punters inside ulcerating against the walls.

A sailor type was slumped across two high-backed wooden chairs, leaning on an elbow, his face sweating, his eyes tearful and his Adam's apple working overtime swallowing bad memories. A girl had a hand in his pocket, massaging his wad. My two girls tried to steer me in there next to him but I sailed on past, heading to the back of the place where there was a big guy sitting on a high stool next to a door. He had to be stoned, the way he was sitting, both legs hanging off the stool, his body doubled over, an elbow on one knee and his head floating in his hand like a nodding dog. He straightened when I hove into his tunnel vision.

'Charbonnier?' I asked.

The guy's lids, heavier than obols, stayed at half mast, so I leaned in on him and gave it to him louder in his ear. He reached over to the door with the speed of a hog-filled anaconda and rapped on it twice, finishing with a flourish and a how-about-that look. I wouldn't have minded giving him a how-about-this elbow in his what-the-hell mouth, but one of the girls had started work rubbing my already sore penis and I shrugged the two of them off.

Inside there was a small-boned Beninois fellow with an accounts book and a calculator in front of him. He stuck a pen behind his ear and folded his arms.

'Le blanc? Il est dedans?' I asked.

He nodded. All these guys had been to some French waiters' school.

'Je veux le voir,' I said

He leaned back and pressed a button on the wall, speedier than his friend. A door buzzed open. A pair of hands was sitting behind a desk. The hands, in a cone of light, were arranging a line of grass on three cigarette papers stuck together. The owner of the hands was in the dark and it took time to get used to the contrast and pick him out and when I did he still hadn't adjusted the astonishment out of his face.

'Hi, Jacques,' I said, getting it quicker than usual.

'What the fuck are you . . . ?'

'I got lucky,' I said. 'Want me to call you Michel now?'

'Take a seat,' he said, going back to his work. 'I hope you smoke.'

'I gave up.'

'Tobacco?' he asked. 'There's no tobacco in this.'

He started to roll the monster spliff which was his bulkhead against a long night of Christ knows what nastiness he had raking through his brain. I took the seat in the hot room across from him, my back to an open netted window. The glow from the desk lamp picked up his thin face, a worn and sweating face that was lined in a way that meant he sneered a lot . . . probably at himself in the mirror of a morning if he could bear it. He'd lost most of his hair, apart from a few strands he'd combed over the creamy whiteness of his pate. He had a tan line across his forehead from wearing a hat, a Panama that was hanging on the wall behind him.

While he finessed the joint I found my gaze locked on to a framed line drawing on the wall which I thought was a still life of a bowl of fruit, but on closer inspection proved to be an Oriental woman weighing a pair of huge balls and about to fellate an impossibly large cock.

'That one gets the girls every time,' he said.

'On the first train out of here?'

'You'd be surprised,' he said, and licked the papers to his joint with a very red and glistening tongue that didn't look as if it could mind its own business for very long. He smoothed off the spliff and put a twist in the end. He tore a strip off a Marlboro packet, roached it and sat back to admire the craftsmanship.

'So what brings you to me, M. Medway?'

'I thought we could have a chat about a mutual friend.'

'Jean-Luc? No. I don't talk about Jean-Luc. You think of something else.'

The sweat stood out on his forehead and I felt my own runnelling down my spine.

'It's hot in here.'

'The air con's broken. It's going to rain.'

He lit the joint, puffing at it to get it going, and then took a huge drag and held it in for so long he squeaked. He let the smoke out slowly and repeated. His eyes glazed and his face softened to a concentrated luxuriousness.

'You don't happen to have any whisky?'

He opened a cabinet, poured me a shot of something and handed over the glass.

'If you want to talk, you have to smoke as well.'

'Too paranoid?' I said.

He leaned over and bug-eyed me.

'Who?' he said, and smiled with as close to a good nature as he could get without borrowing a Ronald Reagan mask.

'Maybe that stuff's good for you,' I said. 'Smoothes you out. Stops your nerves jangling in your ears.'

'In my ears?' he asked, nicely stoned now.

'Whatever.'

'Smoke,' he ordered, and held out the reefer.

I took a tentative drag and didn't cough my heels up. All the pollution I'd been breathing had taken the virginity off my lungs.

'Enjoy,' he said. 'There's not much else around here.'

I nodded at his porno drawing and took another quarter drag from the joint, not wanting to get wrecked in the first minute and waste my time here.

'Not here, M. Medway. Not in Africa. There's plenty of girls to fuck, but, you know how it is for them, fucking the white man *c'est comme un travail de ménage.*'

'You shouldn't knock yourself like that, Michel.'

'Knock myself?' he asked, rapping his head.

'Tu ne dois pas dire du mal de toi-même,' I said. 'There's plenty of other people around who'll do it for you.'

He grunted and leaned back in his chair.

'You need to smoke some more, M. Medway. Take it in . . . deep.'

'Marnier,' I said, sipping the whisky, the strong flavour of the grass like a hay espresso in my mouth. 'Tell me about Marnier. Why do you have to do little jobs for him? Especially when you don't like doing them for him . . . do you?'

'I have no choice.'

'What's he going to do to you if you don't?' I asked. 'Kill you?'

'Kill me. Pah!' he roared, and rocked back on his wooden chair. He fought his feet out from under the desk and put them up on an unopened ream of paper he had sitting next to the phone. He was wearing dirty white plimsolls with no laces. He drew a hand down his gaunt features, picking up some sweat on the way which he wiped on to the thigh of a pair of grey cotton trousers which had been pounded that colour by an African washerwoman. 'What would he get out of killing me?'

'I wasn't being serious.'

'Smoke some more.'

I took a longer drag on the reefer, which seemed to satisfy him. I fitted the joint between his fuck-you fingers and he nestled back into his chair.

'The only reason I'm living is because of Jean-Luc. So why would he want to kill me?'

'I didn't say he would.'

'Non?'

The dope was ungluing the conversation fast. A warm glow emanated from my stomach which was being fuelled by my extremities which felt like frozen chicken parts. My eyeballs prickled. My tongue was lilo size and dry and musty like sun-scorched canvas. The whisky added no lick to my mouth. The silence I was in now felt long and ruminative of such things as the wood grain in Charbonnier's desk, the two missing eyelets in his plimsolls and the crepey quality of the skin on the back of his hands.

'How did Jean-Luc get cut up?' I asked, after a small century of chair creaking.

'Uhn?' said Michel, resettling himself and tilting back in his captain's chair. I repeated the question. Time leaked through my fingers.

'Sierra Leone,' said Michel, while I tried to remember the question. He handed back the joint. I waved it away. He insisted.

'What happened in Sierra Leone?' I asked, the smoke leaking out of me everywhere, the corners of my eyes, my knuckle joints. 'What was he doing there?'

'Buying diamonds,' he said, from what seemed a long way off now.

He eased the joint out of the back of my hand, which was no longer mine, but lay quietly on the desk top ready to be put on.

'He trades diamonds?' I asked.

'No.'

'Why did he buy them?'

'Jean-Luc is an opportunist. He sees a rebel army taking over a diamond mine. He thinks those diamonds are going to be cheap. All I have to do is risk my . . . my life and . . . to get the diamonds . . . and then . . .'

'What went wrong?'

'There are factions in these rebel armies. He bought from one. He headed north to Guinée and met another. They didn't like the white man so much. They cut him with machetes. He was lucky if you . . . *comment dit-on ça: ''chérir''?*'

'Cherish.'

'. . . if you cherish your life so much that you are happy to live the rest of it as a monster.'

'He hasn't always been a monster then?' I asked, the drug drawing together previously unengaged synapses. Michel blinked.

'That was four months ago,' he said.

I blinked back at him with a shutter speed of several seconds and found somebody else inside me asking another question.

'How did you meet Jean-Luc?'

The reefer was now barely a couple of inches long and, after the toke Michel took, red hot, so that he came off it hissing and licking his lips. He slotted it into an ashtray which had a mini Michelin tyre around it and lifted his legs off the desk one after the other as if they were spastic. He opened up a drawer in the middle of his desk and pulled out a pack of old photographs of different sizes held together by an elastic band. He flicked through them and extracted one. He held it face down on the desk top. He threw the rest in the drawer and shut it. He turned the photo up and laid it in front of me as if that was the one that was going to give me a royal straight flush at Binion's Horseshoe, Vegas.

The photo was of a young guy, late twenties/early thirties, with a mane of shoulder-length black hair. He was wearing extremely brief swimming trunks and had the face and body of somebody who could have mod-elled pants *pour homme*, and all the women would have run out and bought the stock thinking the pants *are* the man. He was standing on tiptoe on a beach which I knew was in the front of the Hotel Sarakawa in the Togolese capital, Lomé.

Michel's face just outside the scoop of light across the desk was intense and taut and heavily focused on me.

'Is this you?' I asked.

'*Oui, c'est moi*,' he murmured, as if he'd been in a perfume ad after all.

'A long time ago, Michel. That's what West Africa does to you. It's very unkind to white-skinned Euro—'

He slammed his fist down on the table and roared a spray of spit into the light marking the worn leather inlay of the desk.

'Six years ago!' he said.

He wrenched the head of the Anglepoise towards him and shone it full in his own wreck of a face.

'Look!'

He scrabbled a claw across the desk and tore the photo from me and held it up to his face.

'I've lost everything.'

The paranoia I'd hinted at earlier was creeping up on me. The heat, lack of air, the brain-smacking strength of the grass and Charbonnier's eerie transformation had sent the jitters going in my head like a techno tropical night bird. I wanted out but I was pinned to my seat.

'Four days after this photograph was taken I met Jean-Luc Marnier.'

'What were you doing in the Sarakawa?' I asked, going for the camomile question.

He leaned back out of the light and slipped the photograph back in the drawer. It took some doing, my arms were as heavy as a dead man's legs, but I managed to get the glass of whisky up to my lips and drain it. Michel took a bottle of J & B out of the cabinet and poured me a careful quarter inch.

'I was a journalist,' he said. 'I was planning to canoe the length of the Niger river from Bamako in Mali right through to its mouth in Nigeria. While I was planning the trip up in Niamey I heard there was trouble in Lomé so I stopped the recce and came down to the coast. I filed reports on the troubles from the Sarakawa.'

'And you met Marnier.'

'He was running an alternative and user-friendly bank for expats and travellers. I had my wallet and credit cards stolen in the Grand Marché and he had

84

them picked up off the street in a matter of hours. He saved me a lot of trouble. We became friends.'

Something like chilli from a hot soup got stuck in his throat on the word 'friends'.

'What sort of friends?'

'I was naive . . .'

'Naive people don't always make the best journos.'

'I didn't say I was a good journalist. I was very *sportif*, journalism let me do what I wanted to. Paid for my ideas. I cycled across the Sahara. I've skied down the Himalayas. I've crewed round-the-world yachts. I've ballooned across the Gobi.'

'Did you canoe down the Niger?'

'No,' he said, hitting the buffers in the terminal.

I had a queue of questions in three lanes for Charbonnier but I knew if I asked one of them we'd be gridlocked for the night. He'd rambled across some old painful episodes which hadn't been aired for some years and the spliff had bought them back pin sharp. He looked over the wall by his desk as if it was a surface to which he was about to expose his genius. His hands hung off the arms of his chair above his lap. His tongue, pointed and muscular, came out of the crevice of his mouth in the enquiring way of a mollusc on the slab. His eyelids drooped. I thought he was laying the onion skins over the ugliness until I saw, with a stink of disgust, that he was sporting the contour of an erection in his lap.

'Michel,' I said, which brought him round. He pulled his knees up and rested his heels on the edge of his chair so that his balls bulged graphically in the crotch of his soiled trousers. I was getting the Heike-eye view of Charbonnier now.

'You were saying,' he said.

'I thought *you* were.'

'*Ah, c'est le tour de la sèche fines herbes,*' he said, and reached for the now dead joint and relit it.

'Have you got any advice?'

'Me? Advice for you? Nobody asks me for advice, M. Medway. Do you really think that anyone would look at me any more and say, "I must have that man's advice"? No, M. Medway, advice is not something I keep in reserve.'

'I was talking about dealing with Jean-Luc. He must be one of your specialist subjects by now. I'd have thought you could write . . .'

'*On doit voir ce qu'on regarde.*'

'Well, that *is* the shit talking now, Michel. Come on, give me . . .'

The phone rang, a single piercing trill that stiffened the two of us, tipping Michel back in his captain's chair so that he smacked his head on the wall. He cracked his knees getting them underneath the desk to reach the phone.

'*Oui, allo?*' he said, and then listened for a full minute, his eyes boring into the desk, his smoking fingers trembling with the joint. He handed me the receiver.

'Pick me up at midday at the Hotel du Port,' said Jean-Luc Marnier. 'I'll be around the pool.'

The phone went dead. I gave it back to Michel.

'Do you still need my advice?' he asked.

I got myself to my feet. Charbonnier chewed on a nail, while his other hand drummed the unopened ream of paper. I opened the door.

'What's all that paper for?' I asked.

He bent down and picked up an old typewriter off the floor. He cradled it in his lap.

'I'm going to write a book.'

'What about?'

He gnawed at his lip for a few moments and his eyes drifted across to the line drawing on the wall. I didn't know whether that was his subject or if he just hadn't got that far in his thinking.

Chapter 9

Sunday 21st July, Cotonou.

I sat outside the Hotel du Port in my Peugeot 504 saloon eating a pastry stuffed with a Toulouse sausage. I sipped cold Possotomé between mouthfuls. My head felt as ponderously light as a barrage balloon and I couldn't remember a damn thing about leaving the L'Ouistiti. Had something terrible gone down? It was not something I wanted to come across in dreams or otherwise in the next couple of days.

It was a few minutes before midday. I checked the mirrors to make sure Carlo and Gio were being discreet. After Marnier's call I'd decided not to see the Italians again. I'd sent them to the Caravelle café and had a message delivered by a boy. There was no sign of them out there under the blanched sky, the silent heat. I got out, brushed myself down and walked straight through the reception into a central courtyard where some little *métis* kids were playing in the pool.

It was a Sunday and there were plenty of people lounging on loungers, slumped on towel-covered seats, and I looked at every one of them. You had to admire the courage of the turkey-skinned whites, stripped and sun-factored to the nines, they looked convalescent beside the casts in bronze of the loafing Africans. The kids whooped and splashed and fluttered in their bathing wings. No Marnier.

I sat in the shade of the bar/restaurant and ordered a beer and watched some French people eating *steack frites* and giggling as if their afternoon was taken care of. The waiter brought me a *demi* and asked if I was M. Medway. He handed me a note which said: 'Enjoy your beer and then join me at the Novotel J-L.M.' I reached for my glass, intent on obeying orders, and had an ugly flashback from the L'Ouistiti as I'd been leaving.

I was standing by the door of his office. A girl had come in. One of Michel's girls from the bar. She'd squeezed past me in her lime-green vest and a blue and yellow wrap over the shelf of her well-padded bottom. Had Michel buzzed her in there? I didn't remember. She'd gone to him and sat in his lap, dead-eyed.

'This is Chantale,' he'd said. 'Very beautiful. Don't you think? In a little-girl way.'

I didn't think she was beautiful. Young, yes. But those onyx eyes she had, you didn't see those on a little girl. There was none of the sweetness you see in other girls of her age. She'd seen things she shouldn't have and then done them.

'She's sixteen,' said Michel, as if it was necessary to be legal. '*Regardez la belle fille.*'

The girl pouted. Michel turned the lamp head towards her face.

'*Ouvres ta bouche,*' he whispered, like a lover building up to an unreasonable demand. Her mouth popped open. 'Look inside, M. Medway.'

He pushed the girl forward across the desk with his shoulder. I didn't like this.

'*Vous voyez?*'

He parted her lips and got his two fingers in between her teeth as if she was an animal to be sold. There were white patches on the gums and the insides of her lips and cheeks.

'That's enough, Michel,' I said, and he let her go. He pulled her back and put an arm around her shoulder. He drew her head into his neck as if she were his poor little daughter. Pet-like, she complied.

'Candida albicans,' said Michel. 'Not unusual in small kids. Rare in adults. I think in England it's called oral thrush. Chantale will have full-blown SIDA* in three months unless she's one of the lucky ones.'

'The lucky ones?'

'The strain running around West Africa quite often stops at the VIH stage. The T-cells are depleted so that they pick up these bizarre infections: oral thrush, shingles, diarrhoea, pneumonia . . . but the T-cells never drop so low that they have full SIDA.'

'You've done some reading.'

'I have to,' he said. 'She's been living in my house and I've been fucking her since she was twelve years old.'

'Twelve?'

'Are you shocked? That's not so young for these girls,' he said, stroking her shoulder, shaking his head. 'These girls. A man gives her a pair of sandals, she goes to bed with him. Another a T-shirt . . . she goes to bed with *him. Ach! c'est la culture Africaine.*'

I paid for my beer and drove down the road to the

* SIDA is the French acronym for AIDS.

Novotel, where I was told to go back into town and across the lagoon to the Hotel Aledjo, where it was almost impossible to follow someone discreetly. From the Aledjo I went to the Hotel du Lac and by 1 p.m. I was keen on some hours in the back seat catching flies. At the Hotel du Lac I was told by the barman to head for the Place d'Etoile Rouge via the Nouveau Pont, which meant passing the crowds around the Dan Tokpa market.

At the traffic lights by the south-west corner of the market the back doors suddenly opened and Jean-Luc Marnier appeared in my rearview. An African threw a heavy holdall in the boot, got in next to him and laid a thick arm across the back of the seat. He surveyed people and traffic behind. We drove in silence out to the Place d'Etoile and then on to the stadium and out of town towards Ouidah and Grand-Popo.

At Ouidah there was a police post manned by two armed soldiers and a boy holding a rope connected, on the other side of the road, to a metal rack of spikes on rollers which looked as if they'd seen active service. Marnier handed me his passport, a Belgian one in the name of Bertrand Corbusier, and the African's ID. The soldier leant in to take a look at us and gave a squeak of surprise when he saw Marnier. The soldier looked back at the passport.

'*C'est vous?*'

'*Avant,*' said Marnier, economically.

He waved us on without looking in the boot.

We dropped down on to a causeway across a lagoon. A fishing village, built on an island, wavered in the harsh light. A solitary man stood thigh deep in the flat gunmetal water, still as a heron. He flung a silver filigree net which scarred and melted into the panel-beaten surface.

The walls of the houses close to the road were hand-painted with vivid hoardings but not for Coca-Cola, Camels or Bank of Africa. These advertised the shivering haystack cones of the fetish priests who'd whirl through your village taking the evil spirits with them – VOU-DOUN AGBO, VOUDOUN AGNUNON. We were in a different world now.

The rains had swollen the lagoon and we drove through water up to the sills. A truck had slipped off the road ahead and suddenly Marnier's face was between the seats looking. Kids held out their hands and screamed, '*Cadeau, cadeau,*' until they saw Marnier. He eased back into his seat. The jungle, silent as menace, rolled over the water's edge, thriving, burgeoning and stretching as far as the heat-dazed afternoon would allow you to see.

Marnier sat soldier-straight, the two fingers of his wrecked hand tapping on the seat cover, some music simmering in his head or some wild genius that had got into him before his face, riven by machete steel, had closed back over. The African dozed with his twenty-five-kilo head on his shoulder, the tendons in his neck as thick as primeval lianas.

It was late afternoon when Marnier stopped me from taking the turning to Grand-Popo and told me to con-tinue to the border, where we pulled up ten metres short of the barrier. The African got out and we watched him nod through immigration, customs and the man operating the exit barrier. He crossed the dust-blown and puddled fifty metres of no man's land into Togo, and Marnier and I U-turned and drove back to Grand-Popo.

We dropped off the tarmac on to a long straight beaten track that ran through the village as far as the Auberge. As the afternoon turned, Marnier had me pull up alongside a graveyard. We walked through the stones, some of them simple grey slabs on the ground, others travesties of sarcophagi clad in bathroom tiles of pink and orange. Small black pigs were about their business amongst the graves. We broke through a line of palm trees to a beach. The sky over the sea was now blood-red.

'Very rare,' said Marnier, referring to the sunset.

I said nothing. I was doing some fear management and thinking about what good shape Jean-Luc was in suddenly, or was it only stairs that puffed him out? The heavy smoker of last night had clean air pipes and he wasn't heavy on his feet. For a man in his fifties, who'd taken the beating he had and spent a hot afternoon in a car, he was nimble.

We staggered back through the graveyard in the failing light, and drove to the Auberge and parked up in the darkness. The terrace of the restaurant was packed with a few expats and twenty Australian travellers from an overland truck parked in the campsite, but Marnier went through such a dramatic physical change in mounting the steps that a young French couple vacated their table for us. The place hovered around silence when the company saw Jean-Luc's face, but the Australians sawed through it.

'You thought you were ugly, Micky,' said a ponytailed bum. 'Take a look at that fucker.'

'Shit, Darleen,' said Micky to a girl as broad-beamed as a tipper, 'you haven't been sitting on people's faces again, have you?'

'Why on earth,' said Darleen slowly, 'would I want to do a thing like that?'

They roared. The restaurant crowd pulled itself back together again. Marnier nodded and spoke to me in French.

'Now you see what I have to put up with. Sometimes for a moment I can forget I've had two faces – watching the sunset, seeing the fisherman throwing his net in the lagoon, the jungle – ah yes! What were those lines from the greatest poet of this century?'

'I don't know any French poets.'

'This one's not French . . . T. S. Eliot. He's one of yours.'

'Then you'll be thinking of "The jungle crouched . . ."'

'". . . humped in silence",' he finished for me. 'Bruce, you didn't disappoint me. You have the look of a man who understands poetry.'

'To most people I have the look of a drunken bum.'

'These are people who are only looking at the surface.'

'Thanks,' I said. 'Now you're going to tell me I'm a beautiful human being on the inside.'

'Don't worry,' he said, grinning. 'I won't tell you that.'

'Because you don't think it's true?'

'We all have redeeming qualities.'

'Liking poetry is a very small one.'

'I don't think so. It shows an inclination to examine more than meets the eye. It implies intelligence and a

94

heightened sensitivity to the human condition. These are not small things.'

'But they don't make a man good,' I said. 'I'm sure you could find some celebrated psychopaths with all these redeeming qualities.'

'Such is the nature of a redeeming quality.'

We looked at each other after that unexpected exchange to the point of uneasy silence. Then a waitress came to our table, a white girl in a loose purple shirt, braless, maybe more less. We ordered a couple of beers and the menu. Marnier silenced the Australians to a nervous giggle by struggling past their table on his way to the toilet. Darleen farted, inadvertently, I assumed.

The beers arrived, cold in dimpled pint mugs. The waitress hovered.

'*Tu vas manger?*' she asked in an English accent.

'We'd like to,' I replied in English.

'I thought you were Dutch, the height of you.'

'Not my brilliant French?'

She smiled and we knew we liked each other.

I took a gulp of the beer and ordered another instantly, and one for the waitress. She left and I took my first *pression* down to an inch from the bottom. I looked out across the beach, into the dark beyond the rim of light from the bar. The unseen ocean repeated itself against the shore. Jean-Luc Marnier was reading me easier than a kid's nursery rhyme with pictures. Or was I still paranoid from last night's dope. He was seeing the same things I was seeing. The fisherman's net. The crouching jungle. Mind you, there wasn't that much to look at. I calmed myself with the rest of the beer and blinked away the tears and the strain of having Carlo and Gio on my tail out there somewhere with Christ knows what in store. My second beer arrived.

'You got a name?' the girl asked, startling me.

'Bruce. You?'

'Adèle,' she said, 'but an English one. I'd rather have that beer after I've finished if that's OK.'

'Sure.'

'You could join me if you like.'

'I . . .'

Marnier lowered himself into my vision. Adèle scooted off.

'Don't drink too much, Bruce. I need you to be sharp tonight.'

'What do I have to be sharp for? I don't want any more of your big surprises, especially ones requiring sharpness. Not tonight.'

'Big surprises? I don't remember any big surprises.'

'You calling me at Michel's last night.'

'A small coincidence.'

'What about the dramatic improvement in your health since last night?'

'I have good days and bad days.'

'And your breathing?'

'The country air. Cotonou is very polluted now with all those mopeds . . . and I gave up smoking.'

'Twenty-four hours ago.'

'So, I act a little.'

'I noticed. That's how we got the table.'

'A little bit of fun. I don't get so much these days,' he said. 'She's attractive, no? The waitress?'

I still had Marnier's money folded in its envelope in my pocket, untouched. I had a screaming need to slide it back across the table at him and go and drink beer with Adèle and sleep on a couch somewhere, but even I, with my brain of hot fudge, knew that I had to see this little bit of fun through and do a fair amount of acting myself.

'I think I'll have the *contrefilet*,' said Marnier to Adèle. '*Saignant*. Bruce?'

'The *barre*, please.'

'No, no, no,' said Marnier, so that I thought he was going French on me, controlling my diet, 'not fish tonight. You need something stronger. Something to fill your stomach.'

'I don't plan on any heavy work.'

'Have the *contrefilet*.'

'Why can't he have the *barre*?' asked Adèle.

'Because he needs the *contrefilet*,' said Marnier, firmly.

Adèle tilted her head at me. I had the *contrefilet*. Bloody, too. Marnier found a drinkable Côte due Rhone and Adèle was dispatched.

'So you're an actor as well,' I said.

'An expert in the *comédie humaine*.'

'What sort of range have you got?'

'Just character parts now. I can't lead with such a face.'

'When are you the real you?'

'When I'm in bed with my wife. A good woman won't tolerate liars in her bed.'

'Does acting have to be lying?'

'I think you understand me, Bruce. I act to observe people without being observed myself. As *you* know most people are concerned with surfaces so it is easy to divert their attention.'

'You think people are foolish . . .'

'Unworthy.'

'Is that why you destroyed Michel's life . . . ?'

'Me? Destroyed Michel's life? Is he still telling people that? We make our own choices, Bruce, and when we find ourselves lacking in the vital traits that will see us through those choices, then we seek to blame others for our failings.'

'He says . . . he implied that you took away his youth, his beauty.'

'Michel is wearing on the outside what he had on the inside. That is all.'

'But what happened? He sounded like he had a pretty good life going for himself until you came along.'

'*He* came to *me*, remember,' he said. 'And I didn't force him into his relationship with Gifty.'

'Who's Gifty?'

'He saw with his own eyes what she did to the Indian fellow from Accra.'

'I don't know who the Indian fellow is either.'

'Sudip. The currency kid, they called him. Not any more. He runs a cloth stall in Kumasi now. He started using his customers' money to run Gifty, who was expensive and not what any man would call . . . constant.'

'So Michel fell for Gifty and ran out of money. Enter Jean-Luc Marnier running Lomé's expat bank who found some stolen credit cards and became a friend. Who had the credit cards?'

'Ah, Bruce, you don't know how much pleasure it gives me to find somebody who understands Africa,' he said. 'Of course, you are right, Gifty had the credit cards.'

'Gifty was a friend?'

'I pursued Gifty myself.'

'But you are made of a different stuff to other mortals.'

'Not me, Bruce. In that department I'm as weak as any man. But . . . I do listen. And Gifty, for all her sins, was very fair. Before you dipped into her little bag of delights she would warn you. She would say, and she told me she said the same to every man and I believe her, she would say, "If you put your cock into me I will destroy you. I don't mean for this to happen but it will. So if you want to keep your life . . . keep your life the same . . . put your cock away." '

'And *you* did?'

'I was at an advantage. I had seen Gifty with other men and I had noticed something about those men that I couldn't pin down. I mean, they looked very much themselves, as you'd expect men who were blissfully happy to be, but . . . something was missing. Their real selves had gone to another place. Gifty used that word "destroy" in her little speech. And I realized that was what had happened to them. They had become incapable with love. They'd have had a better chance with heroin in their veins. They'd been destroyed.'

He laughed to himself, a goose of a memory walking over him.

'Ah, Gifty, she wasn't so fair. She would issue the warning lying naked in your bed, looking down at you kneeling between her legs with a hard-on so painful you could faint, her hands framing her open sex, pink and glistening like an open papaya. My God, it nearly destroyed me not to have had her.'

99

'Was this voodoo or what?'

'Gifty was deeply Christian,' said Marnier, horrified. 'This was no voodoo.'

'And she never fell in love with any of these guys herself.'

'At first, of course, but how can you love someone who has gone, who is not there, who is lost? There was nothing for her to love in these men.'

'Maybe she loved you, Jean-Luc. The only one who didn't.'

I'd hit the mark with that. Jean-Luc was going to flatter me with some more guff about 'understanding Africa' or 'having the eye', but he thought better of it and the steaks arrived. He jammed the knife into the corner of his two-fingered right hand and set to it.

'What happened to Gifty?'

'She died,' he said, mincing the steak up in his jaws, his open-plan eating style revolting and transfixing in one. 'She was murdered, in fact, by a Greek who ran a haulage business in Zaire. He stabbed her fifty-two times in the chest. A very jealous type. They still don't use the hotel room where it happened.'

'And the Greek? Is he rotting in a Lomé jail?'

'No, no, no. He got out. Paid his money. But if it's justice you're interested in you might like to know that he had a fall on one of those transport boats on the Zaire river. He was crushed from the waist downwards by two barges lashed together. It took him three weeks to die.'

A mountain of *frites* arrived and Marnier had Adèle spoon a load on to his blood-flooded plate. I liked this girl more. She wasn't disturbed by Marnier, his face was his business, she dealt with him like anyone else. Jean-Luc concentrated on his food, only pausing to throw a glass of red into the mix. I had a feeling I knew who'd given the Greek a shove in the back on the Zaire river.

Marnier insisted on finishing the meal with a *crème brûlée* apiece and strong black coffee, which Jean-Luc sent back twice until it was tarry enough for his taste. His fingers twitched, wanting a smoke, but he didn't light up. A small boy appeared on his shoulder and murmured something in his ear. He stroked the boy's head and gave him a couple of coins. We paid up. Adèle said maybe next time. Marnier replied for the both of us.

We drove away from the restaurant area past the hotel and took a right turn up a dirt track moving away from the sea. The grasses were high after the rains, and the mosquitoes large and aggressive. After a few hundred metres we turned right again into a narrow single-laned track which took us to a small clearing where there was a mud-walled house with a tin roof of *ondulé*.

I parked round the back. Jean-Luc's African was back from Togo. He was waiting for us on the covered concrete stoop at the rear of the house, which was lit by a couple of hurricane lamps. We climbed up on to the stoop. There was a shovel by the back door and a polypropylene sack of what looked like tools.

We went into the house, which had bare concrete floors and consisted of four rooms. The two bedrooms at the back each had a bed and one a broom leaning against a wall. One of the rooms at the front was empty

101

and the other had a table, four rafia-seated wooden chairs and a split-cane lounger. Marnier lowered himself on to the lounger and seemed to go into a doze. I sat at the table.

Our shadows leapt up the walls in the uncertain light from the hurricane lamp we'd brought in with us. Heavy beads of sweat formed on my eyebrows and dripped on to the table top. I listened. There was nothing to hear but the sea breeze moving through the tall grasses and Marnier's steady breathing.

The African returned and cleared his throat. Marnier's eyes snapped open. He brushed the hair away from his missing ear. He sat forward on the lounger. A quiet, well-tuned engine came through the swishing grasses and the room was suddenly filled with white slatted light.

Chapter 10

A vertical line swept across the wall, erasing our shadows, taking the slats with it, as the car swung right and went round the back of the house. Marnier, alert now, looked at me and jerked his head to the door. We left the room. He gripped my arm as we stumbled down the unlit corridor to the stoop. I had nothing to grip.

A black Peugeot 505 saloon drew alongside my car. The driver turned the engine off. The headlights died, sucking the tall grasses into blackness. The boot clicked. Marnier's African opened it and waited for the driver. They lifted something out of the boot, something shiny, black, metallic, a trunk which was extremely heavy by the way their faint silhouettes were staggering. They put it down at the back of the Peugeot and tried the boot, which was locked. Marnier took the keys from me, dropped down off the stoop and opened the boot for the two men. They grunted the trunk into my Peugeot. Marnier shut the boot, locked it and pocketed the keys. He took a billfold out of his shirt pocket and peeled off a note for the driver, who got back in his car.

Light shot out across the bush. Marnier and his African glowed red in the taillights. The car reversed and disappeared round the side of the house. Marnier's face flashed momentarily out of the dark as he lit himself his first cigarette of the day. The man perversely unpredictable down to the last detail, taking the cigarette, which he said he'd given up, just when the tension had left the scene.

'That trunk looked heavy,' I said.

'Let's have a drink,' he said, coming up on to the stoop. *'Felix, amenes le whisky.'*

We went back into the front room. Felix brought in a bottle of Ballantines and a couple of glasses.

'I've got some Possotomé in the car if you give me the keys.'

'We'll take it neat,' he said. 'You pour.'

'That's what I had to be sharp for,' I said, laying out the drinks, 'watching Felix and the driver stick a trunk in my boot?'

'Anything could happen out here.'

'When you're transporting gold across borders, you mean?'

Marnier gave me a teacher/pupil smile.

'Ashante gold,' he said.

'So it's stolen, too. Ashante gold is Obuasi gold is Company gold.'

'*I* didn't steal it.'

'You bought it from all those unofficial miners that hang around Obuasi.'

'I've never been to Obuasi.'

'You wouldn't have to go there. There's thirty per cent of the mine's production that's stolen every year and finds its way across the border to Lomé. A mining engineer told me that years ago, and I know at least one guy in Lomé who buys the stuff. An Indian. Maybe you're another like him.'

'Well, don't you think that's a fairer distribution of wealth than say the Company taking all the profit?'

'Or the freely elected Ghanaian government?'

'*Santé,*' said Marnier, and we drank.

The booze blissed over my nerves, which had been speaking in tongues since we left the restaurant and risen to a clamour when the car arrived. Christ, I was relieved it was stolen gold and not the Italians. Marnier sank back into his lounger, brought his knees up and did some concentrated smoking while staring at a hole in the plasterwork. I tried to come up with conversation pieces that didn't involve Italians, long grass or . . . straight violence, because that, if I hadn't wanted to be sure of it before, I was certain of it now sitting with this smoking buccaneer, was what was coming our way.

'Are you going to tell me something?' asked Marnier. A line which leapt in my chest like a springing cat.

'About what?'

'We hardly know each other. You must have things to tell me. Like things we were talking about before.'

'Like Gifty?'

'Like Gifty.'

'I'm going to be a father,' I said, the damn thing out of me and across the table before I could get something more sensible up and running.

Marnier unlocked his eyes from the wall and turned his head to me slowly as if this was a most surprising revelation.

'Don't tell me, Jean-Luc. I know. I don't look like one.'

'You don't . . . yet.'

'What happens when I do?'

'You look like me.'

'That . . .'

'No cheap jokes,' he warned.

'How many children have you got?'

'None . . . any more.'

'Does that mean they died?'

'They're still alive. I just don't see them, or they don't see me. They wouldn't recognize me anyway. No,' he said, drawing on his cigarette, flicking the ash on the floor, running a finger across his face, 'I'm hurt. Worse than any of these scars. You see, my children were the only two people on this earth who had my *unconditional* love. They are *of* me. And they turned against me. They rejected me. The pain of that is with me and it will stay with me until I'm buried. You know, even when they were hacking at me with the machetes and I thought I was finished, I could see my children. So when you're a father this is how you will be.'

'If I'm unfortunate enough to lose my child's love.'

'No. Once you have given your unconditional love . . . it weakens you.'

'Why did they reject you?'

'Because their mother told them I was a man of violence.'

'Are you?' I asked, the question coming out on a ludicrous croak in my voice so that Jean-Luc and I roared with unconscious laughter, quietened ourselves and roared again.

'*Ah, mon Dieu*, Bruce,' said Marnier, wiping at his left eye with his good hand, the tears running down that cheek only. 'You know something?'

'What?'

'Ach,' he said, rummaging for a handkerchief, 'since they cut me I only cry with one eye. What do you think that means?'

'The tear duct's damaged?'

'Yes, but it must have some significance. A man who can only half cry.'

'Perhaps that is what men are like. Half steel, half . . .'

'Well?'

'Sentimentality?'

'I was hoping for something more noble.'

'Nobility's thin on the ground these days.'

Marnier nodded, refilled the glasses, lit another cigarette and crushed the old one into the concrete floor.

'What can I say, Bruce? I like you.'

'I bet you used to like Michel.'

'Forget Michel,' he said. 'I think you'll be a good father. Tell me something more.'

He fell back on the lounger. I sat on the edge of the chair, the seat frame cutting me across the back of the legs. I rocked with the tension. The violence was getting closer, but this time there was a different pull on it. This time I wanted to tell Marnier . . . but I still couldn't get it out. Still a question hung.

'Go on,' said Marnier.

'My father died when I was sixteen.'

'Was he ill?'

'The smoking killed him, Jean-Luc. Sorry about that.'

'Smoking,' said Marnier, looking at his cigarette, 'is the least of my problems.'

'He gave me some advice.'

'I hope you didn't listen. Deathbed advice . . . pah! . . . worthless.'

'He said never do anything for the money and always follow through.'

'Then he was a misguided fool, his brain maddened by impending death. You should only do things for people for money and you should only follow through if you can win.'

'And he didn't have anything to say about women either.'

'He was English. They don't know anything about women. What do you want to know? Tell me.'

'Of course, the French are experts in everything. I forgot. *L'art d'amour*, *L'art culinaire*, and probably just plain *L'Art* too.'

'We know how to love women . . . and food . . . and, yes, painting as well.'

'Maybe, like food, you love too much at once.'

'To love a woman,' he said, ignoring me, 'you have to give her your undivided attention. She has to feel that she occupies the only important place in your brain. She is above work, above money, above everything else in your life, including your mother. If for one moment she suspects that she has slipped down the ladder . . .'

'You'll never get her into bed,' I said. Marnier laughed.

'Maybe you're right,' he said. 'Maybe that's all we know or want to know.'

'How to act.'

'All men,' said Marnier, refitting his glass on the table, 'are actors. Have you ever thought of this? That the only honest men are the ones who pay for it. The rest of us pretend . . . to get what we want.'

We lapsed into silence. I had no appetite for the argument. I slid my glass round in tight circles on the table top. The sweat stood out on the back of my hand. The heat in the room with the hurricane lamp going should have been intolerable, only the pressure of outside things made it bearable. Something clattered on the outside of the wooden shutters. I stiffened and twisted. A brain-damaged beetle crawled through the slats, fell to the floor and spun on its back. There was no glass, no netting.

'Tell me something more,' said Marnier.

'What more? What can I tell you that you don't know already,' I said, suddenly irritable, the cracks appearing.

'Talk. It will pass the time. Who knows, we may stumble across a universal truth and change our lives and perhaps mankind.'

'Let's just finish our drinks and go home instead.'

'I'm waiting, and anyway, you know better than to drive in Africa at night.'

'You're waiting?' I asked, the sweat suddenly streaming into my eyes, making me blink.

Marnier turned his face on me and I found myself looking into the eyes of the man who was going to kill me. The one eye, the only one with any potential for sadness, was glistening . . . sorry for the fact. I started talking. It was the only thing to do.

'We were followed today,' I said. 'We've been followed all day by two of Franconelli's men. Gio and Carlo, you might know them. They say they want to talk to you, and I don't believe that what they have in mind will be unaccompanied by violence.'

I breathed deeply, not finding the air enough in the

room. Marnier sucked on his loosely packed cigarette, which crackled. He exhaled through his nostrils, looking at nothing in particular, his face unreadable.

'Your child will not be fatherless,' he said. 'Come, it's time to move. Bring the light.'

We left the room and walked down the corridor to the bedrooms. Marnier beckoned me into his. He pulled the holdall out from under the bed, unzipped it and took out a 9 mm handgun and a clip of bullets, a different beast altogether to the .380 revolver he'd had in my office. That was a cap gun compared to this. He shoved the clip up the handle of the gun and worked the slide. He took a torch out of the bag and tested it. Then he threw the bag under the bed and lay down on it.

'Go to your room. Shut the lamp down. Sleep . . . if you can.'

I turned and he added some words to the back of my head.

'One thing about women. Once they have their children you're number two. That's not fair, is it . . . after they've been number one all that time?'

I lay down on the bed in my room and dowsed the lamp. It was brutally hot under the *ondulé* and sleep was out of the question, even if I hadn't a brain full of the choice I'd just made. Mosquitoes whined for blood, the long grass and swamp land around producing a fine pedigree for aggression and prophylactic resistance. I got under the sheet, pulled it over my head, breathed my own breath and started living with my own stink.

A stillness settled over the house. The grasses hushed

to nothing. Night colours came and dissolved in the undiluted darkness. Ideas drifted, merged and disintegrated. My brain rushed towards incoherence until, as crisp as scissors through card, reality cut back in.

From some way off I heard the wind blundering through the trees, scything through the grass until it thumped into the back of the house, charged through the back door and opened a shutter in the front room, which snapped back on to the wall and cracked back into its frame. Fresh, cool air roamed the house. I tore the sheet back and gulped it in. The wind rolled on, dragging the rain after it, reluctant at first – a dash of pebble on the *ondulé* – and then a crash and the rooms were full of noise and a blue/white halogen light.

Marnier was standing at his window looking out, the gun in his good left hand. He registered something and turned before the house imploded to black. I got to my feet with no idea in my head, just a carbon copy of Marnier floating in front of me. I waited. The rain smashed into the *ondulé* so hard that it should have caved in under the five-mile-high clouds full of it. The thunder pounded and the light that came with it burst white and fizzled then burst again. This time there was a figure between me and Marnier. The figure turned to him and took from him the only sound louder than the storm. Then blackness again, roaring blackness. A collision and the feeling of a wet shirt, a warm body underneath, muscle, sinew and something solid, heavy, clipped my cheek, a head, hair on my lips. Then the hard concrete of the floor. A weight on top of me. A weight slipping down my body. A weight wet through. More thunder. More light. Carlo's head in my lap, his

111

mouth wide open, a black hole, a mess on his shirt, high on the chest, another black hole there too, a large nickel-plated gun in his right hand.

'FELIX!' roared Marnier.

I rolled out from under Carlo, kicking his dead weight away from me, suddenly panicked. I crawled and staggered to the door, the percussion of the rain still deafening.

'FELIX!' roared Marnier again.

The lightning showed Marnier out on the stoop, gun in hand, the torch in the other. A wall of white vertical rain in front of him so that nothing was visible beyond the torrent coming off the roof of the stoop. The platform where he was standing was covered in water and, with the rain not so loud outside, I could hear him splashing backwards and forwards.

'FELIX!' he shouted again, but this time his voice rang out into the night. The rain stopped dead. On the back of the rain-rinsed air came not only the smell of wet earth and flushed grasses, but also the sound of two men in some monumental struggle. Marnier's torch found them. A few feet from the back of the car Felix and Gio were on their feet locked together in an impossible octopodial embrace. The tendons of Felix's neck standing out like bridge struts while Gio's agricultural hands encircled, squeezed and crushed.

I grabbed the shovel by the back door and leapt off the stoop and ran at Gio's back.

'Don't kill him!' roared Marnier.

Gio heard me coming and turned in time to take the blade of the shovel a glancing blow on his concrete forehead. He let Felix go but didn't go down. I brought

112

the shovel up again to take Gio out but Marnier roared again from the stoop.

'NO!'

I swung, missed, and, as I staggered round, Gio's stone fist connected with the side of my head and I went down into the mud. Gio moved towards me in triplicate. I tried to scrabble away from him, from the fists he held raised like rock-breakers' hammers. Then he was on me, his breath in my face stronger than a wild dog's, his lips pulled back over the worn teeth. The fists came up, wavered, and wouldn't work any more. The fight went out of him. He collapsed forward, his face as close to mine as a lover's cheek. The shovel blow had just taken that bit longer to work its way down the fossilized synapses to Gio's 'off' switch. Felix pulled him away from me. He now had a knife in his hand. Marnier appeared with some nylon rope and the polypropylene sack, the torch in his armpit. Felix sliced through Gio's sodden shirt, tore it off his back and set to binding the man's hands up behind him.

'Get Carlo,' said Marnier to me, the wind buffeting without moving a strand of his hair.

'Get him?' I shouted, stoking some anger. 'He's bloody dead.'

'Bring him here. Carry him.'

'You shot him. You bring him.'

'Young man's work.'

'Like it's old man's work to shout idiot suggestions during a fight with this complete mad bastard?'

'I didn't want you to kill him.'

'Kill him?' I roared. 'The only way to kill a guy like that is to drop a bridge on him.'

Marnier did that rare thing . . . he chuckled.

'Go on,' he said, giving me some matches. 'It's getting late.'

I crawled around the bedroom trying to find the hurricane lamp. I brought the light up in the room along with the hairs on the back of my neck. Carlo wasn't there. There was a dark patch on the concrete, but no Carlo.

Chapter 11

I crawled on all fours along Carlo's trail of blood to the bedroom door. I've always hated farce – all that painful inevitability before the tragedy. The dark smears went down the corridor to the front of the house. Why hadn't he gone out on to the stoop? He was confused, half dead, a hole in his chest, an animal crawling off to die. The trail of blood came back up the corridor from the locked front door and went into the room with the tables and chairs. I didn't want to stick my head round that door.

I went back to the bedroom and found the broom and hung the hurricane lamp off the end of it. Back in the corridor I eased the lamp waist-high into the centre of the doorway. Three shots of colossal loudness rang out and shattered the lamp, which burst into flames on the ground. See what I mean about farce?

I ran back into the bedroom and tore the heavy horse-hair mattress off the bed. On the way back out I hit Marnier coming in from the stoop and we both went down fighting the mattress between us.

'What the . . . fuck . . . is going on!' hissed Marnier.

'Carlo's in there, alive, with a gun. The place is on fire,' I said. 'That's it.'

'*Putain merde*,' said Marnier, and he left the house via the stoop. I threw the mattress over the flames. Carlo let off another shot, the mattress taking it in the gut, a terrible quantity of horsehair stuffing tore out the back of it as it went down. I slid to the floor by the smouldering door jambs.

'You know somethin',' said Carlo, his voice coming out in little pops and crackles from the blood collected in his lungs and throat.

'Yeah,' I said, 'I know you totally ballsed up this situation. It should be Marnier in there with his chest half out, not you.'

'Fuck you,' said Carlo. 'He was fuckin' waiting for us. You told him, you big fuck.'

'I didn't *have* to tell him.'

'You know what, fucker?'

'I don't know anything any more.'

'You're dead meat. You're dead the worse way you could ever possibly fuckin' imagine.'

'That's not something I spend too much of my time thinking about.'

'One day . . .' were Carlo's last words. A faint light clicked on in the room. Three shots. The noise, loud and continuous, careened around my cranium. The tinnitus staying and staying so that I knew this night would be in my head for years. I looked round the door jamb. The light from Marnier's torch was still on Carlo, who had jammed himself into the corner of the room. His eye, nose and jaw were missing. Marnier was standing by an open shutter, his torso in the room, the gun still extended in his left hand. He looked down at the floor.

'Bring him out,' he said. 'I'll hold the light on him.'

It was a business getting Carlo out. His shoulders,

116

arms and chest were slippery with gore and although he wasn't a big-framed man he must have weighed in at around eighty-five kilos. I got him up in stages, using the chair and table, until I could slide him on to my shoulder. Marnier helped things along with a stream of suggestions from the window until I was half laughing, half crying. I plodded down the corridor and met Marnier out the back, who lit the way for me down into the yard where Felix was standing, crouched under Gio's weight, who was still out cold.

'*Suivez-moi*,' said Marnier, picking up the shovel.

He took us down a path, among the tall grasses, that you wouldn't have known was there. We came to a pile of gravel in front of a wooden shed which was padlocked. Marnier had to go through his pockets a couple of times, with Felix and I grunting and Gio beginning to stir. He opened the shed.

Inside the shed, which was the size of a single-car garage, was a beaten earth floor in which three holes had been dug. Three grave-sized holes. There were maybe twenty sacks of concrete piled on some plastic sheeting at the far end.

'Wait,' said Marnier, checking the holes with his torch. 'Put Carlo in this one.'

I staggered to the graveside with the last of my strength and let Carlo slide off into the watery hole. I collapsed to my knees and elbows, forehead against the cool earth, my whole body coursing with acid, my shirt, slick on my skin, soaked with sweat and blood.

'Glad you had the *contrefilet* now?' said Marnier. 'Imagine trying to do that with a little *filet de barre* inside you.'

He took a camping gaz light off the wall and lit it and a cigarette. He hung the light from a steel crossbeam in the roof, where it hissed. Felix had let Gio fall to the ground and, now that I was unburdened, I realized with some nervousness that, first of all, Gio was stripped naked, and there were three holes in the shed and only two obvious occupants.

But, hell, I couldn't do anything about it. I was weaker than a licked kitten.

Gio rolled over on to his back to take a look at how dark his circumstances were. Marnier stared down at him and smoked.

'*Amenes les machettes, Felix,*' he said, and I suddenly felt like sobbing.

Felix dumped the polypropylene sack at Marnier's feet and retreated to the door of the garage where he picked up the shovel and started filling in Carlo's hole. I slumped on to my side. Marnier took the machetes out of the sack. There were two types. A long thin whippy one for grasses and a short, heavy, thick-bladed version for chopping through anything that was less strong than mild steel.

'Ah, Gio,' sighed Marnier, taking the thin-bladed machete and flicking it so that it walloped in the thickening air.

There was nothing in Gio's features that was translatable into any human emotion. His face was still, composed and huge. If Marnier wanted satisfaction he was going to have to work for it because Gio was as relaxed as if he was on a pool side. With one knee crooked and the other leg straight out, I realized what he was showing Marnier.

118

Most men faced with an ugly death would have had genitals contracted to a pebble cluster in lichen – Gio's sizeable penis slept along his thigh as peaceful as a sun-doped seal. Marnier, with measured disdain, flipped it up on to Gio's abdomen with the end of the blade. Gio lashed out with his leg and caught Marnier on the shin so that he slipped into one of the holes feet first with a splash.

'Felix,' said Marnier, calmly.

Felix helped Marnier out and then turned Gio over on to his front. Marnier, with two swift, practised slashes cut through Gio's Achilles tendons so that the calf muscles snapped up behind his knees. The gaslight hissed on. Christ knows what Gio was biting on, because there wasn't a peep from the man. Two more strokes from Marnier and the hamstrings were gone. Gio's head and shoulders came up off the floor. He bowed his back and lumps of muscle bunched between his scapulae. Deep divots appeared in the back of his arms where the triceps strained against the nylon rope around his wrists, but there was no give in it.

I knelt and went back on my heels and tried to breathe the *contrefilet* back down. Then I saw the state of my shirt, black with Carlo's blood. I tore it off and threw it into the half-filled grave and sent a stream of vomit in after it.

Marnier changed machetes. He put his foot down the middle of Gio's white, sweat-lined back and chopped him on either side of his neck with a heavy-handed knighthood that went down to the clavicle bone. Gio slumped forward. Nothing flowed through the arms any more. Marnier hacked through the ropes and Gio's hands slipped down the side of his buttocks. I crawled to the door.

'Where are you going?' asked Marnier.

'Out of here,' I said. 'This isn't my battle. It's between you and these people talking to each other in the only way you can.'

'Violence,' said Marnier, cigarette in the corner of his mouth, his hair unlocked from his scalp, mad-looking, 'the Esperanto of our century.'

'Right.'

'There's no other language for a man like this.'

'You're going to kill him in the end. Why not kill him now? Be civilized if you can be. Your wife –'

'Shut up about my wife!' he said, and brushed his hair back off his face as if that was enough. 'If I don't do this he will die knowing he's won.'

'And you get what?'

'I will have avenged my face,' he said, and motioned Felix to turn Gio back over.

'Gio did that to you?'

'And don't you believe that he didn't know what he was doing. He could have killed me too . . . quickly. He had a gun. But it satisfied him more to send me out into the world as an example of his work.'

I knew Marnier was right because Gio allowed a squiggle of emotion to play in his face. He looked up and smiled – nigh on beatific – a genius with his magnum opus.

'You lost, Jean-Luc,' I said. 'He knows you've got to kill him. And he knows as you push him into that hole that you're still going to be out there with the face he made for you. Now finish it, for Christ's sake, finish it.'

Marnier looked back at Gio and saw his grin. It triggered something in him – a raw, savage, primitive anger that I'd only ever seen on a man like Franconelli. He slashed at the man's genitals and reduced Gio's face to a ribboned skull. Then, without finishing him off he had Felix throw him in the hole and fill it in. He sat on the cement sacks and watched, smoking cigarette after cigarette while Felix brought the two holes up flush with the floor.

Marnier stamped the two graves down and told Felix to pile on more earth.

'What's the third hole for?' I asked.

'That was for you,' said Marnier, 'if you hadn't told me they were coming. You made the right choice, Bruce. I'm happy for you.'

'Did I? Are you?'

'You'll look into your child's eyes. Think of that.'

'But what will it see in them?'

'Maybe you'll have to learn to act.'

'And what happens when Franconelli comes to see me?'

'More acting.'

'What part?'

'Improvise.'

'With Franconelli?'

'We'll work on it,' he said. 'You must tell him that Gio and Carlo were never here. You gave them the information. They never showed.'

'What about their car? There must be a car.'

'We have to find it.'

'Are you going to dig a hole for that too?'

'Felix will put it in here once he's laid the concrete.'

'What do you think is going to be the first thing Franconelli will do when I tell him they didn't show?'

'He'll ask to see you, which is why – '

'He'll send some troops down here to find out what the hell happened.'

'Then he'll be showing his ignorance of Africa.'

'Don't tell me you rule this town too.'

'I have made some connections,' he said. 'But you are right. Let's find the car and I will teach you something.'

'I always hated school, Jean-Luc.'

'I'm sure, but what I'm going to teach you isn't just to get you through an exam.'

He headed for the door spouting Mina, Felix's language, the words peppered with French like *cailloutis* and *béton*. Felix didn't stop shovelling, filling in that third hole which would have been mine if Marnier hadn't insisted that confession out of me. I didn't know what to think any more. I was glad to be alive, a quick flicker of Heike in my brain confirmed that. But Marnier, the horror merchant, full now of nothing more than building instructions. And Franconelli with that head, those charcoal-smudged eye sockets, the gravestone teeth and atomic anger. The gunshots still whined in my ears and the violence of this night was already branded on me for life. Franconelli would be able to look in my eyes and see it all replayed before him like a private viewing.

'*Viens, viens,*' said Marnier. 'And stop thinking about it. The process of forgetting starts now.'

'Forgetting?' I said, smacking him on the shoulder, spinning him round. 'Forget *that*?'

I was showing him my hands and arms, my bare chest

and torso covered with Carlo's blood, even my trousers bloodied to the knees.

'It'll wash off.'

'You never saw *Macbeth*?'

'That's right,' he said. 'The brain is a different matter. Now let's find the car.'

I followed Marnier into the grasses. Looking at the back of his head I began to feel what Michel Charbonnier must have felt, that with this man you didn't know who you were any more. Anger, hate, fear, awe – were all part of the Marnier experience. But then there was more complicated stuff and I bridled to admit it. I found something to admire in him. He was fearless and tenacious. Even after what Gio had done to him he still had a will to live, a drive.

For a second I had something on Marnier. Something like the germ of a poem which if grasped could be got down true, but it ran away from me, scampered off into the night brain to confuse future dreams.

Chapter 12

Monday 22nd July, on the Grand-Popo/Cotonou road.

'You know what happens when you erase a computer's memory . . . I mean a diskette?' asked Marnier, his elbow out of the window of the car, his face looking straight down the rain-ruined tarmac which the Peugeot sucked in. He took my silence as a negative. 'You don't actually erase the information, the diskette is not wiped clean. All that happens is that the space is made available to be written over again with different information.'

'My brain is not a diskette. It doesn't matter how much you write over what I've got in here, I'm never going to lose it.'

'You've never rewritten a section of your life to make yourself more interesting?'

'We're not talking about bedding women again, are we?'

'The truth can be very dull. All those years spent in London in that shipping office.'

'How do you know about that?'

'You said.'

'No, I didn't.'

'Then how do I know?'

'Anyway,' I said, glancing at his impassive face, 'the "truth" we've just been through is not erasable.'

'Don't be difficult, please. Bruce. I'm trying to teach you something.'

'You're trying to change me.'

'I'm keeping you alive,' he said. 'Now, tell me, what could have been worse than last night?'

'I could have been in the third hole.'

'That would have solved this untidiness,' he said, laughing. 'But I'm serious. I want you to think of something that would make you want to lie more than anything else. What could have happened that would make you want to lie?'

'The fact that I'm hours away from sitting in front of Franconelli should be enough but, Christ . . .'

'You need something else to hold on to. A lie that's stronger than the truth.'

'Like what?'

'Something personal.'

'My life *is* personal . . . to me.'

'Think, man!' roared Marnier. 'Think of the woman pregnant with your child.'

'Heike.'

'Heike. Is there something that could have happened that you would never want to tell her?'

'The truth, for a start. What *actually* happened, Jean-Luc, that would be enough.'

'Something that would irrevocably affect your relationship with her if she found out.'

'It would do that too.'

'But *not* the truth,' said Marnier. 'What was the name of that waitress last night?'

'I don't know. I don't remember.'

'Ah, maybe we have something here,' he said, shifting

himself to more comfort. 'You are a natural liar when it comes to women. Now, what was her name?'

'Adèle.'

'Guilty already, you see? You liked her. I could see that. What's there to be guilty about? You didn't sleep with her. You paid for your beer. Ah, but you did buy her one.'

'Leave it alone. I don't want you messing with that stuff.'

'Would you have liked to sleep . . . ?'

'Forget it.'

'If you weren't involved with Heike?'

'But I am, so it . . .'

'What would Heike do if she found out?'

'There's nothing *to* find out.'

'But what would she do *if* she found out? If there had been something and she found out?'

I didn't say anything. Marnier tapped me on the shoulder with the back of his hand. I shrugged.

'Did you tell her where you were going last night?'

'Maybe Grand-Popo.'

'What?'

'That's exactly what I told her.'

'What sort of an answer is that?'

'That's what she said to me. I didn't know where we were going. You could have changed your plans.'

'Well,' said Marnier, 'if I was a woman I'd be suspicious.'

'We have an agreement not to talk about my work. She doesn't like the types I have to mix with.'

'I'm not surprised if they're people like Franconelli.'

'Or you.'

The road passed underneath us louder than tearing cardboard.

'Do you and Heike have a good . . . have good sex with each other?'

'Private, Jean-Luc.'

'I think you do. That's my guess.'

'Still private, Jean-Luc. Now back off.'

'Not so good at talking about things. Not so good, perhaps, at being honest, for instance. But fucking . . . yes, I think so.'

'Who are you to talk to me about honesty?'

'I won't let you change the subject, Bruce. This is about sex. You and Heike have good sex. So what would happen if she found out you were fucking somebody else?'

'Now?' I asked, getting bloody mad with Marnier.

'Yes, in her state, if that was what you meant?'

I regripped the steering wheel tighter.

'I think we've found our lie,' said Marnier. 'The only one bigger than the truth. Now tell me what happened with Adèle from the moment you went back to the bar for that drink together.'

'I'm not going to play this game.'

'Then you will die,' he said. 'You must learn to live with your choice, Bruce. If you want to stay alive you are going to have to relive last night as a complete and totally believable lie. The only way you're going to be able to do that is to tell me everything as you saw it and as it remained in your head to come back to you in all that time we spend in Africa waiting. Now tell me. Everything. I want every detail down to the size of her nipples, the colour of her pubic hair, the beauty of her labial lips and the tightness of her ass. Go!'

'I don't know about this, Jean-Luc,' I said. 'Isn't this just a little bit . . . ?'

'Don't think, just tell me what happened.'

'I went back to the bar . . .'

'My mistake,' said Marnier. 'Take it from when we left the bar.'

I told him about driving to the house, what the house looked like, what was in the house, how we drank whisky until a car arrived.

'We didn't drink whisky . . . that was later. What did we talk about?'

'Nothing. Marnier dozed until the car arrived.'

'Tell me about the car.'

'I don't remember.'

'What plates?'

'Togolese.'

'Colour?'

'Black.'

'Model?'

'Peugeot 505.'

'You see, it's not so difficult if you play.'

'The driver got out of the car and Felix . . .'

'No Felix.'

'The driver and I lifted a trunk out of the boot.'

'Where did you put it?'

'In the boot of my car.'

'No, in the house. It's gold. I'm not going to let you drive around Grand-Popo with nearly a million dollars' worth of gold in the back.'

'We put it in the house. It was very heavy.'

128

'Did Marnier tell you what was in it?'

'Gold. Ashante gold bought in Togo from illegal mining operations.'

'How much was there?'

'Nearly a million dollars' worth.'

'No. What do you know about gold?'

'It's yellow, expensive and heavy.'

'So you can't tell the difference between a million and five million,' he said.

'The trunk must have weighed seventy kilos. More than a bag of cement.'

'Then what?'

'Marnier gave the driver a thousand CFA.'

'Five thousand, I'm not cheap.'

'The driver left. Marnier and I drank whisky in the front room . . . Ballantines.'

'What did you talk about?'

'A woman called Gifty.'

'That was in the restaurant.'

'I told him I was going to be a father. He told me about his children who he doesn't see any more. We talked about unconditional love.'

'Don't talk to Franconelli about unconditional love.'

'Why not?'

'It's not his line of sensibility. He's a football man.'

'Franconelli's wife died in a truck crash, his daughter died of malaria. He might be ruthless but he's . . .'

'Sentimental too . . . like me.'

'So we talked about unconditional love, about his wife, his kids and how she turned them against him because he was a man of *violence*.'

'*Calmes-toi.*'

'We talked about my father, deathbed advice, how the English don't know anything about women and the French do.'

'We do. I think we do.'

'We talked about acting.'

'No, you didn't. Franconelli is not subtle. You'll only set him thinking.'

'Then he said he was tired. I told him I'd go back to the bar. He asked me if it was the waitress. I said no. Then I went and had the drink with the waitress. She was English, called Adèle. She had red hair, corkscrew ringlets, freckles on her face and the top of her breasts, green eyes.'

'You see?' said Marnier. 'I know you.'

'She was wearing a purple silk shirt, no bra, cut-off denims, leather sandals. She was sitting at a table when I arrived, with a beer and a cigarette watching some Australians playing with petrol bombs in a beach bonfire. I ordered a beer and watched with her until the Australians got bored and went in to start the disco. We talked about England. Not much. She'd been travelling for more than a year and I haven't seen the place for more than five. We talked about crossing the Sahara, the space out there, about time . . .'

'Don't talk too much shit, Bruce. Franconelli's like any guy. He wants the juice.'

'This is important. We talked about the ground.'

'The *ground. Vraiment les anglais.* It's a miracle you do it any more.'

'We talked about the ground. The African ground. How the earth has its own pulse . . .'

'*Ça c'est bon,*' said Marnier. 'I can see where you're going now.'

'Then we bought a couple of bottles of beer and walked down the beach. A long walk beyond the hotel and campsite until it was just the sea and the palm trees. When it was completely dark we took our clothes off and swam in the sea. Then we started playing and we were holding on to each other and then we were kissing.'

'You don't like Hemingway, do you?'

'He's OK.'

'I don't want any of this "the earth moved" shit. I want everything. And when you've had her on the beach I want you to take her back to her room and have her again . . . with the light on so I can see everything clearly. I want those pictures clear in my head.'

'Whose lie is this, Jean-Luc?'

'Please.'

'We got out of the water . . .'

'I just want to be sure, Bruce, that you will be doing it more than once. Because you know how it is with a new woman, you don't just fall asleep after the first time. You do it again and again and again until you can't . . .'

'*Calmes-toi, Jean-Luc.*'

He settled back down and closed his eyes.

'*Je suis calme, maintenant.*'

I told Marnier how we came out of the sea locked together, how I'd fallen and she'd got astride me and reached behind her and taken hold of my penis and slotted it into her. Then she hadn't moved, only her nipples, swollen to raspberries, trembled. She'd held herself above me with just the head of my penis inside her incredible warm wetness until I was shouting at

131

her. Then she'd slammed herself down time and again, her cool buttocks slapping my thighs, her pubis grinding into mine, until we both came loud enough to turn heads in the campsite.

'Excellent,' said Marnier, 'absolutely excellent.'

He talked me through every scene, milking each one for every detail until I was squirming. But by the end I believed that we'd seen the storm coming, grabbed our clothes and run up the beach to the small room she'd taken in the village and we'd continued having each other until we reached a brain-numbing, raw-genitaled standstill. I knew I believed all this because, as Jean-Luc insisted on the refinements to each scene, I felt a terrible weight settling on me, in fact not a weight, just the opposite, an emptiness. The emptiness of infidelity, of guilt, of self-disgust, of humiliation.

'Then,' said Marnier, after I'd fallen silent, having turned in a performance that would have left an Olympic athlete slack-jawed and trembling.

'Then nothing,' I said.

'Nothing?'

'Nothing else happened.'

'But there has to be something. There has to be that something extra. That new . . . *frisson* to recharge your . . .'

'It's finished, Jean-Luc, nothing else happened.'

'You've left out one detail.'

'I don't think so.'

'You've told me everything except . . .'

'There's nothing left to tell.'

'Except . . . your cock. How big is your cock?'

'Piss off, Jean-Luc,' I said, the disgust strong as the taste of shit in my mouth.

132

'No. It's important. It's the only thing left.'

I could tell he wasn't going to let it go.

'Not as big as those guys in the blue movies.'

'But they are impossible. They are freaks.'

'Normal size, Jean-Luc. Normal size.'

His eyes opened. The good one nearest me was brim full.

'What is normal size?' he asked.

Chapter 13

We drove into Cotonou's mobile phone footprint at around midday. Marnier called Carole and told her to bring a car to the Hotel Aledjo, organize a room. We got caught in lunchtime traffic coming across the bridge and arrived at the hotel at 1.30 p.m. Carole had taken a bungalow right out down by the sea, away from inquisitive eyes, and, being French, she'd arranged for some food and drink.

It was Carole and I who hefted the trunk out of my boot into hers and she made light work of it. All that gym time paying off for fifteen seconds. I wouldn't have minded talking to her, making some kind of connection, but I had no vocabulary for it, and her body language was coming across in Sanskrit, stuff, no doubt, she'd learnt from Marnier and his readings of the Upanishads and his greatest poet of the twentieth century.

We went back into the room and found Marnier cracking crab claws and slugging back the cold Chablis that sat in a bucket at his feet, one bottle already upside down in the melting ice. Carole sat by his side and I opposite to watch her give a passable rendition of 'pretty French housewife welcomes home the bacon bringer'. This involved a little bit of shoulder stroking, some head kissing and the occasional morsel feeding. Marnier rewarded her with a constant view of the mash of sea-

134

food revolving in his mouth. I didn't eat so that I could put my full concentration into some Chablis drinking and I was still chugging it back while Marnier was sucking up thimbles of tar poured from a cafetière that never left Carole's hand. The Marniers' was an ordered household.

'You owe me two hundred and fifty thousand CFA,' I said.

'Of course,' he said, closing his eyes at Carole, who produced an envelope and slid it across to me. I pocketed it. Marnier dug in his trousers and came up with a lump of something small and dirty which he laid in front of me.

'A bonus,' he said, 'for a good night's work.'

It weighed a good half pound.

'Why should you want to give me a couple of thousand dollars' worth of gold?'

'I told you. I'm not cheap. And . . . you made your choice. One that I'm glad you made, but it will cost you. This, I hope, will go some way to covering those expenses.'

'Then you *are* being cheap,' I said, getting up from the table, leaving the lump.

'Don't be like that,' he said. 'You're well prepared.'

'What if I tell Franconelli what really happened? That you brutally murdered his two men and . . .'

'If you think that's a risk worth taking . . .' He trailed off. 'It's not me sitting in front of Franconelli telling him that.'

'It won't be me either. I'm not going to *see* Franconelli.'

'You will. I can assure you of that. He will demand it.'

'I won't go.'

'Don't be a kid about this. He'll make you go.'

'He hasn't been able to make *you* go.'

'I'm not so vulnerable. I keep moving. I'm used to it.'

'What did you do to Franconelli that he had to send Gio to . . . rearrange you like that?'

Marnier was instantly furious.

'Yes, exactly my point. What crime did I commit to deserve such a penalty? Did I kill his wife? Did I thin his daughter's blood with malaria? No. None of these things. I merely spat in his food. Not what you would call a serious offence.'

'Depends how much he liked what he was eating.'

Carole stroked Jean-Luc back down from the towering inferno.

'*Calmes-toi, chéri, calmes-toi.*'

'You did more than gob in his *stracciatella*, Jean-Luc. Come on. Let's have it.'

'All I did was a little churning.'

'Buttering your own bread, not his.'

'It was small change. All local currency.'

'And you did some local investment for him up and down the coast?'

'I always gave him a good return.'

'And you turned his money round for your own account.'

'*C'est normale.*'

'How did he catch you?'

'He asked for his money back. It was otherwise engaged in tyres in Ghana at the time. Tyres weren't moving.'

'Just tyres?'

'There were other things.'

'How much was out?'

'Half a million.'

'Half a million what?' I asked. 'Not cedis. He wouldn't have done that to you for a few hundred quid.'

'Dollars. Half a million dollars.'

'That's not spit, Jean-Luc,' I said. 'How long was it out?'

He didn't reply. I looked at him hard and saw something at the back of his dark little peepers.

'You're lying.'

'That's right,' he said. 'You'd never have known if I hadn't given it away.'

'There's not much point talking to you, is there?'

'Then ask Franconelli. He'll tell you. He's a man of *honour*.'

'Looks as if I'll have to.'

'And when you do,' said Marnier, 'watch him. Look into his eyes. See if you can see *his* lies. He's not as good as me, he never had the training, but he's better than Carole. I always know when she's lying. She always looks up into her head to select the lie. Useless. But I'm grateful for it.'

'Perhaps she has other talents which she's more proud of.'

'She's a talented manipulator. Women are. Do you think a man is capable of creating an intolerable atmosphere in the home? No. But lying. Men lie for a living.'

'Speak for yourself.'

'Now, M. Medway, don't come talking to me in your pristine white communion gown. You would have had me killed if I hadn't squeezed the truth out of you.'

'You knew they were coming. You didn't need me to tell you.'

'A matter of intelligence, greatly lacking in the Italians.'

'How *did* you know?'

'Charbonnier has girls who work for him out of La Verdure. The slap on that Nigerian girl's leg still hadn't gone down the day after.'

I looked down at the lump of gold on the table.

'Take it,' said Marnier.

'Maybe you should be using this to get your face fixed up.'

'My face has gone. I don't want a rebuilt face. I want my own, not some surgeon's idea. And anyway, what can I use it for now?'

I walked to the door, leaving the gold.

'Something to remember about your night with Adèle,' he said.

'There *was* no night with Adèle.'

'*That* is a bad sign, Bruce. You must believe me that for Franconelli to believe you ... you must believe it yourself. And if you are to believe it yourself, then others close to you must believe it of you too.'

'What the hell is that supposed to mean?' I said, the booze tanking up the anger quicker than usual.

'You've been unfaithful, remember that.'

I went back to the table and leaned over it to within an inch of Marnier's ghastly face.

'This isn't *au revoir*, Jean-Luc. This is goodbye. That's *adieu* to you because you need His help more than any-one I know.'

138

'I think you'll find it's *au revoir*, Bruce.'

I pushed myself off the table.

'You need me,' he said.

I walked to the door and opened it.

'You're going to need that gold too,' he said.

I left.

'Don't forget to call the Hotel de la Plage,' he shouted after me.

I went back to the office and called the Hotel de la Plage and asked for Carlo and Gio. I was told they'd checked out the day before. I sounded surprised, left a message and my name and number in case they returned. Another round of lying had begun.

The thought of phoning Franconelli brought me out in a cold sweat, so I went back home and caught up on some sleep. Terrible sleep. Deep, traumatic sleep where dreams came thick and fast and combined hideously graphic sex with faceless people and, of course, with blood. In the final moments of this hell ride I found myself rutting madly with a nobody who I knew was Adèle, the sand of the beach smoothing my knees as I held the hips of her raised behind before me. We were snorting, like pigs troughing, and when I withdrew, the shaft of my penis was a bloodied stump. I woke with a shout, rolling and yawing in the sweat-drenched sheets and pillows.

It was dark. I was not alone in the room. Heike's smell was there. Her silhouette, vague through the mosquito netting, held a glass of water.

'You should drink this,' she said.

'Christ,' I said, wringing the whimper out of my voice. 'What time is it?'

'Ten o'clock. You've been wrestling with yourself since I got back a couple of hours ago. The noise you were making I thought you had a woman in here.'

There came a nanosecond of frost-brittled silence.

'Six hours' sleep,' I said. 'And I'm bloody exhausted.'

Heike came in under the net. I drank the water and sank back.

'You stink of booze.'

'The client bought me lunch.'

'The gout's going to come back on you again and I'm not going to have any sympathy.'

'I don't remember much the last time,' I said, a little more brutal than I intended.

She hardened on me but not for long. She ran a hand through my sodden hair.

'Ugh, is that sweat?'

'I think it might be Chablis, or a distilled version of it.'

'You've got to stop this . . .'

'Don't start, Mrs Clean.'

'Ms Clean. It's still Ms Clean.'

'Well, I can recall a few sessions Ms Clean has had in her time. I'm sure you could have got on a national team. The German one, maybe. Not the British.'

'Don't be so brutish.'

'What was that?'

'Brutish. Not British. I said don't be so brutish.'

'OK, I won't be,' I said. 'Neither of those things.'

'You haven't asked me how I've been.'

I felt stabbed by that, but rode it out and thought for one clear moment I might tell her the whole thing. Vomit it into her lap and lie back feeling clean and empty of the trouble. But I couldn't do it. Not to her.

140

'Did you hear me, Bruce?'

'How's it been?' I said, rubbing her tummy, my sweaty hands catching on her skirt material, awkward.

'We're fine,' she said, and stood up.

She told me to take a shower and left the room.

I stripped and got under the shower and washed myself as clean as I could without flaying myself with the pumice. I stayed under, comforted by the rush of water. Heike came into the bathroom. I heard her clothes drop to the floor.

Something was missing.

The sound of her skirt falling, the flutter of her knickers down her slim legs and I'd get the prickling at the base of my spine, the weakening tingle in my groin as the blood started thumping down there. There was nothing. I was as flaccid as shop-tired celery. I faced the wall as she came in under the shower. I felt her breasts on my back, the nipples hard. She ran her hands up the back of my thighs, over my buttocks, over my hips.

I was in a panic. The automatic desire had gone. By now there should have been some roaring down there, the bellowing of a provoked bull sea lion with mating rights. Her fingers found me and I felt them question what they'd found. She turned me round and dropped to her knees, running her hands up my stomach, down my loins. Still nothing. She gripped my buttocks and the darting, flickering flame of her tongue gave me the first squirm of desire, the first draining moment.

I felt saved. Guilty but saved.

I pulled her up and she excited me further by refusing. Then she stood. She was ready and trembling, her throat and cheeks flushed as usual. Another stab of guilt.

I lifted her off her feet, pushing her back against the wall, and eased into her. I thought I was ready now, thought I was back to my good self and went to it, but overkeen and frenzied so that I shot my bolt weakly and fizzled out to nothing. I dropped my head on to her shoulder and found myself looking at the vortex of water twisting down the plug hole. I let her down and whispered a lame 'sorry' in her ear. She said nothing.

I got out. She stayed in and washed herself off. I dried myself, looking at her fogged form in the steam beyond the shower curtain.

'Bruce?' she asked, and I felt a bad question coming. 'Bagado called. He left a message on the answering machine while you were asleep.'

I was disappointed not to get the question. Sorry not to get a more intimate enquiry.

'Did you hear me?' she asked.

'I heard you,' I said, and lost her in the mist.

I called Bagado, who sounded burnt out, frayed at the edges. He wanted to speak to me, it had to be tonight and it had to be private. I said I'd be in the office in half an hour.

Chapter 14

I was examining a wood knot through the bottom of a whisky glass and contemplating the nature of infidelity, infidelity of the mind. Wasn't there a president of the United States who said: 'I've committed adultery many times in my mind but never in my body'? That must have cheered the First Lady no end. I had to amuse myself with this kind of thought to prevent the seepage of unhappiness, to try and cling on to that moment after Heike had told me she was pregnant.

Bagado barged into the office shortly after 11 p.m. He was clenched in his mac and stood in front of me, his forehead ridged and troughed with a deeper geological worry.

'José-Marie is missing,' he said.

'Your daughter, José-Marie?'

'The nine-year-old. She's missing.'

'Since when?'

'Since four o'clock this afternoon. She didn't come back from school,' he said, knots tightening in his throat, the man unable to swallow, having to stroke his Adam's apple to get the lump down.

'Is this . . . ?' I started. 'Look, you'd better sit down, old man. Get this out right. I'll start work on it now. Don't worry. But just take a seat for the moment.'

'I can't sit,' he said, and began pacing the room. 'Since

143

we found the girl on the sand bar we've had reports of two other girls who've gone missing. A seven-year-old and a six-year-old . . . again both schoolgirls, we think picked up on their way home. José-Marie is the third. I think that makes it eight in total. One dead, seven missing.'

'Did you get anything from the autopsy on the girl off the sand bar?'

'I haven't seen the report, if that's what you mean. I'm picking up crumbs from anybody prepared to drop them. I saw for myself that the flesh was eaten away from the underside of her forearms, the palms of her hands and around her knees.'

'What does that mean?'

'I think she climbed a wall topped with broken glass. The fish did the rest.'

'Any signs of abuse?'

'She'd been caned across the back and buttocks. I suspect to show the others that trying to escape would not be tolerated.'

'Sexual abuse?'

'No, thank God for that very small mercy.'

'Cause of death?'

'Strangulation.'

'What with?'

'Bare hands.'

'Jesus Christ,' I said. 'Do you think they beat her and strangled her in front of the others?'

Bagado stood in the middle of the room and pinched the bridge of his nose, his eyes screwed tight to block out the horror.

'I don't know,' he agonized.

'Have you spoken to the parents?'

'I'm not on the investigation team. I have been told to stay away from it.'

'Bondougou?'

'Still with a very close personal interest.'

'Why haven't the parents been storming the police station?'

'They have. They sent the riot police out to break them up.'

'What does that say to you?'

'Powerful people.'

'Why do you think they're picking exclusively on schoolgirls? I mean, these are kids who will be missed. There must be plenty of street girls who could be taken . . .'

'I think, Bruce,' said Bagado, a tortured plexus on the other side of the desk, 'I think it's because they're more likely to have their virginity intact. You know the fear of AIDS is very great, but the need for sex in Africa, as you've seen with Moses, is even greater. Politicians, businessmen, aach! . . . You know how it is, Bruce.'

'*La culture Africaine.*'

'And now it's a dangerous culture.'

'You don't think these girls are going to be exported?'

'I have no idea. I cannot get involved. I cannot even get my resignation accepted. I'm locked in.'

'Drink this,' I said, and filled a glass for him. 'It'll help you think because if I'm going to help you you've got to give me everything you've got and all the direction you can think of.'

Bagado tipped the glass back. I refilled my own and his. Bagado sat down, retreated into his mac and let the whisky do the work it knew best. I started to ask questions but Bagado held up his hand.

Now *I* wanted to talk. Talking was like walking for the mind. I didn't have to think. When silence yawned the horrors started, the stitches of old wounds split, the pus leaked and the gangrenous stench of unhappiness flared my nostrils.

'Bondougou's purpose,' said Bagado, just as I'd decided that drinking was as good as talking for the mind, 'is not just to suppress this investigation and hundreds of others because of the bribes he receives for doing so. Although the money is an important factor, there's something else that's pushing him.'

'He's just a bad-ass, Bagado.'

'He wants to break me, Bruce. He wants to break me as a human being.'

I started in again but Bagado backed me off with his hand.

'This is not . . . and I've thought about it very carefully . . . This is not my own paranoia. When I first lost my job some years ago, or rather, when Bondougou sacked me, for telling the media about the unpleasant death of that young Frenchwoman, he knew that this should have made my life very difficult. I survived through your charity, leaving the Cotonou scene for a while to do that job in the Ivory Coast and then more work from you and, of course, Heike.'

'Heike?'

'She has been very generous too. So you see, he knows that he can't break me financially. So what does he do? What is the worst that he can do?'

'Break you professionally.'

146

'Yes. But this isn't just a professional's job. In the best policemen, as my old English detective friend used to say, there is a moral drive.'

'The good versus evil stuff.'

'Exactly. So what's the worst that Bondougou can do? The worst is that he can embrace me. Bring me back into the fold and then render me useless to watch the crusade trampled underfoot . . . under the feet of his corruption. And *you* know . . . I know, because you saw it on the *Kluezbork II* the other day . . . *you* know he is succeeding. These girls disappearing and now my daughter. This is breaking me, Bruce. I can feel myself cracking.'

He sat and reached his hand across the table. I took it. It was fragile, bony, each joint a sharp but tender pressure in my palm. He brought his other hand round and gripped the meat of my shoulder. He stared into my face with the eyes of a man who knew he was falling.

'You're still young and strong. Bruce. I'm getting to be an old man with all this. You have to help me but I'm not sure how much I can help you. I'm confused. I've lost that ability for straight, clean thought. It's as if the wiring's burnt out. I can only get so far . . . and then I think of José-Marie. I've stopped being a policeman. Bondougou,' he said to himself, letting me go, walking off around the room again, 'Bondougou is winning.'

'Are you telling me that you think that Bondougou was responsible for having José-Marie lifted?'

He stopped by to sweep up the glass and dash the contents down his throat, then he took two strides and hurled the glass against the wall with such force that

147

diamonds of it rebounded and skittered under the desk.

'That,' he said, 'is the extent of my powerlessness. Bagado, the great detective brain, is reduced to throwing glasses.'

He brushed his hand across the larger and whiter dusting he had in the hair on the top of his head.

'I've been walking in the Jonquet,' he said, setting off again, crunching through the glass, 'and I heard some Americans talking. Peace Corps workers. They are under pressure. The US government is cutting spending. You know how Americans can talk so that you wonder whether it's English. These two were throwing up various situations: "win-win" and "lose-win". At the time these things meant nothing to me. But now I see it. I am in a lose-lose.'

'Lose-lose?'

'You know that time we were heading north and I told you that Bondougou had recalled me to the force ... split us up? You told me not to go. You said I wouldn't just end up on the shit heap this time. I wouldn't just get fired. You were right. I underestimated your powers of perception.'

'Part of the problem with being a good man is that it makes you predictable. Somebody said that to *me* once.'

'He's turning me ... turning me into something I couldn't bear to be.'

Bagado opened the door, leaned his arm up against it.

'When I said that about you not just getting fired, Bagado, I don't think I was perceiving anything. I just didn't want you to go. You've been important to me and since you've gone there's been some falling apart.'

'I know,' he said. 'I've seen it. Heike and I have talked. We've talked since she told you what I thought of you. She probably shouldn't have done that, but I understand why she did. I also know you're a good man and I know you will do the very best for me.'

'I will, Bagado. But what's this lose-lose business about?'

He sighed and I thought he might be about to tell me, but he lost his energy. The talk just went out of him and without a word he left. I went to the door, but he was off and away and down the stairs. I crunched out on to the balcony in time to see his shrinking frame melt into the shadows.

'I know someone in the Jonquet, Bagado,' I shouted down to him. 'He'll be able to help. I'll find her.'

He waved at me without turning. He reached the streetlighting on Sekou Touré, looked left, turned right and was gone.

Chapter 15

I slumped back into my chair. Lose-lose. Lose-lose. I'd never seen Bagado so low, so helpless, so stifled. That quality about him, that quality of goodness had dimmed to a candle flicker in an ocean. His children were everything. What had he said to me that first time? More children than trousers, that was the way to be. But lose-lose . . . what did that mean?

I stabbed the 'play' button on the answering machine, just to jog myself out of the lose-lose groove and got message after message from Bagado searching for me. Then a different voice. No name but an unmistakable inflection.

'Call me.'

There was only one voice that could turn my bowels to water with a single amoebic order. Franconelli. It was 11.30 p.m. Too late. They were an hour ahead. It wouldn't wash. I had to call him. Tomorrow would be suspiciously late. I dialled the number and got no reply for a long time until an answering machine kicked in. I left a message, thought I was home free but someone tore the phone off the hook and cut the tape.

'Wait.'

Some brutal Italian followed and footsteps retreated. Seconds ticked into minutes, expensive minutes. I fingered the 'fast forward' button, wanting to zip myself

150

through this patch of time, get out the other side of the nastiness. Then the phone was picked up.

'Franconelli.'

'Bruce Medway,' I said, and felt the tension wrap round my throat. 'What happened?'

It came out as a shout, overcompensating. I didn't want to croak it. The static on the line roared back.

'What happened?' asked Franconelli, as if he hadn't heard me ask it first.

'What happened to Carlo and Gio? We had an arrangement. I organized a meeting with our friend. They didn't turn up. I called the Hotel de la Plage when I got back. They checked out yesterday. So what happened?'

More static. Voices in the ether squabbled.

'You'd better come to Lagos,' he said. 'Explain it to me.'

'I can explain it now. I went out of my way to set this thing up for them. I kept them fully informed about where we were going. I admit I didn't see them on the day. I wasn't aware of being followed but when I tried to tell Carlo that he had to be discreet he gave me some shit about not telling him how to do his job, so I assumed he was out there. I did the job that was asked of me by our friend. I wait. Nothing happens. Carlo and Gio don't show up. In the morning we leave. I get back to Cotonou for lunch. I call the hotel. Nothing, *nada, rien du tout*. I get some sleep and I've been trying to call you for the last hour. So that's why I'm asking what happened. You don't have to tell me. I don't need to know. I just want you to be sure that I kept up my end of the deal.'

'Come to Lagos.'

151

'When?'

'Now.'

'I can't.'

'You can.'

'I've got some important work to do . . . for a friend of mine. His daughter . . .'

'*This* is the most important thing.'

'Does this mean you don't know what's happened to Gio and Carlo?'

'You come to Lagos now and make everything clear.'

'I've told you. I'm not being difficult but I can't come right now, not immediately.'

'No, Bruce. You will come now.'

'I *will* come, but not yet.'

'Now, you *stronzzo*, you will come NOW!' he roared down the line.

'Mr Franconelli . . .'

The line went dead. I put the phone down slowly. Round One. He was going to be back with something bigger, have me hauled off the street, maybe, and taken to Lagos in a boot. Lose some weight that way. Or perhaps he'd get Bondougou to do it. We'd see.

I went out on the street and stopped one of the stream of *taxi motos* in the sodium night light. He took me to the Jonquet and the bar L'Ouistiti.

The girls were still there in their red cave. They bristled and shimmered as I walked in, all tongues and eye contact. I strode through and past the moribund guard into Charbonnier's inner sanctum. I buzzed myself in, the accountant giving me the swivel eye over his shoulder, and walked straight into the usual incense. Michel was sitting with his shins up against the edge of the desk, his joint held in prayer. I took the spliff off him and dowsed it in the tyre.

'Are you moving in?' he asked, fitting his legs under the table. 'Marnier's new boy.'

'Is this his top job?'

He blinked at that, trying to compute whether he'd had enough toke to get over that depressing little thought.

'I want to ask you something,' I said.

'Me?'

'That's why I'm taking it slowly, because I know how long you need to filter stuff through that sludge you've got between your ears.'

'You know I don't talk about Marnier.'

'This isn't about Marnier. It's your other specialist subject. Sex.'

'You want some? You didn't have to come this far. It's all at the front door.'

'What if I wanted you to supply me with a virgin?'

He laughed.

'They're all virgins . . .'

I leaned over the desk and smacked him with the open palm of my hand across the side of his head hard enough so that he had to put a hand out to stop himself falling to the floor. He came back up looking more poisonous than a coral snake and I smacked him on the other side of his head, rocking him the other way. He wasn't so quick to come back up.

'I can do this all night,' I said.

'OK, OK, OK,' he said. 'You didn't say it was urgent.'

'Do you think I'd come into your burrow if it wasn't?'

'*Comment?*' he asked holding his head in his hands,

the bells ringing in his ears all the way from Chartres.

'Where can I find a virgin? *Une vraie vierge, Michel.* None of your shop-soiled goods.'

'You don't look the type.'

'What is the type?'

'There are all types . . . but you don't have the look.'

'Maybe it's not for me.'

'You'll have to come back later.'

'Give me the name of the supplier and tell me where I can find him.'

'*Impossible.*'

I hit him three times, bounced him back and forth like the rubber man in the rage room. His eyes went. His ears were red and throbbing. The full carillon ringing in his bonce. I sat down and oozed some more threat at him. He tore off an old sheet from his desk calendar and wrote the name Wilfred Agbabu on the back.

'Nigerian?'

'An Igbo.'

'Where?'

'He has a *friperie* business across the other side of Sekou Touré and a warehouse up north of Dan Tokpa where he rebales the clothes.'

'Where would he be now?'

'The bars.'

'Which?'

'Work your way through the Jonquet, I don't know.'

By 4.30 a.m. I looked and felt like a tranche of the stinking, black accumulation in the gutters and storm drains of the city. It hadn't rained but the pressure had built and the jauntiness had gone out of the whores' footwork. The dim yellow interiors of the bars down

Rue des Cheminots barely lit the bruised purple night. Only God and the lucky voyeur knew what was going on out here.

I'd let 7000 CFA slip through my fingers trying to find Agbabu, but he was either very elusive or more likely a phantom. I thought I'd give it one last round, telling myself this was for José-Marie while the big emptiness in my guts tut-tutted that I just didn't want to go home.

I trudged the bars. Names flitted, amalgamated. A la Tienne, La Grande Joie, Bar Ravi, Avec Entrain. All exhorted fun, but the faces on the street weren't buying it or had bought too much of it. I drifted into a place called the Jouet Doux and got hit on the way in by 100 kilos of white man on the way out. I staggered back on to the pavement with my new friend hanging off my neck. I shook him off and he came at me, fists flailing, and I didn't have to reach too deep to find the ugliness to hit him hard in the flab he had over his liver. He went down on all fours, gasping, muttering to himself in German.

'This isn't the place to get fighty,' I said, not giving a damn whether he understood. 'Unless you like long, hot nights in a malarial stink hole. There's a wagon up the street full of policemen waiting for your kind of custom.'

'*Engländer?*' he asked, looking up, passing a dog-sized tongue over his lips.

'I can't say that in German. You'll have to live with the English version,' I said, and moved off.

'Wait,' he said, and got himself up. I kept moving. 'Wait.'

He came alongside and hooked a hand around my elbow. I turned and shrugged it off. He was a short, stocky guy who had to look up a long way to anyone. He passed a hand through his jagged hair and patted his face with a handkerchief. He wasn't drunk.

'What are you looking for?' he asked.

'What do you mean, *what*?'

'Who then?'

'And who are you?'

'Someone with experience.'

'The experience to come horizontally out of a bar?'

'Yes, well, I went too far. They're not as understanding as they are in Thailand, don't you think?'

I twigged it then. A sex punter. I shuddered. Now I really was getting down and dirty, in the street mulch with the paedophiles and necrophiles, the sodomites and catamites, the flagellators and fustigators . . . all of us having fun.

'I'm looking for somebody.'

'We're all looking for somebody,' he said. 'But who for what?'

'Agbabu. Wilfred Agbabu.'

'What does he do?'

'He supplies virgins.'

'Ah, yes-s-s,' he said, his eyes alight with possibility.

'You know him?'

'No. But I understand the problem. Myself, I avoid all that. No exchange of bodily fluids.'

'Is that your motto?'

'I'm sorry?'

'Nothing,' I said. 'Good night.'

'Wait, don't be so . . .' He didn't finish. 'Have you

156

tried the L'Ouistiti. There's a Frenchman there. He's very knowledgeable.'

I gave him a long steady look.

'It's a bar up there . . .'

'I know it,' I said.

'I'm sorry. That's all I know, but . . .'

'But what?'

His damp handkerchief slowed on his cheek and he fixed me with a gleaming eye. I realized he was going to share one of his proclivities with me.

'You wouldn't beat me up, would you?' he asked, balling his little fist.

'I'm saving myself for somebody else,' I said, and barged past him.

Michel's hophead guard had been replaced by two more responsible-looking individuals. I backed out and went next door to a bar called La Gloire du Matin and paid a thousand CFA to get myself into the toilet where I'd have paid five grand to get out. I found a back door down the corridor from the stinking cubicles and beyond it a beaten earth courtyard with a solitary, diseased tree, some broken furniture and three high mud walls. I got up on to the wall via the tree and dropped down into the L'Ouistiti's back yard.

Through a crack in the back door I could see the anteroom to Michel's office was empty. The light was still on behind the blinds at Michel's window. The man was there in his customary position, plimsolled feet up on the desk, spliff in hand, but he was not alone.

Marnier's claw was wrapped around a tumbler. They were talking to each other in rapid French with southern accents. Michel was reliving my visit, showing

157

Marnier the *paf, paf, paf* of the beating he'd had to take. Marnier flicked questions at him. Agbabu didn't exist but somebody like him did. Michel didn't give Marnier a name, the man not interested in that.

A different opportunity was presenting itself. A chance to follow Marnier to one of his Cotonou hideaways. Something that might help me in my Franconelli negotiations. I was torn between getting ready to follow him and listening in some more to see how interested Marnier was in my sudden and inexplicable requirements. But then he threw back his drink and stood up and I got up and over the wall, through La Gloire du Matin and snapped up the first *taxi moto* I could find.

Marnier was on the same kind of transport, his chauffeur wearing the yellow numbered jacket of a licensed *taxi moto* driver. I noted the number. The streets were too empty for tailing and I was too tired. I followed as far as the Nouveau Pont and saw him turn left up into the northern part of Akpakpa.

I thought about going back to L'Ouistiti to thump the toke-bag for being so smart, but I'd used up my reserve tank of ugliness and anyway, the sky was a flamingo-pink in the east and the first fishermen were paddling out on to the dark lagoon. There was a moment's peace up there on the apex of the bridge, a moment when the air was nearly fresh with a saltine zest coming in from the sea. Then the traffic cleared its throat, the gears of the day ground through the synchromesh and the monoxide gargle began again.

Chapter 16

Tuesday 23rd July, Cotonou.

'Where have you been, for Christ's sake?' asked Heike, whipping back the shower curtain on me, standing there in her T-shirt and knickers, a fist in her side and a rash of anger going up her neck, dark rings around her eyes.

'Out and about,' I said, turning my back on her. 'Getting a bit too close to street level even for my liking.'

'It's six in the morning. What the hell have you been doing all night?'

'Is that rhetorical or do you want to know?'

'I want to know. I want to know what's so important that you can't spend ten seconds to call me.'

'José-Marie . . .'

'José-Marie? Who's she?'

'Bagado's nine-year-old daughter, remember?'

'Well, thank Christ for that. I didn't think even you would do that to me.'

'What?'

'Will you *look* at me while we do this?'

I turned. Heike reached in and cut the shower.

'Do what?' I asked, Heike still a blur in my water-filled eyes.

'That you'd give me something like that full in the face with your backside turned to me.'

'Like what?'

'Do what? Like what? What is this?'

'You tell me.'

'I thought you were off with somebody else.'

'Who?'

'Another woman, *Bruce*.'

'I just told you José-Marie is Bagado's nine-year-old and, if you'd have let me bloody finish, I'd have told you . . .'

'Don't give me any shit, Bruce Medway,' she leaned in with the finger. 'Don't give me any shit.'

'I haven't and I'm not going to. So stop winding yourself up.'

'I've been lying in bed all night, not sleeping, waiting for you to come home . . .'

'Winding yourself up about "other women".'

'Waiting for a call from the father-to-be of my child . . .'

'*Our* child. Let's start that off on the right foot.'

She hit me, quite hard, a hatchet thump on the chest which boomed through me. I grabbed her wrist and the other one before it managed a repeat. We wrestled for a moment until I let go and got an arm around her shoulders and pulled her into the shower, her face pressed hard into my chest. The fight went out of her and she started sobbing, her lashes blinking on my nipples, hot tears on my skin.

'Come on now, Heike,' I said. 'Don't do this to yourself.'

'I got worried,' she said, holding me round the waist

now, turning her head to one side. 'I've got all these hormones crashing around inside me. I didn't know where you were. I started thinking and thinking and I couldn't get myself out of it.'

'Hormones, Heike. You just said it. You're pregnant. Your body's changing. You want to feel secure. You don't want to take on too much thinking when you're in that kind of state.'

I manoeuvred her out of the shower, grabbed a towel and we crushed through the bathroom door, awkward as hell, the jamb taking skin off my back. I got her on to the sofa and she put herself back together again.

'I'm being stupid.'

'You're not. Somebody just swizzle-sticked your chemicals.'

'Yep.'

'And I should have called.'

'So it *was* your fault?'

'It usually is.'

'Give me a kiss.'

I kissed and cuddled her and we fell sideways on the sofa. She ran her hand through my chest hair and spoke to my belly.

'I don't know how I started thinking like that. When you didn't come home I started thinking you'd been killed and I went through the whole process of telling your mother, sending your body home, the funeral arrangements and feeling sad.'

'For a couple of minutes before . . .'

'Shut up. Then I thought you didn't want me any more, and you were off with another woman and I drove myself mad with that. I remembered how we

161

were crazy for each other's bodies when I worked up in the north. Then I thought, we're not doing it so much, and I didn't know whose fault that was.'

'Even if that's true, which it isn't, it's nobody's fault.'

'I know, but it didn't stop me thinking it had happened. And I couldn't believe that would happen to us. *After* the baby, maybe, but before . . .'

'We're in Africa too, remember. A long way from home.'

'Yes,' she said, 'and I started thinking about that too. About home and Berlin. I got homesick. For Berlin. Me.'

'I think if we had a baby manual this would all be under the chapter called "Nesting".'

She stroked my belly and snuck a hand down underneath my towel. She palmed my flaccid penis.

'He looks tired.'

'Been out all night.'

'Not in places he shouldn't though.'

'Just down the Jonquet. It doesn't want to go down there too often either. Puts it off the whole business.'

She toyed with me in a desultory fashion. Not interested, vaguely proprietorial.

'What chapter heading would you appear under?' she asked.

'There might be a section called fatherhood . . . we get involved somewhere along the line.'

'Shouldn't there be a little subsection about you under "Nesting"? Like "Holding on to your Man".'

She gripped me, vice-like, threatening and clinging in the same fist. I ooched. She kissed me. Helen arrived and we floundered like teenagers. She looked across with half-lidded eyes of total disinterest.

'Mornin', sah, madam,' she said, and slopped into the kitchen.

We went into the bedroom. I fell on to the bed naked, exhausted. Heike looked at her watch, stripped and went for a shower. I heard it come on. It mingled with the sea snarl of the traffic. I tried to do some thinking about change and got as far as the rains. How the rains in Africa changed everything.

I woke up at midday with the side of my face flatter than a spade and a map of creases down one side from deep, immobile sleep. I ironed out over coffee and popped my face back. I hit the office at 1 p.m. with two slices of cold pizza and a beer. I wasn't going out after the *taxi moto* driver. He was on a night shift and, even if he wasn't, downtown traffic was no place to be for a man with my sensitivities.

No Leads Medway, I thought. Not an unusual state to be in. I cradled the beer and put my feet up, hoped the blood would run to my brain more easily. But, as was so often the case in Africa, I found that someone was thinking exactly what I was, and at the same time, and the man doing it chose that moment to come into my office. It occurred to me that the collective unconscious worked a lot better in Third World society. The first world spent too much time tapping into it on the Internet rather than doing what they should do, which was to let it come to them.

The man, an African, wore a simple yellow cotton knee-length shift, matching trousers and oxblood loafers with tassels. He came in hunched low, about four feet behind an ingratiating smile. He wanted to sell me something – no honours degree needed to read that body language. I summoned one hundred and twenty per cent disinterest, achieved by thinking of chiropody.

'Excuse me, sah,' he said.

Heel skin and hard pads.

He nudged his smile forwards, tweaked it at the corners.

'Please, sah, may I sit down?' he asked, in English, Nigerian.

Corn plasters and mycota powder.

He sat right on the edge of the chair, maybe even hovered in case I decided he couldn't.

'I have something for you, sah.'

Verrucas and ingrowing toenails.

He stuck a forefinger and thumb in each nostril, pinched the septum.

'I unnerstan' you looking for something, sah.'

I turned my head with t'ai chi slowness. Not slow enough. He knew he had me.

'Agbabu?' I asked, forgetting for a moment that the man didn't exist.

'Agbabu?' he repeated, the name careened round the back of his head, pinballed between his ears and went straight down between the flippers – no score.

'Not Agbabu,' I said.

He leaned forward off the chair and placed a tentative elbow in the middle of the desk. He said something in a voice so low that only a wild animal with nothing else on its plate could pick up.

'What?' I asked.

'Girls,' he breathed.

'Who sent you to me?' I snapped, and he leapt back like the goalie off his line who'd seen the lob.

'No, sah, no one, sah.'

'What are you doing here then?'

'I heard.'

'What sort of girls?'

'Young girls, 'swat I heard,' he said, getting sly now, the smile on a stick being reeled in.

'There's young girls everywhere.'

'Virgins,' he said in a tiny little voice no bigger than a hymen itself.

I had a rise in the gorge then, the cold Napolitana frothing in beer came up warm and acid. Now I knew what all those guys in bars were doing – breathing back their own self-disgust. The African sat back and crossed his legs, more comfortable now he was in the right place.

'Where?'

'Here . . . in Cotonou,' he said, examining his long little fingernail, which told the world he didn't have to labour in the fields under the hot sun.

'Where they from, these girls?'

'They Benin girls.'

'Good girls?'

'They virgins, sah. They don' know nothin' bad.'

'Have they been to school?'

The African smiled the horrific smile of a man who's seen another's deep corruption. I tensed, singing tight as a wire guy in a hurricane.

'They been to school,' he said.

'How much?'

'For the firs' night . . . five hundred thousand CFA.'

'Five hundred *thousand*?'

'Guaranteed virgin, sah. You never goin' get sick from her.'

'Five hundred *thousand* . . . I could . . .'

'You don't need condom, sah . . . you never get sick.'

'Do I get a choice for five hundred thousand?'

'Oh, yessah.'

'Where and when?'

He leaned forward again, so far that I could see his knees on my side of the desk. He examined its surface with the forlorn look of a man who was going to have to ask for money upfront. I got the whiff of a set-up, strong as a fart in a two-man lift.

'No money upfront,' I said, so he knew he wasn't dealing with a greenstick. He nodded back his disappointment.

'You come to Restaurant Guinéen, opposite the motor park for Lagos. Eight o'clock.'

'You got a name?'

'Daniel,' he said, got up quickly and left, no hand-shaking in this dirty business, don't know what you'd catch.

I ran out on to the balcony and hissed at one of the boys from the tailor's. I nodded down at Daniel as he appeared beneath me. One of the boys fell in behind him. They walked up through the swirling dust to the main road where Daniel hailed a *taxi moto*. My boy got one too and they disappeared up Sekou Touré.

I shuddered and rubbed my arms until I realized the goose flesh was on the inside. I ran on the spot trying to get rid of that crawling, seething sensation. I thought about how he could have found me – Charbonnier, Marnier, the sex punter German. The phone rang.

'Where've you been?' asked Bagado in the dead and tarnished voice of the clinically depressed.

'I was out all night trying to get a lead.'

'And?'

'I started to get somewhere but it went cold on me.' Bagado lowed like a team of oxen on a windy moorland. 'But . . . it came back . . . just now. I've got a meeting at eight tonight.'

'With who?'

'I don't want to get your hopes up. Let's just leave it at that.'

'Where?'

'The Restaurant Guinéen . . . but don't show up, Bagado. I don't know who knows you down there.'

Silence. Bagado's oilless brain seized.

'Have you got anything for me?' I asked.

'I don't know whether my instinct's anything to rely on any more, but I think they're going to ship these girls out.'

'Any reason?'

'The girl on the sand bar tried to escape. It makes me think they're holding them temporarily . . . collecting more before shipping out.'

'And holding them in Cotonou.'

'At the time she tried to escape, yes. But I think they would have moved them by now, taken them into the lagoon system and that's a big problem. You know you can go from twenty kilometres west of Cotonou all the way to Lagos without leaving the water?'

'Interesting,' I said, 'there could be something in

that. Is there any record of a trade in girls out of West Africa?'

'Not, as far as I know, from Benin, but other countries, yes . . . to Europe, the States, South America.'

'Have you got friends in the port?'

'Some.'

'Anybody on the container side who could look out for you?'

'Yes, but it'll need some money.'

'If I give you more money than you need do you think you could buy your way into some good information?'

'It's very tight here,' he said, and the phone went dead as if to confirm it.

Bagado was not thinking well, his head in a spin over this, his professionalism out the window, Bondougou's magic working on him. As soon as I'd thought it, I knew I was right. Magic. Now this *was* going to cost. Finding a medicine man stronger than Bondougou's was going to take some heavy change. Bagado wasn't going to like it either. He'd been a Christian all his life and didn't hold with Voudoun, but there was no denying the power of it. The president had just made it Benin's official religion and I'd seen enough of it at work along this coast to know that it wasn't just men dancing around in hayricks. I'd been told never to take a Beninoise housegirl because they were great poisoners and I'd pooh-poohed the -ism, whatever it was. But . . . I've always had Ghanaians in my house, didn't want to risk it with that stuff.

I went back to thinking about how Daniel got to me. The German sex punter was not out of the question.

Information did its rounds in the Jonquet, especially when there was money in it. And as for finding me, a 6' 4'' white man in a piddling little city like Cotonou, no problem.

If it wasn't the sex punter, if this was something put together by Marnier or Charbonnier, then that had a more interesting slant to it, a slant worth a good slice of my time.

I was giving it the slice when Bagado showed up looking grey-skinned and as torpid as the late afternoon. I gave him 50,000 CFA to use in the port and he might have drifted straight back out into the pollution if I hadn't made him sit down.

'You know what you need?' I asked, but he didn't look up, lost in some circular thought. 'You need a witch doctor.'

His head clicked up, muddy brown eyes locked on.

'You know better than to talk about that to me.'

'Get one. You can bet Bondougou's got one.'

'I'm depressed. I've lost one of my children. That's all.'

'Your brain's gone. You look terrible. There's no fight in you. Where's all that professionalism you're so proud of?'

'I don't know.'

'He's working on you. Find a man. A good one. I'll pay . . . but do it now. Tonight.'

He nodded. I didn't know whether I'd got through. He stood and went to the door and wrenched it open.

'Bagado,' I said, and he stopped, stared straight out down the stairway, 'remember all that good versus evil

169

stuff? This is part of the battle. Get some of the dark forces on your side.'

A gust of wind fluttered his mac. He walked into it and left.

Chapter 17

Night fell and I locked up, wondering where the boy I'd sent after Daniel had got to. I found him curled up in the tailor's shack. He said he'd lost Daniel in the Dan Tokpa market. I didn't believe him. I especially didn't believe him when he refused my money. I got down to his level and saw the fear in his eyes. I gave him a little rub on the head, pressed a 100-CFA coin into his hand and told him not to worry about it.

Back home I waited for Heike until a quarter to eight, then wrote her a note. I loaded myself up with a couple of hundred thousand CFA and headed for the Restaurant Guinéen.

No rains for a couple of days and it was hot out there, hot and still and thick with pollution. I was nervous and sick and this kind of unrefreshed atmosphere of pillaring pressure gave me breathing difficulties, made me panic that the motor would miss a few beats and not restart.

I took a seat in the restaurant and ordered a beer. I hadn't eaten since the pizza slices, but strong liquids were the only things that were going to stay down. The clientele was mainly African, the few other white people were travellers on a peanut budget, their clothes so faded from the sun and washing they were diaphanous.

Eight o'clock slipped by and I filled the minute after

171

it by ordering another beer and a plate of cashew, my guts improving with time and the hope of a no-show. The travellers full of rice and sauce, left. An electric fan tried hard but couldn't cut it. Thunder rumbled a long way off and the remaining Africans approved, confirming the release to come.

By nine o'clock there were three of us in the place and only one of us a customer. I'd taken some yam pâté and sauce for the feeling of something solid in there with the butterflies, and the beer around it was starting up some secondary fermentation. I belched and gave myself hiccups. The waiter sat down to his meal. I left money on the table and got out into the sallow light on the pavement. A Mercedes pulled up with Lagos plates. Daniel got out of the front passenger seat wearing the same clothes as this afternoon. A big guy got out the back and there was another one in there in the dark trying to encourage me with a smile you wouldn't trust from your sister.

'Who're your friends?' I asked.

'They lookin' the same thing.'

'I'll take a window seat.'

'We air-conditioned in there.'

'I like the view.'

'At night?'

I took another look at the big guy who was leaning against the boot of the Merc, arms folded, dressed European, shortsleeve white shirt hanging outside black trousers, no socks, black scuffed lace-ups. Muscle.

'Let's take a look at the guy with the smile,' I said.

Daniel leaned in and said something in Yoruba. The guy got out into the road, put his arms up on the roof, the smile still there and I could see what was so trust-worthy about it now. A gold tooth in the middle. Heavy, rudimentary cicatrices on his face. More muscle.

'These two can go and do some window shopping.'

'Uh?'

'They're out or the deal's off.'

'They . . .'

'Do it, Danny boy.'

He spoke to them in Yoruba at some length, no doubt making more arrangements with my comfort in mind. They shoved themselves off the car and seeped into the night.

Daniel and I got in the back seat. I was relieved to find the driver thin as hanger wire and the seat leather cool. We drove out of the Jonquet, heading north. The driver, with the lightest of touches on the steering wheel, only moved his hands. Our eyes connected in the rearview three times a minute until the streetlighting ran out and the tarmac cratered – the Francophonie rehab not getting as far as this.

The driver eased us in and out of the potholes which were water-filled to within an inch of the brim. Then we were on to a beaten mud piste, moving swiftly over the bumps and the odd stretch of washboard. We could only be heading for the lagoon. There was nothing else out here apart from jungle and, beyond the headlight cone, the thick dark which came alive every so often with lightning crackling up and down the high-stacked cloud in the eastern sky.

We made a couple of turns and came out at a collection of houses at the edge of the lagoon. All the houses were made of wood and on stilts, most of them up to

173

their knees in water. We turned back on ourselves and went up on to some higher ground where there was a concrete and brick building with a walled compound. It was the only house with lighting and there was a continuous whine from a small petrol generator at high revs. We parked in the compound and Daniel spoke for the first time since leaving Cotonou.

'Five hundred thousand.'

'I haven't done anything yet.'

'Pay me the money, go into the house, do your business and we take you back.'

'What if I don't like the girls?'

'You like them. They ver' sweet.'

The driver leaned forward and took something from the glove. He shifted sideways in his seat and looked at me mildly over the headrest. I went to open the door.

'The money,' said Daniel.

The door wouldn't open, child locks on.

'You said I had a choice.'

'You do, when you pay the money.'

'I want to go in there see if I like what I see. If I don't I want to come out, get in the car and go home. No money.'

'Show me your money,' he said. 'Just want to see. Make sure you got it.'

The driver clicked the courtesy light on. I fanned the couple of hundred thousand I had on me and put the roll back in my pocket. He nodded. The driver let me out. After the air con the night's breath was all over me like a dance-floor flirt. I walked to the building, resisting the urge to turn at the steps up to the verandah for encouragement.

I opened one half of the cracked and peeling double doors and walked into a steel blue glow which was not chilly but stifling. It lit an anteroom and a long corridor which ran the length of the building, the blue light not quite making it to the back wall. A large woman in an African-print dress struggled to her feet from one of two easy chairs up against the wall behind a coffee table which had a spray of plastic flowers in an old gin bottle on it.

This was my first time in a bordello. I'd been in hotels which turned out to be bordellos if that was the service you wanted, but a purpose-built bordello, never. I was expecting some false *joie de vivre*, giggling girls in basques and garters running from room to room, pursued by fatties in string vests, knee-length boxer shorts and sus-pendered black socks. If I could have heard anything above the howl of the tortured genny it would have been grim silence broken by tears.

The woman stepped into her flip-flops and slouched over to me. She didn't speak but set off down the corri-dor, her behind kissing the walls with each stride.

'*Il m'a dit que tu as des vierges ici,*' I said to the hair she had plaited in rails on her head.

She threw open a door on the left and turned to me.

In the yellow light of the table lamp lay a small girl in a little white dress undone at the back. She was sleeping curled up with her hands to her mouth. The tragedy of this terrible business hit me hard then – the little girl needing her sleep, the only ministration re-quired was a parental kiss on an unconscious cheek. She stirred, knowing she was being observed.

'*C'est tout?*' I asked.

The girl came awake on my question and I saw the first thing in her eyes. Fear. The next thing was nothingness. The lights went out in her. She disengaged from the world. The one thing certain – she wasn't a virgin.

The woman closed the door and crossed the corridor. The story was different in this one. The girl was screwed up tight as a ball of paper in the corner of her bed furthest from the door. She was darting fast animal looks about her and shivering, even though the room was hotter than an infected wound. This feral kitten might have been a virgin about a week ago but she still hadn't found the way to detach the brain from the body. I stepped back into the corridor.

'*Il m'a dit que tu as des élèves ici.*'

The woman shot the girl a mean look which almost completely unravelled her and closed the door. We went to a room at the end of the corridor. The girl lay flat on her back, stretched out, taller than the others. She wore pink pants and nothing else. She covered the nubbins of her young high breasts with her hands and looked at me as if she was remembering my face to take with her to eternity. The madame pointed to the wall. Hanging off a nail on a crippled hanger was a small brown uniform.

'*Comment t'appeles tu?*' I asked.

'*Veronique,*' said the woman quickly, the improbability of the name straightening me.

'*Tu es en école?*' I asked, looking at her face, knowing now she didn't understand French.

'*Elle est élève,*' said the madame.

'*Je crois que non.*'

'*T'as vu ça,*' she said, pointing at the uniform.

176

'Elle ne comprend pas français.'

'Tu es professeur ou bien quoi?' asked the woman, so I had to check her for irony. I stormed back down the corridor, past the doors with their veneer of tacky varnish, and into the steel lighting at the front of the building.

'Où vas-tu main'nant?' she shouted after me.

I didn't answer. I wanted to get out of there now. I was on the last rung over the abyss, one more room of that place and I'd be falling. I got out on to the verandah and found myself looking at the muscle I'd told Daniel to fade to black back in Cotonou.

'Il n'a pas payé!' hollered the woman, gasping up the corridor.

'Je n'ai rien fait.'

The gold tooth winked at me. The bigger guy stood with his hand up his shirt stroking a flat hard belly. Daniel stood at the bottom of the steps. The car was pointing out of the compound. Lightning flickered far to the north of the lagoon.

'Now you pay,' said Daniel.

'I didn't like what I saw,' I said. 'No bunny, no money. That was the deal.'

'We not goin' nowhere 'til you pay.'

Gold tooth stepped forward to reinforce the situation. With what I had boiling inside me I felt no fear but I yelled in his face, a high-pitched scream, and waved my hands in the air like a lunatic. It did what I expected – got him on to the back foot and rooted him. Then I swung from a long way off, from way back behind my knee, over my shoulder, over my head and hit his friend full on the solar plexus with getting on for 200 lbs behind it. Even over the whine of the generator I heard the air go out of him. He doubled over, fell back, ricocheted off the roof support and fell the two feet off the verandah to the beaten earth of the compound. That put gold tooth in two minds, neither of them his own. My wave of anger started curling and breaking now, so that the kick I unleashed into his crotch lifted him on to his points and must have left him adenoidal for life.

Daniel backtracked to the car, a wild look on his face that said, let's get away from the bully boy. I shuffled down the steps after him, cocky, and nasty with it. He joined the car whose motor was running. The driver's window was down, which does little for the air con, and I noticed his arm was out straight. I was almost on it before I saw it. In the driver's hand was an old revolver, a long-nosed job right out of a forties 'noir'. I stopped about three feet from it, close enough to know it was real.

'The money,' said Daniel, his voice going a bit F-sharp with panic and fear.

The driver resighted his aim from my belly to my chest, which made no difference to me – gut shot, cardio shot, I wasn't into either. I handed over the money. Daniel got into the car, sweating, relieved. He badgered the driver to get on with it and the car pulled away very slowly. Slowly enough for me to see the mozzarella smile in the bony features of the pipecleaner driver. Never trusted those thin guys.

The muscle was still scrabbling in the dust, one trying to get a bite of air, the other on all fours vomiting off the verandah, back arched like a dog after green meat. I found the little Yamaha scooter they'd arrived on and went after Daniel and his handyman, my rage still clean and focused, wanting to finish this more than I'd wanted to do anything.

I was glad of the driver's arrogance. He purred back to Cotonou without ever taking it above forty m.p.h. I followed with no lights on until we hit the city and I could join the anonymous peloton of a thousand other mopeds.

We went past the Dan Tokpa, over the Nouveau Pont and joined the main Porto Novo road, direction Nigeria. I'd have followed them all the way to Lagos if I'd had to, but they came off at PK 12 and went up to a cheap and unfinished beach hotel called Le Paradis. The driver dropped Daniel off with a small holdall, turned the Merc and floated back past me on his way to a cheaper joint.

I parked the Yamaha and took a peek in the empty concrete bar. Daniel was at the foot of the stairs swinging a room key and ordering some food and drink from a solitary barman, asking him to bring it up to his room. Daniel went up the stairs taking slow nonchalant steps, a little celebratory bounce on each one, the fear forgotten, pleased with himself now.

The barman went into the kitchen leaving the grim neon-lit bar empty. In reception, room eight was the only missing key. I gave it five minutes and went up to the first floor. I found room eight along an untiled corridor with electric wire hanging from the ceiling between the lights. I knocked on the door. Daniel opened it so cool and happy he didn't even bother to check it wasn't his dinner. He was already stripped and heading across the dark blue tiles to the bathroom, a towel round his waist. I padded up behind him and gave his head a slight change in direction so that it hit the corner of a built-in louvre-doored wardrobe. He dropped to his knees, shouting, both hands over his eyebrow. I grabbed him by the back of his neck and slammed him forward so that his head cracked through the wardrobe door and he came to rest with his windpipe crimped against the louvre slats, unconscious and choking. I yanked him out and massaged his throat. I went through his clothes and found my roll of 200,000 CFA amongst another 100,000 or so and a bunch of niara. I was tempted to cover my expenses from the remainder, but got a little flash of Heike and Bagado giving me a finger-wagging. I checked the holdall, which was even juicier, the CFA all blocked off, five million of it, getting on for $10,000 and the revolver on top. I hauled Daniel away from the wardrobe, dragged him over to the bed. I ripped his towel off, soaked it in cold water and cleaned his face up, which was covered in blood, the eyebrow bleeding like a stuck pig's throat. He started moaning and I got up and closed the door to the room, locked it.

I dabbed his face some more and got him up on to the bed. I sat on the other twin bed and waited for him to stop making a fuss, the guy with a head of glass to let a few louvre slats knock him out. He wasn't happy coming back into a world of red-flooded pain, which pleased me. His black skin was tinged green too, so I got him a bucket from the bathroom and he puked his headache up.

'A few questions, Danny, before I leave you to your dinner.'

He focused on me and modestly covered his genitals with a hand. Blood leaked through the fingers of his other hand from the eyebrow. I leaned forward with the towel. He flinched. I tossed the towel at him.

'You're in this business, aren't you? I can see from the money,' I said, nodding down at the holdall.

'What business?'

'Don't make it too slow, Daniel, or your level of suffering's going to angle up sharply. You understand? Now, you're in the business of procuring young girls, isn't that right?'

He nodded.

'Those girls I saw tonight, were they your girls?'

'Not any more.'

'Explain.'

'I buy them from the villages. Take them to Cotonou. Sell them.'

'You sell them to the woman?'

'No, no, she jus' run the place.'

'You know these schoolgirls . . .'

'You and schoolgirls. You sick in the head . . .'

I inched off the bed and slapped him hard, twice, with the front and back of my hand. He drivelled and sank back on to the pillow.

'You're forgetting you're the asshole pimp, Daniel. You're the one peddling little girls into a life of misery and pain. You keep your opinions to yourself and answer my questions and I might not be inclined to leave you pulped in the bath, because, I tell you, with what I've got humped up inside me I could do a lot worse than that.'

He put the cold towel compress to his face, shivering with twitchy fear, the room sauna-hot.

'You know who sell me the girls?' he asked, quietly.

'Who?'

'The parents,' he said. 'You like that?'

'And I suppose you tell the parents that their daughters are going to short happy lives of torn pudenda and diseases? Don't justify your shitty life to me.'

'I'm jus' tellin' you . . .'

'Tell me something else. These schoolgirls who've gone missing off the streets of Cotonou over the last few weeks. Eight girls, seven still alive, one found dead on the sand bar in the lagoon. You know what I'm talking about?'

He nodded. There was a knock at the door, his dinner arriving.

'*Ça peut rester dehors*,' I shouted, and I heard the tray go down on the floor and the flip-flops retreat. 'Now tell me what you know about the schoolgirls.'

'You know,' he said, taking the towel away from his face for a moment, to see if the blood still ran free, 'you know you a dead man.'

I probably was too, but I was so crazed I didn't care, not a trace of ice in my veins, not the slightest tremor in my gut. I just leaned over to him and slapped him again, a downward stroke that fattened his lip nicely.

'Someone told me that the other day, Daniel, and he's six foot under concrete now with most of his face blown off. People are telling me all the time how they're going to hang me by the gizzard and feed my entrails to the dogs but, look, I'm still here, still here with the task of slapping you about until you tell me something sensible. Now get on with it, my hands don't need this much work.'

I could see he was confused. The beating he'd taken

and a lot of English he didn't want to understand. I calmed myself down and a couple of things occurred to me. The first was that Daniel was a middle man, low down in the chain, the boy not having any presence of mind at all. That meant a boss in Benin for him to report to, and, probably, a Mr Big in Lagos above it all. I saw how I could give him a problem, a big problem which, with any luck, would get him killed well before the cross-hairs landed on me. The other thing that came to mind was the first squirming wriggle of an idea like an elite sperm heading for the egg. The only problem, I didn't understand it – my mind operating faster than my brain. I shrugged it away. Daniel flinched.

'Who do you work for, Daniel?'

No answer.

'Who do you pay the money to, Daniel?'

'He comin' soon. Bring you some trouble.'

'I don't know anybody who doesn't bring me trouble. What's he do with the money you give him?'

'He tek it to Lagos.'

'Who in Lagos?'

'I don' know.'

I opened up the holdall and took out the revolver. It really was an antique with a hammer and everything. Daniel froze. I placed the nozzle of the gun on the back of his hand covering his genitals.

'I don't know how to work these things too well but I know it's something to do with pulling back the hammer.'

I eased it back.

'But you know, Daniel, I had trigger thumbs when I was a kid. Doctor said it might weaken them.'

'Madame Sokode,' he said, quickly so that he could pretend he hadn't.

'Tell me where I can find her,' I said, and brought the revolver back into my hands where I examined it further. David gave me an address. 'Talk to me about Madame Sokode.'

'I don't know her,' he whined. 'I jus' take the orders, pay the money.'

'You do anything else for her?'

'What you mean?'

'Maybe you do drugs too. You got five million CFA in the bag. That's money.'

'I don' do drugs. That's Lagos business. I only work in Benin.'

'What about these schoolgirls? What do you know about them?'

He shook his head.

'Is Madame Sokode involved?'

No answer.

I leaned over him like a bad sky and gave him a look down the pipe of the revolver. I hit him with the heel of my free hand in the forehead and his head cracked back against the wall. Once, twice, three times.

'I don't think you know how angry I am, Daniel,' I said and eased back the hammer again. He started blubbing. 'Where are they keeping the schoolgirls?'

'I don't know. On the lagoon. I don't know the place.'

'Where are the girls going?'

'Lagos.'

'Are they going to be sold in Lagos?' I said, sitting back down.

'They already bought.'

184

'What sort of money do they fetch?'

'Thirty, forty thousand dollar.'

'That's a hell of a lot more than five hundred thousand CFA.'

'If they virgin. Genuine . . .'

'Sounds like good business, Daniel. What sort of people can afford that kind of money?'

'Big people,' he nodded.

'When are they going to move the girls?'

'I don' know the time. It soon. But I don' know the time.'

'Do they need more girls?'

He shook his head.

'You think this is good business, Daniel? Taking girls off the street and selling them to die?'

His eyes slitted at that. Revenge already in there. Don't get moral with those that don't have it unless you want a lapful of spite. My translation.

'You got any children?' I asked, standing up and pacing away from him, suddenly nervous about the money man due tonight. He didn't answer me but I knew he had them. I picked up the holdall and took out three blocks of CFA and tucked them down the front of my chinos. I threw the holdall down by the side of the bed. Daniel was blinking fast, wondering if he was coming to his time and thinking if he wasn't, how he was going to explain that all the money hadn't been stolen.

'Keep your kids indoors, Danny,' I said. 'Now stand up and turn around.'

I got him to the end of the bed. It was hard because he thought that this was it and his legs wouldn't work properly and there were tears. I tapped him on the head and he dropped on to the bed and bounced. I made sure he could breathe. I brought his dinner in from outside, scraped it down the toilet and poured the drink after it and put the tray on the table.

It wasn't until I got back on the scooter that I realized I still hadn't found out who'd sent him, a question that fidgeted on my mind all the way back to Cotonou.

Chapter 18

Wednesday 24th July, Cotonou.

It was just after midnight when I dragged myself back up the stairs to the house, having put the money and the revolver in the usual hiding place in Moses's ground-floor flat. Bagado was lying asleep curled up with his head on the front step. My first thought – where was Heike?

I let myself in and went for the answering machine. No messages. Bagado came in and shut the door, still not looking good, thin, wasted. I checked the bedroom, knowing she wasn't there.

'She's not here,' said Bagado.

'You know where she is?'

'I've been out there since ten.'

I went back to the answering machine. Still no messages. Panic crept in and made its house. I flipped through the address book by the phone. Then I smiled. Heike getting back at me for not phoning her last night. That didn't work though. Not in her nature, and gone midnight was stretching the tease. I leafed through the book past Gerhard Lehrner, Heike's boss, to Traudi Linke, a work colleague, an insomniac vegan who read Brecht and ate carrots until she snatched an hour of sleep between four and five in the morning.

I dialled the number. Traudi picked up the phone, breezy, fresh from a couple of hours with *Mutter Courage*. Her voice went flat when she heard it was me. We didn't get along. Something to do with my ostentatiously wearing shoe leather in her company and telling her that vegetables have families too.

'Have you seen Heike tonight?' I asked.

'Have you been fighting again?' she replied, a barbed question guaranteed to snag my dander.

'She left this morning. She hasn't come home. No messages.'

'She went for a drink with Gerhard after work. That's all I know,' she said. 'And you shouldn't fight with her in that condition, you know? If she has a miscarriage . . .'

'Thanks, Traudi.'

The phone went down on me hard. I called Gerhard, not an enjoyable call to have to make, as he'd been holding a candle for Heike since he took up his post and the news would definitely boost. The phone rang for ever until I was blinded by irrational jealousy and panic, livid if she was there, mad if she wasn't. Gerhard finally answered. He'd clearly been in a deep, possibly booze-induced, sleep.

'Gerhard. Bruce. Do you know where Heike is?'

'Heike? She left hours ago.'

'From your place?' I asked, unable to resist the question.

'We were drinking in the Beaurivage. She said she was going back to Cotonou. That was seven, eight o'clock, something like that.'

I dumped the phone. Blind panic leading by a full lap

now. Bagado took the phone and dialled a number in Porto Novo. He spoke rapidly in a mixture of Fon and French, giving Heike's car description and registration. He got nothing back, no accident report, no sighting. He did the same with Cotonou and got the same response.

Then it hit me. The final admission of the truth, of the irrefutable evidence, like giving up on rechecking your pockets looking for the wallet you knew had been stolen all along. Marnier's voice came back to me.

'He will *make* you go.'

I dialled Franconelli's number in Lagos. The usual hard-boiled Italian answered. I gave my name and waited, thinking, damn Franconelli and his bloody respect. I should have known he'd think up a suitable punishment for my refusal to come, bundling me off the street too easy.

'Franconelli,' he said, calm, clear, nearly sing-song.

'Medway,' I said. 'Is she with you?'

'Not yet. The traffic's been bad,' he said. 'Tell me.'

'You didn't have to do that, you know. I was coming.'

'You don't show me any respect. I don't show you none. Not you. Not your family.'

'She's pregnant, Mr Franconelli. I'd appreciate it if you'd be careful with her. I'm coming now.'

'Nothing's going to happen to her. You're coming now. That's all.'

He put the phone down.

Bagado stared me down to my core, which felt gaunt and haggard.

'What do you want?' I asked.

'You'd better go.'

'What are you doing sleeping outside the door if it's not important?'

'I wanted to speak to Heike.'

'You're the only man she trusts, you know that? Including me.'

'This isn't about that. I need money. A lot of money.'

'Like how much?'

'Half a million CFA.'

'Come with me and don't ask any questions.'

We went down to Moses's flat. I stripped off a half million from one of Daniel's blocks while Bagado sat on the bed.

'There's more and I'd give it to you,' I said, handing it over, 'but this is just about the dirtiest money you've ever laid your hands on.'

'I'm not asking questions any more. Lose-lose, remember, and anyway, what you said about the forces of darkness . . . maybe you're right . . . maybe the light's not strong enough for this.'

'What does all that mean?'

'You were right.'

'How do you know?'

'My wife told me.'

'I thought she was a Christian.'

'But she's a Beninoise too. She knows the power of Voudoun when she sees it. She never dared talk to me about it. She's tried going to a doctor on my behalf, without telling me, but the medicine was too strong.'

'Or the money too weak?'

'C'est ça,' said Bagado, managing a smile.

I told Bagado about Daniel, about the little-girl bordello outside Contonou and the schoolgirls in a hideout somewhere in the lagoon system before shipment to Lagos. He swallowed hard and took the half million out of his pocket and looked at it in the dim light of Moses's room. For a moment I thought he was going to give it back, the stuff too tainted, but he just nodded and rerolled it and put it in his mac.

'This should do the trick. Strong money,' he said, trying to brighten himself. 'You see how I'm changing, Bruce?'

'I can see how you're going to win.'

'I don't think so,' he said.

I turned the light off and locked up. I swung myself behind the Peugeot's steering wheel. Bagado opened the gates.

'What is all this lose-lose stuff?' I asked.

He shrugged as I reversed past him.

'You'd better stay away from me unless you need more money,' I said. 'I think there are some bad things going to happen.'

'Bad things have already happened and will carry on happening,' he said. 'I'll be here when you need me.'

I pulled out into the street. Bagado closed the gates. I leaned out across my elbow.

'Are you going to bust up that bordello?' I asked.

'I don't think it's going to be as easy as that. Not yet.'

I left him, hands jammed into his pockets, his head turned sideways, looking off into the night as if he was expecting to be followed. I gunned the Peugeot to Sekou Touré, took a right down to the cathedral, ran the red light and crossed the lagoon on the Porto Novo road to Lagos, where I tried to wring a dew drop of hope out of Bagado's 'not yet'.

191

It was fast going to the border and I was through all that in half an hour and a few thousand. The fifteen or so roadblocks on the Badagri/Lagos stretch took some time but I cruised on to the Expressway into the city at a cooling fifty m.p.h. which was a miracle. The traffic situation even at 3 a.m. could be as bound up as a cancerous bowel.

It was a lava crawl across the bridge on to Lagos Island. The place never changed, still stank because the rubbish was never collected but left to accumulate and degrade under the violent rains and triturating heat. At least there wasn't the stench of putrefaction you sometimes got from bodies floating in the harbour and nobody shoved a shotgun up my nose, took my all and blew my face off anyway. Lagos could be like that.

I crossed Five Cowrie Creek on to Victoria Island, through embassy land and into the smart residential zone where piefingering businessmen, politicians and customs officials snuggled together. Franconelli lived in a secure street, one with armed guards at both ends with radio phones and visitor lists. They let me through and down to Franconelli's oversized pillbox of a house. One of those structures that hadn't been built but poured. The gateman made a show of opening the armour-plated gates and I did my bit by tipping him extra.

I drove up the short driveway. No light came on in the barred and shuttered house. I felt a sense of doom stronger than those night frights that thump you awake into the black freezing roar of the first leg to hell, but somehow I didn't think I was going to get the reprieve of finding it was just lousy air con.

The doom wasn't just because of Franconelli. Heike was in this now. The Italian's move had been shrewd and calculated for maximum damage. He'd done his research. Heike would not forgive this easily, being taken off the streets by the mafia, for God's sake. I could feel the hurricane building. What I didn't know was that this was the least of my problems. When I look back on that moment I gave myself, parked outside Franconelli's house in my dark, heat-racked bubble, I realize it was a final moment. The last seconds before any residual innocence, any smattering of the real child-hood stuff, finally burnt out.

A crack of light appeared at the front door and a figure. I shouldered my carcass out of the Peugeot and went to meet it. The figure moved to let me past, the steel door was thicker than a ship's bow. One of Franconelli's boys shut it behind me. We didn't say anything. These guys never do. I followed his short, wide frame up the stairs to where Franconelli kept his office for security reasons. I looked at the muscles working in the man's legs and banished my last wincing recall of Marnier's machete at work to submerge myself in the lie. The bigger lie that was going to save my hide.

The guy let me into the harsh, neon striplit office and shut himself out of it. Heike was sitting on the sofa, legs crossed, foot nodding, a finger in her mouth. The only thing keeping her from smoking was the concentration required to distil her anger down to one hundred per cent pure.

Roberto Franconelli was parked up behind his desk to the right of his computer. He was wider than I remembered, his head bigger, the jowls jowlier from the weight of his concerns, even his wire hair looked heavier. He looked at me with his dark, charcoal-smudged eyes, sleep not the sweet visitor it had been since his wife and daughter died. He wore a long-sleeved white shirt with cuffs pinched by heavy gold studs, no tie, his neck at his throat ageing him. His hands were clasped, a thick finger tapped a signet ring. It didn't look as if there'd been much chit-chat.

I went to kiss Heike and was given the back of her head. Franconelli nodded me into a chair in front of his desk. I sat down with Heike still in my peripheral vision but my eyes fixed on the Italian's mouth, the dark, full-lipped mouth which went white-rimmed with anger.

'Tell me,' he said, leaning forward, so that I knew why we were in the striplit neon. He wanted to see every facial nuance.

'I don't think there's any need for my wife to be in the room.'

'I'm not your wife,' said Heike. 'He keeps saying that . . .'

We both looked at her.

'. . . but I'm not.'

'Tell me,' said Franconelli. 'From what you said to me on the phone you've got nothing to hide, not from me, not from your . . . from her.'

'I don't think this is woman's talk, that's all.'

'Fuck you,' said Heike. 'These people dragged me out of my car at gunpoint, Bruce. Did you hear that? Gun-point. That's not women's talk either. So you've involved me and I want to know what this is all about. Now tell him and let's get the hell out of here.'

Silence.

'Maybe you should give her your trouser, she gonna talk like that,' said Franconelli, smirking.

I leaned an elbow across his desk and bolted my eyes on to his.

'I'm not saying a word while she's in the room.'

A spear of light traversed my vision from left to right, the noise, louder than a shotgun blast, span me. The desk, PC, wall, ceiling, Heike's feet, the rug on the tiled floor flashed through my head. I lay still and blinked at the clawed feet of the desk and registered that Franconelli had swiped me off my perch. A handful of my hair was grabbed from above and I found myself looking at Roberto's raised hand and white-rimmed mouth. He slapped me a tearing backhander across the face and my mouth flooded metallic and warm.

'By dawn, maybe . . . just maybe you gonna understand the word respect,' he said. 'I don' care about your woman. You know what I mean? I will hit you in front of your woman. You will talk to me in front of your woman. You will give *me* respect.'

He dropped my head. I got up on all fours and crawled up the corner of the desk and back into my chair. Heike was moulded to the sofa now, her hand up to her mouth, eyes wide and unblinking. The violence up and running, close to, and real. It had rubbed some of the brass off her, taken the blade off her edge. My ear was ringing hot, and my lip torn and fat. I rolled my head on my neck, a crick in there from the first slap, and started.

I got as far as sitting outside the Hotel du Port, waiting to go in and find Marnier, when Franconelli stopped

195

me and said he didn't want diagrams, he wanted oil paintings. I started again, this time I threw in the stuff about the sausage-stuffed pastry, the cold Possotomé. He nodded me on, watching me all the while, careful as a pro poker player. He asked me to go over things occasionally, let other things drift. He liked the Australians, what they said about Marnier's face. Heike didn't. He was interested in what we ate. Heike wasn't. He was mesmerized by my description of the waitress, Adèle. So was Heike. Her legs twisted so tight her toes went white.

The screw turned in the room. The air-conditioned air didn't feel so conditioned. The glare from the neon shot my eye whites to blood. Franconelli was crouched, his chin not far from the desk, looking up into my skull, waiting for it.

I told him about the house, the Togolese car arriving, the heavy trunk the driver and I put in the house, the 5000 CFA for the man's trouble, his leaving, the drink with Marnier, what we talked about and then his going to bed.

'And you didn't go to bed?' asked Franconelli.

'I was too nervous. I told Marnier I was going back to the Auberge for a drink.'

'With the waitress, Adèle? Like you said you would before?'

'That's right. And I wanted to see if Gio and Carlo were out there. I hadn't seen them all day. And anyway, even if I didn't see them it was none of my business what they wanted to talk to Marnier about. I didn't need to be there. I didn't *want* to be there.'

'But Marnier let you go?' he asked, frowning.

196

'Why shouldn't he?' I asked, feeling a chasm starting to open.

'What was in the trunk?'

'I told you, it was gold. He didn't make it clear where it had come from. I put it to him that it was illegal mining . . .'

'That's the point. You left him on his own with the gold. He asks you down there as his bodyguard and you leave him with a trunk full of the stuff under the bed.'

'Wrong. I was his *driver*. I was never his bodyguard. He didn't tell me we were going to pick up gold. He said he didn't want Carole to have to drive him down there. And look at me. I don't carry firearms. I'm not violent. What use am I to him as a bodyguard?'

'Did *he* have a gun?'

'He might have. In the holdall. I didn't see it, if he did.'

'So you went to the Auberge.'

'I drank beer with Adèle. We watched the Australians playing with petrol bombs in the bonfire on the beach.'

'What did you talk about?'

I shot a quick glance at Heike. She was riveted. Franconelli saw it too.

'We talked about England, not much. She'd been on the road for a year and a half. I haven't seen the place in five. We talked about Africa, the Sahara, about the big open spaces in the desert . . . we talked about the ground.'

'The *ground*?' said Franconelli.

'This might not be something you know about Africa, Mr Franconelli. The earth has its own pulse. You can

197

lie on the ground and feel its energy, the force of nature . . .'

'Yeah?' he said. 'You're right. I wouldn't know that. I sleep on a bed, on the floor, in a house like normal fucking people do.'

He leaned back and looked across at Heike. He didn't quite understand what was in her face. To me it was as if it was carved there in her bark. Betrayal. She felt betrayed by the intimacy, our intimacy, that I shared with another woman. It interested Franconelli. He couldn't take his eyes off her and I knew I was winning, had that hook firmly in his gullet, but Jesus Christ, what a cost.

'So you had your conversation about the *ground*. Then what?'

'We bought a couple of bottles of beer and went for a walk down the beach.'

Franconelli got it then. He saw what was dropping through Heike, what that look had meant. He turned back to me. His tongue went right to left, taking the relish off his lips.

'How far?' he asked.

'Quite a long way. Beyond the hotel and campsite. Way into the dark. I remember a graveyard off behind the palms.'

'And?'

'We stripped and went swimming.'

I heard the sharp intake of breath from the sofa, not just cold water on the genitals but a stab in the heart.

'And after that?' asked Franconelli, knowing it was coming.

'We had sex on the beach.'

Heike gasped, lurched forward in a kind of vomit of breath that brought her to her feet. Franconelli span to look up at her. I couldn't *not* look at her. What I saw was a deep hurt in her eyes, black and deep as a mine shaft. It put a fear in me, a fear of something profound like the fear of swimming in a fathomless lake. I didn't know how we could ever be the same again. I felt damned.

'Mr Franconelli,' she said to my face, drawing on her reserve tank of dignity, 'do you have a driver who could take me back to my car?'

Franconelli looked at me, then back to Heike. He didn't have to have any culture to know that this wasn't acting.

'Sure,' he said, and buzzed up one of his guys.

We waited in silence. The air in the room suddenly went cold and splintered into slivers. Heike's breath came out in pants. The man arrived. Franconelli gave his instructions. I stood to face her, to try and communicate something.

'Heike,' I said, with nothing further to add.

She reached back and wheeled round, uncoiling an arm to full stretch, and landed a stinging slap on the same side of my face as Franconelli's blow. My head snapped round. The eyebrows jumped on the face of the guy at the door, not used to domestics round here.

'Look at me,' said Heike.

I brought my head back round and looked into her glazed eyes.

'I don't want to have to look at you ever again,' she said. 'I just want to make sure you've seen it.'

I don't know what I had on my face at the time. I

don't know what could have possibly come through but I saw the hurt again and, on top of the hurt, a small, quizzical frown, as if I was the rarest specimen she'd seen. Then she was gone.

The door closed. Footsteps receded. I was left with a fluttering in my chest like a frightened, caged bird beating against bars.

'One more thing,' said Franconelli.

Chapter 19

I sat back down, my hands clenched and twisted between my knees, my face alive with the slap, and the shame. I asked for a drink. Franconelli took a bottle of whisky out of a mini bar and poured me a good measure. I sucked it in and let it burn through me. I stared into the floor, a sucking black hole opening wide and dark in my gut. I spoke on automatic.

'There was a storm coming and we didn't want to get caught out in it so I went back to her room. In the morning . . .'

'You fuck her some more?'

I nodded.

'I wouldn't want to think you gone through that just for one little fuck on the beach.'

'In the morning I walked back to the Auberge and drove back to the house. Marnier was still sleeping. When he got up we loaded the trunk into my car and drove back to the Aledjo where his wife . . .'

'His wife?'

'Carole. I mentioned her before. He didn't want her to have to drive him down there, to Grand-Popo, in the first place.'

'His wife? The only wife I heard about died,' he said, fingering a cigar he'd just slipped out of a tube and weighing up whether to smoke it at this godforsaken hour of the morning.

'Marnier the Mystery Man,' I said. 'Anyway. We ate something. Carole and I transferred the trunk into her car. I drove back to the office. Called the Hotel de la Plage – no Carlo, no Gio. End of story. What happened? Do I get to know?'

'I don't know what happened,' said Franconelli, sliding the cigar back into its tube.

'What's the one more thing?' I asked. 'You want me to find out what happened to them?'

Franconelli opened his desk drawer and threw the cigar in there. He swivelled his chair a quarter turn and put an ankle up on a knee. He tapped the desk top with his ring finger.

'When I first saw you, you know, I was impressed,' he said. 'That party. Gale's party. You didn't drink the champagne, didn't fight for the caviar. You dumped that guy in the pool who was beating his wife in public even if she was a fucking whore and deserved it. Yeah. I thought you were OK. Someone to trust. Reliable. Then you lied to me.'

'I lied to you for a good reason.'

'No. You underestimated me. You thought I wouldn't help you out. That was wrong. You made a mistake.'

'OK. I made a mistake.'

'You lied to me. You showed me disrespect. And now I can't trust you.'

'You can't trust me? You mean you don't believe what I'm saying?' I asked, my insides congealing to a frozen jelly.

'You have to show me you can be trusted.'

'Well, I don't know how I can do that. I gave Carlo and Gio all the information they needed. I've just given myself a big problem . . .'

'You're the only guy I know who can get close to Marnier,' he said, holding up his hand, seeing me going off on a tangent.

'If Marnier had anything to do with Carlo and Gio's disappearance you think he's going to tell me?'

Franconelli stopped tapping his desk. Our eyes connected.

'I want you to kill Marnier,' he said.

Silence. I unclenched my hands which were now freezing cold. I snorted and laughed, horrified and relieved.

'I've never killed a man in my life,' I lied without thinking, but still got the flash of the man's face as I'd hit him with the toilet bowl all those years ago. What was his name?

Franconelli didn't say a word, but resumed his desk tapping.

'I haven't got a gun,' I said. Jesus, another lie. 'I'm not a man of violence.' Another one. The lies popping like bubbles.

'I'll have a gun delivered to your office,' he said, his lips barely moving, so that I panicked myself into a stupid question.

'And what if I won't do it?'

He swivelled round in his chair, dismissing me, and would have looked out of the window if it hadn't had a steel shutter across it.

'Have you seen Lagos harbour?' he asked, as if it was a tourist attraction or a marina full of yachts worth oohing about. I didn't stumble into any more stupid questions. I tried to rein back, slow things down, but the team of horses dragging me through this bad patch were in a lather.

'And I don't want to hear from Cotonou that you've disappointed me.'

I rummaged around my brain trying to find reasons not to run this errand.

'You can go now.'

I stood and he whipped round on me as if he'd seen me giving him the Vs in the window's reflection.

'And when you've killed him, I want you to bring me something.'

I saw myself at a border post, the boot of my car open, a gaggle of policemen around and Marnier's severed head staring up from an old wine box.

'Marnier has a tattoo on his back. One he had done in prison in Marseilles. It's a kind of joker, like you see in cards. I don't know what you'd call it. A harlequin, that's it, a harlequin. That's what I want.'

'You want me to cut it off his back?'

'That would be easiest.'

'What the hell did Marnier do to you that . . .' I stopped myself before I got into machetes and such, '. . . that you have to have this . . . this . . . ?'

'You don't have to know.'

'But maybe I need to,' I said. 'To have a reason.'

He pondered that while cleaning his teeth with his tongue.

'The gold . . . half of it's mine. That reason enough?' he said, and looked at his watch. 'Seventy-two hours. You be back here with the harlequin.' He winced as if

204

he'd had a shot of pain through him. He massaged his chest and stretched his jowly neck up as if reaching for breath. There was nothing more going to come from him. I made for the door, thinking he was lying about the gold. I heard him open the desk drawer and the rattle of a pill bottle. Then I was out and down the stairs and the same man was opening the steel door again, letting me out into the lagging night.

I sat in the car with the dawn coming up and tried to think my way out of the spiral, breathe back the hysteria. The only man who could tell Heike what really happened on that terrible night in Grand-Popo was the one I was going to have to knock off to save my own skin. A perverse and grunting laugh coughed out of me as I thought about flaying Marnier's hide to save my own. Then the hieroglyph of that idea I'd had at the Hotel Paradis wriggled into my brain again. I snatched at it, nearly getting it whole, but found that somehow it was incomplete, that I wasn't ready for it. I realized that the only way was forward, to run with events, let things muddy or become clear, resolve themselves or not.

I eased down the drive, through the steel gates. The chassis rocked as the car climbed on to the street. The guards waved me through the barrier. The further away from Franconelli the less the bird fluttered in my chest, until by the time I'd got to a nearby hotel called Y-Kays my chest was still and I'd decided that responsibility for whatever was going to happen lay with the same powers Bagado was summoning against Bondougou.

At Y-Kays they weren't too concerned about the exhausted white man who'd come in at the wrong end of the night asking for a room. I got up there, showered and was surprised to sleep a clean, dreamless sleep until 11 a.m. when I woke up with Daniel on my mind, face down on the bed, in the Hotel Paradis, a golf ball growing out of his head. I reached for my trousers and pulled out Madame Sokode's address. I flicked through my little black book and found the name of a man who was going to help me with some local information, an Armenian businessman I'd done some work for in Cotonou and Lagos – Dic Zangelian. I called him and arranged to meet at his office on Lagos Island.

From the outside Dic's offices were small and shabby. He spent nothing on the exterior. Inside looked like an Armenian's idea of an English country house with leather sofas, patterned carpets, repro furniture and bad art on the walls. Dic was sitting in his office with the door open looking like a horticulturist presenting a variety of rare palms to an unseen TV camera. He was obsessed with these palms as he was with things English. He always served Earl Grey in tea cups with saucers and offered shortbread on small flower-bordered plates. He smoked Marlboros constantly, dressed himself in four-ounce grey lightweight suits and did his best to look like Omar Sharif after an all-night bridge tournament.

'I need to know about a woman called Madame Sokode,' I said, sipping the Earl Grey.

'Madame Sokode,' he said, parting his moustache with a thumb and forefinger.

'You can tell me the dirty as well as the clean.'

'Is there any dirty?'

'What's her business?'

'Construction,' he said, 'and supermarkets. She buys corner sites in residential areas, builds a block of flats with a supermarket underneath. Nothing big. Three floors, that type of thing.'

'So she's well connected.'

'I would think so. She had a very powerful mother who died a few years ago.'

'Does she do anything else?'

'She trades.'

'What?'

'Anything. Tyres, sugar, palm oil, timber. She likes making deals. I'm told she's very open-minded, tough too, but with more of a European mentality when it comes to doing business. You know, things happen around her and . . . she always makes money, which usually means you don't.'

'Would she be interested in gold?' I asked, bearing something in mind.

'I don't see why not. It's the heaviest money there is. Have you got some?'

'A little in the bridgework of my teeth.'

'She might not be that open-minded,' he said.

'Can you get me a meeting with her?'

'If you've got something just turn up at her office,' he said. 'You're white. She'll let you in.'

I had lunch, a piece of fish in a hot pepper sauce and the usual lump of starch. I sent a beer down after it and felt it swill and eddy like frothy sea in a rocky inlet. I bought a *Guardian* newspaper and a half bottle of Bell's, which was all they had, for the traffic jam that I knew was out there waiting for me. It was going to be a crawl over to the other side of Lagos Island to get on to the

Third Axial Road up to an area called Shomulu which butted on to the lagoon where Madame Sokode had her office – four hours minimum.

Out in the creaking heat people looked unusually happy given that Lagos is one of the most punishing cities in the world to live in and the rains don't make it any better with a quarter of the population living on the street. The newspaper filled me in. The Nigerian football team were in the Olympic quarter finals heading for gold. A solid, tangible ray of golden light pierced the heart of darkness. The rest was not such easy reading. Still no democracy. Oil price depressed. Niara in free fall. Crime wave – tidal. There was nobody I knew in the death notices which was cheering.

The newspaper done, the nerves came back. I didn't know what I was going to say or offer to Madame Sokode, and there was still a good chance that Daniel had not been beaten to a pulp for dropping a few mil from his float. I could just be walking into the mincer. Breathing exercises would have helped or a personal stress manager to suffer for me. I reached for the Bell's.

I found the offices around 4.30 p.m. A small concrete block of three floors, just like Dic said but without the supermarket underneath. There was a parking compound in the front and a security guard who for a note let me in, told me Madame Sokode hadn't arrived and said her company, called Nexim, was on the top floor.

I shook the jam out of my legs, unstuck my shirt and made for the entrance looking like a bum. There were brass plates on the outside for three companies: Nexim, Bortran and Finlan. Just inside the door was a guard with a leg-length truncheon and army boots who looked at everybody who went past him, daring them to make eye contact. I walked in giving him a balls-out look that had him checking outside to see who was holding my train. A black Mercedes arrived which interested him more and I went up to the first floor.

Through the reinforced glass doors of Bortran Co. Ltd I saw a keen-eyed receptionist with a complicated hairpiece and Western clothes. She had her eyes closed, holding her blouse away from her breasts, getting some cool air circulating. I ducked into the office. Her eyes snapped open. She dropped her blouse front.

'How may I help you?' she said in a frosty Americanized voice.

I asked her if it was Nexim and she pointed me up.

'Did you study in America to get an accent like that?' I asked.

'Yeah, I did,' she said, still cool.

'And now you work for Madame Sokode?' I guessed.

'Yeah,' she said, disappointed. 'It was my dad got me the job, you know, like it's not so easy to find jobs in Lagos.'

'Unless you know people.'

'Right,' she said, keeping her eyes on me, not quite friendly yet.

'And what do Bortran do to keep you interested?'

'Shipping. Containers. Stuff like that.'

'So you do all the shipping for Nexim?'

'Not so much. We clear their containers for them. Building materials from Spain, supermarket goods from England –' She stopped suddenly.

Three people walked past the glass doors. The first, a very beautiful, tall, thin and poised woman dressed

209

from headscarf to ankle in blue and white Dutch Wax African print. Her head was completely still on top of her loping body, so still that the three-inch gold-drop earrings she was wearing did not swing with her motion. She was a cat, a stalking cat. The man behind her was a different animal, a short squat bull rhino in dark-green robes with a very black and shiny face. The third was the driver, carrying two large Samsonite suit-cases and a face as glum as a gun's. The zoo team filed past and continued up the stairs.

'Madame Sokode?' I said to the receptionist. 'Was that her husband?'

She threw her head back and clapped her hands at that one.

'That was her father,' she said, amazed at me. 'Madame Sokode isn't married.'

'She must have to work at it to stay that way.'

'They say she only likes white boys,' she said, giving me a flirty dare-you look, the accent slipping towards Nigerian.

'I'm tall enough.'

'I don't think that matters.'

'Well, that's a shame because I'm not weighed down in the money department.'

'She is.'

'So what is it?' I asked, and she tapped her forehead. 'Brains?'

'That's what I hear,' she said.

'I always hated school,' I said, and she gave me a tough-shit look. 'If she kicks me out I'll buy you a drink.'

'As for me,' she said, wagging her finger, 'you'd have to be . . .'

'Black?' I asked, turning at the door. 'I don't do black.'

'Oh, no,' she said, 'but you *would* have to be . . . what was that you said . . . "weighed down in the money department"?'

She tinkled a little wave at me and I went upstairs.

The receptionist at Nexim was one of those large, impassive, obstructive African women in full gear with a 'the eagle has landed' headpiece in cobalt blue and maize yellow. I asked to see Madame Sokode and she asked if I had an appointment, knowing damn well. I shook my head, which pleased her. She asked for a business card and I gave her one with just my name and phone number on the card. She reversed out of her desk like a forklift and trolleyed down the corridor.

A few moments later I was shown through a waiting room containing father, driver and two suitcases and on into one of those rare African offices where the desk didn't take up half the room. Madame Sokode looked me in the eye and I put her at 6' 2'' in her sandals. She extended a featherweight hand, knuckles up, which asked for a papal kiss. I shook it and sat down on one of two repro chairs on my side while she paced the office as if she had a dictionary on her head.

The room was tastefully decked in African art, Italian table lamps and English furnishings. There was no connection between this woman, this setting and Daniel's bordello of six-year-olds. She stopped at the window and looked out through the slim grey blinds. I wiped a trickle of sweat off my eyebrow. There was no air con in the room.

'I think it's going to rain very hard tonight,' she said in

perfect English, without the slightest trace of a Nigerian accent.

'It's that time of year,' I said.

'Yes,' she said, turning back into the room. 'Do you like the rainy season? Don't you miss your British four seasons?'

'Yes and yes,' I said.

She walked round the back of my chair and sat in the one next to me, cool, not a hint of perspiration. She crossed her legs under the ankle-length skirt and a one-inch slim-heeled gold sandal flashed. She flipped away the corner of her jacket so that I could see she had a sleeveless top on underneath with an inch of bare, flat, uncreased torso showing at the bottom of it. She folded her hands and gave me the benefit of her very dark eyes which were all pupil and no iris. She drank me in some more and I felt the pressure of those black limpid wells sucking me in.

'What are you doing in Africa?' she asked.

'Making a living.'

'Not a very good one,' she said, introducing a little edge early on.

I didn't respond.

'Your Peugeot looks a little sad,' she said.

'I leave her out at night. She's resentful.'

She smiled, which didn't ease my mind. Her teeth were brilliant white but a little pointy from the front to the canines and she zipped up quick as if she'd been told this was off-putting.

'My African business theory,' I said, 'is that if you're white and you drive around showing your all you're just inviting people to come and take it off you.'

'Not something practised by the Africans themselves.'

'How right you are,' I said, and she nearly smiled again.

'So how do you make this ... unostentatious ... living?' she asked, sidling up to the point, not getting to it, not just yet.

'Africa is full of opportunities –'

'Yes,' she interrupted, and then dropped it, worried that I might be rushing it.

'You've got a very expensive English education on you,' I said, taking my turn to flee the nub.

She notched up her accent and gave me the name of an English girls' public school where pocket money came on Amex gold cards.

'And they still teach deportment there,' I said, and she really liked that but didn't want to show those teeth again so she stood and stripped off her jacket and laid it across her desk with long slim arms with only the BCG blemish.

'Just hockey and lacrosse,' she said.

'And rounders in the summer, I'll bet.'

'Useless game,' she said bitterly, and sat back down.

'How long were you over there to get an accent like that?'

'I was sent away when I was five,' she said, looking at the door, hoping her father overheard.

'University?' I asked, to get away from that little darkness.

'Bristol.'

'Your father must have made some money to –'

'My mother. She sold cigarettes on the street singly when she was six and built up from there to make one of the biggest drinks and tobacco distribution companies in West Africa.'

'And where's that now?'

'We sold it after her death,' she said. 'You have a lot of questions, Mr Medway.'

'I thought we were just talking.'

'I thought you came to see me . . . What did you come to see me about?'

'An opportunity.'

'For you or me?'

'The two of us.'

'Why should I want to do business with you?'

'I'm here. We're talking the same language.'

She leaned across the desk, picked up the phone and yabbered away in what I thought was Igbo and sat back down again.

'I've just sent my father back to his house in my car so you'll have to take me to mine in yours. Is that all right?'

Chapter 20

Now *I* was nervous we weren't getting to the point. I thought for a moment I'd had my hands full of initiative but it was just sweat and soggy chinos after all. Madame Sokode wanted to talk. She'd just picked her father up from the airport where he'd flown in from London after some treatment or other she didn't want to talk about. Now he was dispatched, she wanted to rack up some tongue miles. I didn't have that much of a point to get to so for me dawdling with the yakety-yak didn't seem a bad option except ... this went on for *three hours*.

In those three hours we covered the ground Dic had in fourteen seconds. We also changed location. I took her up to her new house, just recently finished, at the back of an almost American-style middle-income housing estate in Ikeja.

'I like being near the airport,' she said. 'I don't want to be down there on Vic Island a five-hour traffic jam from anywhere. The air's better too.'

Interesting stuff.

She didn't get to talk to too many interesting people by the sounds of things, or at them, even. She told me how much she disliked Lagos society and the expectations of family and friends. She didn't go out much, maybe up to the Sheraton for a drink, but that was it. She talked about her family, trashed them heavily, including old rhino. The friends didn't cut it either. The girls were all sluts and the boys . . . well, just as you'd have thought given the girls.

'And, as *you* know, Mr Medway,' she said, 'that's a very dangerous state of affairs in this day and age.'

I didn't know why that 'you' had to take such a heavy stress.

A watchman opened up the steel gates to let us in on a short, straight drive up to the house which was a big neo-colonial affair with a red-tiled roof and long shuttered windows. It had a pillared and netted veran-dah out the front overlooking a garden with mature palms and plenty of building detritus. She led me up long wide steps to the front door, which was not opened by a servant.

'The furniture hasn't arrived yet,' she said, as if this explained the lack of staff.

She unlocked the door and leaned into it. It was hotter inside than out. She flipped the light switch and a monsoon of cut glass lit up in the roof above a double staircase which went up to what she was already telling me was eight bedrooms with bathrooms en suite. Look-ing forward to having all those family members and friends she liked so much.

'I couldn't wait to get out of my father's house,' she said, showing me into a living room with a three-piece suite, a table and nothing else but acres of parquet flooring. 'Drink?'

I'd been inches off flipping the glove and chugging the Bell's all the way out here so I went for the drink and let her know the kind of measure required, but not the amount of paranoia it had to quell. What was I doing here? She told me to wander the house, tell her what I thought. I said she could turn on the air conditioning if she liked, but she didn't like . . . she didn't have.

She then unnerved me by leaving from one door and reappearing through another with a large whisky, then floating off again and coming up behind me soundlessly on bare feet in a lime-green minidress. I lagged a few yards behind as she led me into yet another stately-home-sized room and found that she'd vanished when I got in there. Snuck into some double-doored closet built into the wall, only to shiver me down again by ghosting into the corner of my eye in a tiger-striped top and ankle-length skirt ensemble.

The whole performance put me in mind of the great white hunter pursuing the cunning cat only to find himself getting manoeuvred into the killing spot.

After the seven-bedroom tour (all empty, the eighth was hers and private) she took me back downstairs to the living room and we sat on the hot easy chairs opposite each other, the sofa vacant between us. I drank. She didn't. She didn't open any of the shutters on the windows in the room, either, and the one thousand cubic feet of brilliantly lit space around us was as thick as New York subway air.

'I lied to you before,' she said.

Here we go.

'About what?'

'The furniture.'

'When it's coming, you mean?'

'I cancelled it. Do you think that's strange?'

217

'Only if you *like* clutter.'

'I had a German boyfriend once,' she said, as if the word 'clutter' had reminded her.

'What was his name?' I asked, trying to get into the spirit, wanting to get out of here badly.

'Helmut,' she said, as if I'd just questioned her integrity.

'And Helmut was into squash-court living?' I asked. 'Or was his name Klutter?'

Wrong sense of humour. Her mouth hardened up on me.

'No.'

'I mean did he like space? Clean lines? Freedom from the trappings of consumer society?'

'No. He was a homosexual,' she said, derailing the clutter conversation.

'Madame Sokode,' I started and then decided to do some derailing myself. 'Why are you called "Madame" if you're Nigerian?'

'I'm not "Mrs", I can't stand "Ms", nobody's going to call me "Miss" at my age and "Sistah" is out of the question. I did some business in Francophone West Africa, they called me "Madame". I liked it. You can call me Elizabeth if you want,' she said, as if this wasn't her real name but would do for the evening.

I'd painted myself into a corner with nowhere to go but the point, but how to start? Do you do virgins for export? No. Mine's another double and then I must get going. A question like that gets out into the open and nothing stays the same. There was also the fear that Daniel had shot me some shit about Madame Sokode, that she was just as Dic had painted her and I was going

218

to drop a stink bomb from which all we could do was sprint.

'Mr Medway?'

'Bruce, Elizabeth,' I said, snapping out of it.

'Bruce, I wanted to tell you about Helmut.'

'I wouldn't want to invade your privacy,' I said, a tad Victorian, but I really didn't need to hear about Helmut.

'It's easier to talk to strangers.'

'As long as they stay that way.'

'What do you mean?'

'You don't want to reveal your inner life and then have it paraded around your family and friends.'

'Oh, I see, I thought you meant you didn't like being intimate.'

Maybe I didn't.

'Surely Helmut was bisexual,' I said, thinking, we're not going to get away from the guy so let's do him and quick.

'No. He was homosexual. He always preferred boys. It didn't bother me. Our relationship suited each other. He liked to be seen with a beautiful African woman on his arm and . . .' I knew I had to look her in the eye for this, '. . . and I didn't like sex. Still don't.'

The relief was substantial.

'So what happened to . . . ?'

'Everything in Africa is sex,' she said, bitterly and with disgust.

'It's the only fun there is if you're living in grinding poverty.'

'You were going to ask me something,' she said, not enjoying the concept of a billion people hoeing their way to a night's satisfying rut.

'So what happened to Helmut if you suited each other so well?'

'He died.'

'I'm sorry.'

'Don't be,' she said. 'Helmut was a great card player and I can assure you he had a very good understanding of probability.'

'AIDS?'

'He was very reckless.'

My drink was over and I'd just sent the instructions to my legs to get up and out of there when Elizabeth whipped my glass off me and set off across Lake Parquet. She came back with the tumbler half full. I took it with both hands.

'Unfortunately,' she said, sitting down, legs underneath her, 'I was too. One night.'

'Not reckless, I hope.'

'That's why I cancelled the furniture.'

Conversation not derailed after all, very much on line. The whisky glass rattled on my teeth making an idiot of myself. She laughed, out came the pointy teeth, snapped shut.

'When I first saw you,' she said. 'I thought we had something in common.'

'I'm not HIV positive if you're asking.'

'I didn't mean that,' she said. 'I thought we'd both lost something valuable to us.'

'Well, I might have just lost my wife,' I said, the whisky talking now. 'I mean my girlfriend.'

'Which?'

'Girlfriend. She's pregnant. That's why I keep calling her my wife. She corrects me . . . every time. She would have if she were here. She's German too,' I finished like a complete asshole.

'Why do you say "might"? You *might* have just lost her.'

'I told her I'd been unfaithful.'

'That usually works.'

'But I lied.'

'Then you're *very* strange.'

'It was a *very* complicated situation.'

'That wasn't what I meant about losing something.'

'I lost my car a few months ago,' I said. Avoidance tactic.

'You mean *that's* new?' she said, and smiled without opening her mouth.

'Your sense of humour's coming along.'

'What about your innocence?'

'Fresh out.'

'Me too.'

'I was joking.'

'I don't think you were.'

Here we go with the inner child stuff.

'Where did you lose yours?' I asked.

'I'm not talking about virginity,' she snapped, the last word tripping over her teeth, annoying her.

'Then what *are* we talking about?'

'I told you. That's what we have in common.'

'Lost innocence? Well, there must be a hell of a lot of people like us. Most of Lagos for a start. You want to go wandering the streets downtown see how much . . .'

'You think so?'

'I don't know what you've done to lose it.'

'What *I've* done,' she said, savagely, beginning to get shrill.

'Nobody loses it for you.'

'I didn't even *have* a childhood,' she said, her tight fist beating on the arm of the chair.

This was getting screechy. Her mouth was open nearly all the time now and those teeth with the lips curled back snapped and snarled in the jam-packed air of the room. The sweat sprung out of me, and the chair clung as if I was its last possible chance at happiness. I gripped the arms while Elizabeth Sokode went off on a rant.

'I'm not African, I'm not white, I'm not even halfcaste. I'm a nothing. I don't belong anywhere. I take the bits I like from both cultures but none of it is me. Do you know where I went for my school holidays?' she asked, thumping her stomach with her fist as if she'd just knifed herself.

'No.'

'School.'

I nearly laughed at that. It was just too damn tragic. And if I had it would have come out high and hysterical like a vixen on heat barking to the full moon. But for her, with her black shiny eyes flashing over me, the horror was still fresh, the abandonment a blight that had ruined her.

'I'm surprised you still see your father,' I said.

'He was a weak man.'

'And your mother?'

Her limbs were folding back down again now having been wildly overextended and she lapsed into silence. I dropped a couple of gulps to keep the glare down in the room.

222

'You have no idea,' she said after some time.

An aircraft took off loudly overhead. I had the whisky down to half an inch. My face felt hard and fat like whale blubber.

'That'll be the last plane out tonight,' she said.

I saw her spending night after night in her empty palace counting aeroplanes and imaginary slights.

'The rain's coming now,' she said.

'I was thinking I've got to be going.'

'Not for an hour or two. The rain's coming. Listen.'

The palm trees were wilding outside, hissing and clapping. Elizabeth got up and opened some French windows and the shutters out on to the verandah. Cool air blasted into the room. She shuddered and left, taking my glass from me on the way. I went out and up to the mosquito netting. The garden was floodlit now and I could see the dog runs around the high walls, the angled razor wire on top.

The brushes started on the snare – the unmistakable sound of a line of heavy rain moving across the city.

Elizabeth reappeared in designer blue jeans and a fat, cream rollneck which came up to her nose. She handed me my refill. Another three inches. The wind drove the rain over the walls, through the palm trees and it crashed on to the house. The lights in the garden blurred. Madame Sokode looked out like an animal but not one that felt safe or protected by the rain, rather a predator that could see rich pickings after. She hugged herself and spoke without taking her eyes off the rain.

'I get cold very easily,' she said.

'Maybe you're more African than you think.'

'I can't eat fish-head soup or grass cutter,' she said, 'I can't stomach manioc or cassava.'

'You've got to be brought up on that stuff.'

'Why did you come and see me today?' she asked suddenly, as if I'd had romantic intentions or regretted a bust-up.

'A proposal,' I said.

'How did you hear about me?'

'In the business community in Benin. Names get thrown around. I don't remember where I heard yours. The High Commission told me where to find you.'

'What is this proposal?'

'Can I just use your lavatory before we get into this?'

'You'll have to go upstairs in one of the bedrooms. The downstairs isn't plumbed in yet.'

I ran like a madman up the stairs, eyes bugged, tongue out on its stalk, trying to shed some of that unbearable tension. I saw on the landing that her bedroom door was ajar and I couldn't resist a peek.

It was the smallest room in the house. The walls bare apart from a poster of a young white movie heart-throb. The bed was single and on it were cuddly toys – two dolls, a wild-haired troll and four plastic ponies with lurid tails. There were books, lots of them in a floor-to-ceiling bookcase. A nightmare read of romantic slush – table settings and princes, linen and love.

A door slammed below. I got out and took a long shuddering leak. I found my face had set in a plastic half laugh in the mirror.

Elizabeth was pacing the verandah, arms folded, thick

mountaineer's socks on her feet. I sucked a half inch off the whisky.

'Are you interested in gold?' I asked.

'Is this a business proposal?'

It's not a marriage proposal.

'I wanted to know if you'd be interested in buying some Ashante gold,' I said.

'How much?'

'Around two thousand ounces, just under a million dollars' worth.'

She stopped and stared into the floor for a moment. The business brain flickering. The number of emotional cripples and close to certifiably insane people who hold down top jobs and run business empires – it's amazing. Maybe that's what it took . . . being a kid without the innocence – single-minded, total aggression, fuzzy concepts of good and bad, right and wrong, and a desperate need for total playground dominance. Was that the only way I could justify my own failure?

'Yes,' she said, and the rain stopped so suddenly she turned around. 'That could be very interesting, depending on the price, and the usual quality and delivery.'

'Where do you want it delivered?'

'Here in Nigeria.'

'When?'

'Immediately as possible.'

'Quality?'

'I have someone who can help on that.'

'And price?'

'It would be interesting for me if you could accept part money and part goods in kind.'

'What did you have in mind?'

225

'Perhaps that depends on your principal's interests.'

'Maybe *I'm* the principal.'

'I don't think so,' she said.

Arguing with that kind of shrewdness was just going to wear out my tonsils.

Chapter 21

Thursday 25th July, on the Lagos/Cotonou road.

I followed the storm back to Cotonou. Always on the edges it sucked me on, but not into the hard four-inches-a-minute stuff, just squally, windscreen-slashing rain. I set up some thought programmes to shut out the clips of Heike's hurt which were replaying in a continuous loop. Marnier and Sokode – the physically maimed, the emotionally crippled – an interesting love match if she'd liked sex more, not that Marnier was a performer these days but he did like to talk. My great non-plan – selling Marnier's gold to Madame Sokode – where was that going to get me? Looking stupid or, worse, badly exposed. The seven schoolgirls – huddled together in their brown uniforms, wincing under the roar of the rain on the corrugated-iron roof of some shack out in the lagoon system – headed for Lagos and what?

None of it worked. Heike's pain and the pointlessness of her feeling it tortured me all the way back.

Cotonou was bruised, battered and blacked out after the storm but refreshed. Home was deserted. There was a leak in the kitchen. I poured a Red Label. It was 3 a.m. Heike's clothes had gone. All her possessions. No note. I sat in the dark with the bottle in my crotch and drank steadily, but the long drive had taken the edge off my drunkenness and nothing could numb me now. I lay down on the floor and drank even more. Then I slept. Badly.

I woke with my fingers round the glass and Helen's flip-flopped feet inches away. I rolled and felt the world roll with me. Nausea lurched. I breathed and stabilized.

'She gone away, Mr Bruce.'

'Did she say where?'

'I axed her. She woul'n't say,' said Helen. 'She comin' back?'

'I don't know.'

She rested the sheaf of reeds she used for sweeping on her shoulder.

'Mebbe is time,' she said.

'For breakfast?'

'Breakfas'? No. Time for me go home. I'm tired this place. I wan' be with my people again.'

'Don't be hasty.'

'Sistah Heike gon' come back?'

'I don't know, Helen. We're going to have to try.'

'Swat I'm sayin'. I don' wan' go through this no more. I don' wan' see you fightin', I don' wan' hear you swearin', I don' wan' see you drinkin' strong dring, I don' wan' . . .'

'I'm going to take a shower now, Helen.'

She went back to her sweeping.

'Rain come in the kitchen,' she said.

'Thanks, Helen.'

I did my business, picked up a sandwich and headed for the office. The *gardien* said I'd had visitors, the same one and three times that morning, a white man.

I stood in the middle of the office, ate the sandwich and drank bottles of Possotomé. I sat and studied the empty square left by a broken tile kicked out of the floor. The afternoon heat herded itself into the room. I slept and was woken by a polite knock from the *gardien* who told me the white man had arrived.

A big solid guy came in behind him. He had a heavy beard in which the sweat beaded so that he had to squeeze it out every once in a while.

'Where you been?' he asked, drying himself off with a small white towel he kept for the purpose on his shoulder. Lebanese, American accent.

'I didn't know we had an appointment.'

He cocked his head at the *gardien* who was still bent round the door.

'You wanna give him a pen and a book so we can make our appointments.'

'He can't write,' I said, waving the *gardien* out. 'That's why I have an answering machine.'

'I don't think you'd appreciate my message being left on it,' he said, and sat down. The man liked himself a lot, liked talking tough, too.

'You're not in the business of giving me money, by any chance?' I asked.

'Nope.'

'You don't want to be a client of mine?'

'You're *my* client.'

'I am?'

'That's what I been told.'

'I'm not buying.'

'It's already paid.'

'What?'

229

'Your name *is* Bruce Medway? I mean, I don't wanna be rude but you're not sounding like the right guy for the job.'

'What job?'

'Whoah!' he said, and put his hands up. He took the towel off his shoulder and wiped himself off. 'That's nothin' to do with me. I'm just the supplier.'

'Tell me what you got.'

'A .380 Browning with a spare clip,' he said, pleased with himself to get the line out like that.

'You've come from the Italians.'

'You don't look like the kinda guy with a loada these jobs stacked up.'

'What do those kind of guys look like?'

He dropped his head and put two fingers up to his eyes.

'You like the movies?' I asked.

'I *love* the movies,' he said. 'Gotta satellite dish cost me twelve thousand bucks, I watch them alla time. You?'

'Yes. I like them too. Beer?'

'Coke. I don't drink alcohol, don't like the taste.'

I dispatched the *gardien*, told him to bring food as well, Lebanese pastries.

'Where are you from?' I asked.

'In Africa?'

'You're Lebanese.'

'Yeah, from Beirut.'

'And here?'

'Lagos.'

'You know the Italians pretty well?'

'We've done business before.'

'I imagine they have a lot of demand for your kind of service.'

'It's the nature of their business, you know. Africans need a lot of control sometimes.'

'Don't want them running off with their own ideas.'

'Right.'

The drinks arrived and the pastries. We ate and drank.

'Do you ever talk to these Italians?' I asked. 'About work.'

He shrugged.

'Did you ever talk to Carlo and Gio?'

'You gotta be kidding.'

'Gio's interesting,' I said. 'An interesting guy.'

'Gio never said a fuckin' word.'

'That's right, he only spoke Italian.'

'I don't think he spoke much of that either.'

'I haven't seen those guys in a while.'

'I heard they got whacked,' he said, not often he got to use that word.

'Somebody *killed* Gio?' I said, impressed.

He gave me a furtive look and I nodded him on.

'I heard that's the guy you're gonna deal with.'

'You found a talkative Italian.'

'They get bored. They like to talk to someone different.'

'Did they tell you why I've got to deal with this guy?'

'Because of Carlo and Gio,' he said, the ground feeling a little swampy underneath him now.

'No.'

'Oh, right,' he said, nodding at his lap.

'It's something to do with the boss . . . Mr Franconelli.'

'I didn't hear that,' he said, fear glimmering now.

231

'What *did* you hear?'

'I mean I didn't hear you say his name.'

'What did you hear?'

'This isn't gonna go back to the guy you just mentioned?'

'That you know things about his business and his associates that you shouldn't?'

'Hey, look, they tell me. What can I do?'

'Keep your mouth shut.'

'OK.'

'Tell me what you heard about this job,' I said, playing the hard-on, 'and it won't go out of this room . . . any of it.'

'I heard it was something personal.'

'Definitely not business?'

'I don't know. I just heard it was a personal thing. Now I gotta . . .'

'Show me the gun,' I said.

He laid a cloth-wrapped weight on the table and pulled a clip out of his pocket. He opened the cloth and ran through the niceties of the Browning .380. He was not a happy man any more. I let him know he was safe with me as long as he didn't blabber. He left a few minutes later, that towel on his shoulder sodden, heavy with fear.

I hefted the gun. Guns and me did not go together. Whenever someone gave me a gun, someone else always took it away. People could see that guns didn't belong to me. Maybe this time, though, there was no way out. Maybe this time I was going to have to use it. Then rather than Marnier, Bondougou came to mind – Bagado, Bondougou and the words lose-lose.

The cleaned and well-oiled gun shone dully in the late afternoon light. I sipped La Beninoise – as Heike once said – the only woman who'd ever got close to me. Yes, I'd done some lose-lose recently. I'd told my lie, lost Heike and I had no doubt I was going to lose something else by killing Marnier. And if I hadn't told the lie . . . the big lose. The biggest lose there is.

That's when I got it. Lose-lose. If Bagado did nothing, Bondougou would slowly crush him to death; he wouldn't be a policeman any more, just a husk of a policeman. If he 'got rid' of Bondougou, killed him or had him killed, he'd lose that moral integrity so precious to him and perhaps do a life sentence too.

I called Bagado at the Sûreté. He wasn't there. I wrapped the gun in the cloth and stuffed it down my chinos. I drove back to the house, put the gun with Daniel's revolver and his money and tried Bagado again. Still not there, but not gone for the evening either.

At 6.30 p.m., I called Traudi. I had nothing to say to her and Heike wouldn't be talking, but I had to know she was all right.

'*Kann ich mit Heike sprechen?*' I asked.

'You don't fool me, Bruce Medway. Not even in German on the phone,' said Traudi.

'I wanted to make sure she was OK.'

'I wouldn't know.'

'You haven't seen her?'

'She's not here and I haven't been in today.'

'When's she coming back?'

'To you?'

'No, to you.'

'She's not staying with me.'

233

'Who's she staying with?'

Silence.

'Are you still there, Traudi?'

'I'm still here,' she said, weighing something up. 'She's staying with Gerhard.'

A little fanfare of triumph came down the line. I slammed the phone down, didn't want to hear any of Traudi's crowing, and collapsed on the sofa writhing as if a kidney stone had come loose.

There was a knock on the door.

'*Entrez*,' I roared, and headed for the kitchen and the fridge. I poured a whisky, downed it and poured another. I went back into the living room. Carole was standing by the door in a black sheath that just about covered the gusset of her panties. She was on some black stilettos so high she didn't dare look down.

'What do you want?' I asked her in savage French.

'Same as you,' she said.

'How would you know?'

'Whisky. I like whisky,' she said, and with a practised sashay she tok-tok-tokked to the couch, 'with soda.'

I turned back into the kitchen and laid out a whisky with ice and Perrier. She'd managed to sit down somehow without her dress snapping up around her waist. Her muscly legs were crossed tight. I handed her the drink, noticed the lipstick, red this time, and the heavy eye make-up.

'What are you doing here?'

'I came to see how you were.'

'For Jean-Luc?'

'No.'

'I heard an interesting thing last night.'

'Oh yes?'

'This person said the only wife of Jean-Luc's he knew about died.'

'Jean-Luc means wife in the broadest sense of the word,' she said. 'Where's yours?'

'I'm not married and she's not here.'

'Still working?'

'No. She's not coming back.'

'I'm sorry.'

'That lie I had to tell about what happened in Grand-Popo, I had to tell it in front of her. She wasn't happy.'

'I'm sorry.'

'You don't sound it.'

'Why don't you sit down?'

'Just tell me what you want.'

'I came to see you,' she said, putting her drink down. She stood up and walked over to me, shoulder height to me in her heels.

'I'm not seeing anybody,' I said. 'Does Jean-Luc know you're here?'

'He doesn't control me.'

'He controls most people.'

'You know,' she said, her finger in the corner of her tiny mouth, 'he can't do it any more . . . since his accident.'

'I guessed.'

'But he still likes me to have fun.'

'And report back . . . with all the details.'

She smiled up at me, glossed her lips with her tongue and then dropped her eyes. She hooked a finger in my trouser belt. I locked my hand on to her wrist. There was a knock at the door. Everybody crowding round to see me all of a sudden.

'*Entrez,*' I shouted.

Carole didn't move.

The door opened. Bagado walked in and took in the tableau. Two uniformed policemen appeared behind him. Carole unhooked her finger. I let go of her wrist.

'I was just leaving,' she said, and tottered away from me.

The dress had ridden up at the back over the lower part of her buttocks so she had to tug it down as she walked deliberately past the three men at the door, one of the policemen tracking her all the way out and down the stairs.

'I've been trying to call you,' I said.

'We've just come from your office,' said Bagado.

'We must have just missed each other,' I said. 'Do you want a drink? Your friends probably do. Take a seat.'

'Not this time.'

'I see.'

'I'm taking you in for questioning. I've been *ordered* to bring you in for questioning,' he rephrased.

'And these two?'

'They're going to search the premises,' he said, motioning them forward.

'Up and down?' I said, but he didn't react. 'What are you looking for? What's the questioning about?'

'I'm just bringing you in.'

'And the questioning?'

'Commandant Bondougou.'

'And these guys?'

'They're looking for a weapon. A murder weapon. That's all I know.'

'You'd better get on with it then,' I said, and socked back the whisky.

Chapter 22

The uniformed boys, and they were on the brink of puberty, tossed the place into a heap, making free use of the army-issue boots they were wearing and enjoying themselves as much as any adolescent in an amusement arcade. Possessions for the possessionless African were fascinating and all my things were handled, sniffed, squeezed and bunged on the central heap. Bagado looked into the void, his head still, his mind ticking, his jaw muscles working over his spearmint thoughts.

'Who did I kill?' I asked.

'I don't know,' he said, without looking round.

The boys went into the kitchen. Bagado's eyes followed them. Pans cascaded on to the floor. He shook his head. Ice trays and precious amber bottles followed.

'Happy Hour,' I said. 'Don't take them downstairs, Bagado.'

'Is it down there?'

'Something's down there. Something they could make something of if they wanted to . . . but it's nothing. I haven't killed anyone. I don't even know who I'm supposed to have killed.'

'I know, I know,' he said. 'My sense of humour's warping with my circumstances.'

'Bondougou must have enjoyed sending you.'

'Have you got any insect repellent?'

'Not on me.'

'You're going to need some where you're going.'

'Where's that?'

'The locals call it *La Boîte de Nuit*.'

'The Night Club?'

'Because it's hot, sweaty and dark and unspeakable things can happen in there. They hope the name takes the spike out of the horror. I'm told it doesn't.'

The boys crunched out of the kitchen and into the bedroom. The mosquito net tore. The mattress shot out into the dining room.

'How long?'

'Depends how badly he wants to speak to you. Anything from six hours to six days. You'd better give me your watch if you want to see it again. Put some money down your underpants.'

'This is getting a little Devil's Island for my taste.'

'We learnt a lot from the French. How to soften men up. But Africans are very hard. Maybe you won't have to be down there for so long.'

'A night out of my own bed and I'm all aquiver.'

'Two hours off the whisky . . .' said Bagado, leaving it open ended, giving me a sad, sleepy look.

'That medicine man of yours is working.'

'I'm trying not to let it show.'

'Maybe you should get him working on Bondougou.'

'We haven't got that far yet,' he said. 'Now put your hands behind your back, I'm going to have to cuff you.'

The pre-pubes came out of the bedroom with some of my clothes stuffed down their tunics.

'*Rien.*'

'*Allons y,*' said Bagado, snapping the cuffs.

We went down the stairs. The boys looked at Moses's flat. Bagado told them to take me to the car. Carole's Renault 5 was still across the street. They folded me into the back seat. Bagado came in after me. Carole's headlights flared and swung across the back of our heads as she turned the Renault towards Sekou Touré.

We drove to the Sûreté. Bagado tried to lighten my load with some chit-chat. The boys' ears wagged in front but didn't understand.

'I didn't tell you about the postmortem on those five stowaways we found on the *Kluezbork II.*'

'No. No, you didn't,' I said, my mind trying to veer off *La Boîte de Nuit.*

'They suffocated.'

'I thought we knew that already.'

'It's been confirmed.'

'That doesn't sound very interesting. What about the fresh timber?'

'The postmortem budget for stowaways doesn't extend to minute examination of lung tissue to find toxic and volatile traces.'

'So we'll never know?'

'We'll never know,' he said, and looked out of the window with the bland face of a man who's added another blank to his ignorance.

At the Sûreté I was taken down into the basement where a jailer uncuffed me and told me to strip to my underpants. He put his hands down there, up under my balls, and came out with the roll of money. He nodded at me and put it in his pocket. He picked up a truncheon and walked me down a long corridor of cells to a door at the end. He put the key in the lock, readied the truncheon, opened the door and pointed me in.

It was like walking into a sick animal's pen, or up its arse, more like. The heat was double what it was outside and the stink of shit as strong and thick as if they were burning it. I coughed back the gag that rose in my throat. I had time to see four men sitting with their backs to the walls, all of them naked with their eyes screwed up to the light. Two bodies lay on the floor. The door shut behind me.

The floor was wet and slippery. All the men in the room were coughing. I found a wall. It was wet too, dripping with what felt like recently spat mucus – bubbly, slimy. I trod on another body which groaned. A hand, hard and tight as a manacle, snapped around my wrist and jerked me down fast. My feet slipped away from me and I landed on the point of my shoulder, my lips making contact with the sludge on the ground.

'*C'est un blanc*,' said a voice.

Hands went down my pants, rummaged my balls, the crack of my arse. I had a wild moment of panic that gang rape was going to be added to my CV, but that wasn't the African way and these men hadn't been without sex for that long. They were looking for the money the guard had already taken. They let me go.

'*Il est trop petit*,' said a voice close to me.

A few men managed a laugh.

I crawled to the wall and was pushed around to an empty section. The men fell silent apart from the coughing – Cotonou's high-water table oozing through the walls clogging the bronchials.

The mosquitoes whined. The sweat poured off me. I

241

wiped the shit off my mouth, calmed down. Everybody in here was keeping something back for themselves. Violence was for another place. I brought my knees up, dropped my head and let the stink creep into me, become a part of me like another membrane until it didn't stink any more.

Friday 26th July, Sûreté, Cotonou.

At dawn the light seeped into the room from three barred slits fifteen feet up in the metre-thick outside wall. There were fourteen men in the room, which was four by three metres. Two open buckets were filled to the brim with piss and faeces. As the light came up the men who could stood. Four remained lying in the middle of the floor. They'd taken some heavy beatings. The one nearest me looked out from his one eye that wasn't closed and bloody. The eye said nothing to me. It had no fight in it, no interest. It was just hanging on in a face that was going to get broken some more.

Last man in, I was on shit-bucket duty. Then I was on cleaning up the piss and shit that overflowed from the buckets down the corridor. Later a hose was put through the grill of the door and we hosed ourselves down and the men on the floor, one of whom was moved, groaning in pain, off the drain hole.

Breakfast came. A calabash of thin millet gruel. We ate from the communal pot. The injured men were force fed by the others. Then it was backs to the wall again and think your own hollow thoughts, keep your strength for the questions and the beatings.

It was the middle of the afternoon when they sent for me. I was weak from the insufferable heat which had built through the day. The jailer cuffed me and took me into the toilet where he hosed me down. He prodded me up the stairs to another corridor where a solitary woman was working her way down, scrubbing the floor to a dull sheen. The jailer told me to get down on my haunches. He knocked on the door and rested his truncheon on the back of my head, telling me to keep it down and not to get up from this position. A voice called us in. I waddled in after him. My eyes at desk level saw a uniform. The jailer tapped my head down again and left the room.

Under the desk were some well-shined black Oxfords and a pair of legs in some dark-blue trousers crossed at the ankles. There was nothing in the room except the desk and the man's chair and the smell of lino. I was not comfortable. The crouch was breaking my knees.

'You know why you're here,' said the deep and unmistakable voice of Le Commandant Bondougou speaking in French.

'Is there any water?' I asked, and bang, the edge of the desk cracked me across the forehead. I went over on my back and beetled there until Bondougou called the jailer back in to right me. He told him to bring some other guy along and to wait outside. Now that I'd seen the huge, fat, sinister head – the eyes angled down to the nose that spread across his face as thick and as soft as a boxing glove – I got into a more sensible frame of mind.

'You know why you're here,' he said again.

'You think I killed someone.'

243

'Tell me what you were doing the night before last from about eight in the evening.'

'I went down to the Jonquet, had something to eat in the Restaurant Guinéen.'

'Do you normally spend your evenings in the Jonquet?'

'No. My wife's pregnant at the moment. She's not interested in sex. I was looking for girls. Clean girls.'

'Did you find any?'

'There aren't any in the Jonquet.'

'Does that mean you went home?'

He knew things. I knew he knew things. I shut up. There was a knock on the door.

'*Attends*,' he roared.

I breathed in the refreshing lino, inspected the shiny shoes.

'Did you meet a man called Daniel Ayangba?'

'Daniel? Yes. A German guy sent him to me.'

'Did you meet him that night?'

How did Bondougou know all this?

'Yes. He took me to a brothel outside Cotonou near the lagoon. I looked at his girls. I didn't like any of them. They were too young. When I came out his driver pointed a gun at me and they stole two hundred thousand CFA.'

'And after that?'

'They drove off.'

'What did you do?'

'I borrowed a moped and went back to Cotonou.'

'Where in Cotonou?'

The lino had been laid in tiles, square tiles. They were green with cream flecks. They offered no assistance.

'Where did you go?' he asked again.

'Home.'

'You didn't go to the Hotel Paradis.'

'Where's that?'

He wrote something on a piece of paper. The pen creaked across the desk, gave a dull thud for the full stop.

'It's a hotel on the coast just off the Porto Novo road. You don't know it?'

'I might do if you took me there in daylight.'

'And at night?'

Back to the lino tiles. Nothing for me to say.

'Face the door and read this out,' he said, giving me the paper. 'Shout it out.'

'*Ça peut rester dehors*,' I shouted.

'*Entrez*,' said Bondougou.

Behind the door was the barman from the Hotel Paradis.

'*C'est lui, c'est lui*,' he said, as if he'd been paid.

The door shut. I turned back to Bondougou.

'You were seen leaving the hotel. The barman heard your voice. You are white, tall, people don't make mistakes about you.'

'OK. I followed Daniel to the hotel. I went up to his room, beat him up and took my two hundred thousand CFA. Then I left and went home.'

Bondougou nodded.

'Why did you lie to me?'

'I forgot the name of the hotel.'

Bondougou roared something incoherent. The door opened. The jailer rushed in and clubbed me across the shoulders. I went down. He started laying into me. I

245

had a flash of the broken men lying in *La Boîte de Nuit*. The blows rained down.

'*Arrêtes, arrêtes!*' I shouted.

Bondougou called the guy off. The jailer righted me on my haunches and left the room.

'You said you beat him up?'

'That's right.'

'How?'

'I knocked him into the wardrobe, split his eyebrow, put his head through the wardrobe door, slapped him about a little.'

'Was he still conscious when you left?'

I shut up again. No sense in going on about hitting him over the head with a gun which was still in my possession.

'He wasn't conscious, was he?' said Bondougou. 'You left him naked in the bath, his face beaten to mince meat . . . barely recognizable . . . then you shot him in the head.'

'No.'

'You've been positively identified by the barman. You've admitted you were there. You said you beat him up. Now I want you to admit you shot him and I want you to tell me what you have done with the gun.'

There was no way out. There was nothing I could say to persuade even a free and fair court that I hadn't killed Daniel Ayangba. I'd give it one more try and then I'd have to call on a friend.

'Commandant Bondougou,' I said, 'there's nothing I can say to you to make you believe that I didn't kill this man. But I think you know that I'm not a killer. I think you know that Daniel Ayangba was a pimp and in that line of business you deal with difficult people. I was there. I beat him up. I took the money he owed me . . .'

'Did he have any other money?'

'Yes. In a holdall. Maybe four million CFA . . .'

'We didn't find it. Where has it gone? Tell me what you have done with the money *and* the gun. And tell me now or I will have you beaten again.'

Who said truth never hurts the teller? I'll kill him. It was time to call in the artillery.

'We have a mutual friend,' I said. 'I think our friend can help explain some things to you. I think he can help you understand my situation.'

The change of direction wrong-footed Bondougou for a moment. Mutual friends was not something he was expecting to have with me.

'Who is this friend?'

'Roberto Franconelli,' I said.

'Franconelli?' said Bondougou. 'What has Franconelli to do with this?'

'I think you should call him. I'm doing a very important job for him and I think you should call him and let him explain it to you.'

I looked over the lip of the desk. Our eyes connected. Bondougou's were intense and astonished. A realization crept into them that perhaps he hadn't got me in the bag. Franconelli was not a man he could dismiss. Whatever Bondougou was doing for him, and I only knew of that one cover-up some months ago, he was taking some heavy cream. Bondougou left the room. The jailer came in and stood over me.

'*Ça va?*' he asked.

247

I nodded and clicked at the same time that the money he'd taken off me had worked. The beating he'd ladled out had left me barely bruised. He'd held back on the full meat.

'*Merci*,' I said. '*Je vais arranger quelque chose pour toi.*'

He tapped me on the shoulder with the truncheon and smiled.

Bondougou was back in ten minutes. He bustled into the room in a nervous flurry, sent the jailer out and sat down, his feet working overtime under the desk. He told me to stand up. His slit eyes were blinking a lot, his finger and thumb up his nostrils thinking, thinking.

'You spoke to him,' I said.

'Yes, yes, yes.'

'He explained things to you?'

'Of course.'

'Can I have my clothes back?'

Bondougou shouted out an order to the jailer whose footsteps retreated.

'He told me he has sent you to *find* Jean-Luc Marnier.'

'That's right,' I said. 'I understand it's a personal matter.'

'You must do something for me when you find Jean-Luc Marnier.'

'Anything, M. Le Commandant, please, tell me.'

'You must report to me before you talk to M. Franconelli.'

'No problem,' I said. 'Is there any particular reason?'

'I want to speak to him. He owes me money.'

'Perhaps I can help . . . if he owes you money.'

'Yes, but –' he started, and changed his mind. 'Just tell me.'

248

'I heard there was some trouble on a ship called the *Kluezbork II*. Some men found dead. Stowaways, I think.'

'That's enough,' he said. 'You can leave now . . . but when you find him tell me before you . . . before you do anything.'

Bondougou walked to the door and opened it. The jailer was standing with my clothes, about to knock. He was surprised by the turnaround. Bondougou took the clothes and waved him away. He handed them to me with a long reappraising look, a look which told me that the firm ground he thought he'd been standing on was on the shake now. It was an uncertainty I thought I could use.

Chapter 23

Nobody would ever tell you that Cotonou air was sweet, cut with two-stroke fumes, dodgy drainage and an accumulation of sweat it would never win a clean city prize, but that day, beyond the Sûreté gates, it was ambrosia.

By the time I got home it was dark and I got the free-fall gut feeling at what was behind the doors. But the place had been cleaned up. Bagado must have stroked Helen into a stupor to get it done. He'd left my watch in the kitchen for me too, but no whisky. I cleaned myself up, put some money in my pocket and went down to the office, buying a couple of beers on the way.

The day *gardien* was sleeping on some breezeblocks. The night *gardien*, a Muslim, had spread out a length of cardboard pointing east and was preparing to pray. I nudged the day *gardien* awake. He looked over his shoulder at me like a dog in the sun who's not moving for no one unless it's a thirty-five-ton truck. I asked him if anybody had dropped by.

'*Deux hommes.*'

'*Blancs?*'

'*Non, non, noirs, de Nigeria. Ils ne parlent pas français.*'

'*C'est tout?*'

He fell back to sleep. I nodded at the Muslim, who dropped to his knees with the suddenness of a man who'd seen a 5000-CFA note, and prostrated himself to Mecca. I went upstairs and sat in the streetlight crossing the floor of my office and drank beer and whisky chasers until the Night Club was a distant speck on the horizon of my memory.

I put a call through to Dic in Lagos. No answer from the office so I hit him at home. One of his children picked up the phone, roared over the battle on TV and dropped the phone out of the window. Dic's wife was still in hospital in Beirut after an operation and the kids were out of control.

'Visitors?' I asked.

'I wish they were but they're all my kids and they stay here and this is the noise they make and I pay for the pleasure. Don't do it, Bruce, you got the right idea.'

'How many did you say you've got now?'

'Eight.'

'Look, Dic, you remember we talked about that woman, Madame Sokode? You told me about Nexim and the construction business and it all sounded very nice. But now I need some different information.'

'Like what?'

'The real thing. The dirt. I've heard things about her.'

'You have?' he said, as if this was a big surprise.

'Maybe you already heard something.'

'Me? No.'

'Did you hear she ran girls? Prostitutes. Whores.'

'I didn't hear anything,' he said. 'But I haven't been listening. Leave it with me. Let me look into it. I'll call you. I can't talk with all this . . .'

We hung up. More cold beer. More whisky. My heart thumped magnificently. Maybe I should eat something.

251

I went down to the street with the second cold beer and ordered a kebab and ate it in front of the guy. It was good. I had another with extra chilli, felt my insides kicking in.

I stopped a *taxi moto* and headed for the Jouet Doux in the Jonquet. I had a couple of things to do here. Find the German sex punter and hunt out the moped driver who'd taken Marnier home the other night.

Business was slack in the Jouet Doux. I ordered a beer and slumped. Girls came and went but no whites slid in. I started tramping the bars again.

I went down an unlit sidestreet where there were cheaper bars, shacks with thatched awnings and blue and white painted tables outside. The clientele was African. The music, some Afrobeat stuff, was loud and distorted from high amps and bad speakers. The Africans didn't mind, they liked being buried in sound. I had a drink by candlelight but couldn't see anything in the street so upped and moved on.

I got to a point in the mud road where it widened and there seemed to be nothing more of the bars and nightlife. There was a building site with bricks piled up inside a skeleton structure and slag heaps of sand and gravel outside. I'd just decided to give up on the sex punter and concentrate on finding Marnier when I saw him. He was crossing the road back down towards the bars and heading for the Rue des Cheminots, stumbling over the rough puddled road. I caught up with him.

'Remember me?' I asked.

A car rocked and rolled down the road towards us, lighting his face. He'd taken a little more hammer since I last saw him.

'*Der Engländer,*' he said. 'Did he find you? The man. I don't know his name. The one with the young girls.'

'That's what I wanted to know. You sent him to me.'

'Yes,' he said. 'And who are these people? Are they friends of yours?'

Out of the dark came two men. A big, reinforced concrete type and a slimmer version carrying the brains for the two of them. A fist the size of a small lintel came out of the night and connected with the already sensitive tissue on the German's face. There was a crunch which did not sound like the concrete man's knuckles breaking up. The German hit the ground faster than rubble down a chute and went foetal, holding his face.

The big guy turned to me, the slim one behind him looking over his shoulder as if he was operating the levers.

'You owe us some money,' said Slim, in a silly high-pitched voice.

'I don't even know you,' I said. 'And I'm not giving you *anything* if you want to knock me around like that.'

'We're friends of Daniel.'

'Maybe you're the same friends who shot him.'

'Mebbe we are.'

The German was making a terrible noise at our feet and it was winding Slim up some. He fluttered his hand at the big guy who leaned down into the dark and with a short jab there was silence. Slim breathed out with relief and that's when I hit him. Not even I was drunk or stupid enough to try my fragile metacarpals on the other guy.

Slim went down with a whinny and I hurdled him

and sprinted back down the street to the building site, the big guy after me, the ground shaking. I got into the concrete cage, picked up a breezeblock and waited with a trampolining heart.

Mr Big wasn't so sharp without his friend. He rounded the pile of bricks and walked his face straight into my breezeblock swung from yards back. The breezeblock shattered. The man stood up straight. I hit him with another across the jawline, which turned his head a good fifteen degrees and probably knocked everything back into focus. He put one foot forward and winched back his arm. It was time to do some more running.

I leapt through the concrete cage and kneed my way through the pile of gravel and took a tumble down the other side. That side swipe must have slowed Mr Big down. He didn't seem to be following but I ran anyway. I ran past the German, who was still lying in the road, and Slim who was on all fours spewing black. I got into the streetlights down Rue des Cheminots and started walking, trying to get my heart back behind its ribs. I crossed the road at a traffic light and saw the *taxi moto* I wanted, the yellow jacket with the right number, but he had a ride. The lights changed and I was off down the road towards Sekou Touré after him, my eyes bursting out of my head, my tongue streaming behind me, a vapour trail of beer and whisky chasers in my wake.

The phalanx of mopeds stopped for the red light. I was fifty metres away when they changed to green and I had to put some beef into my legs to get across the lights myself. The moped crossed the road and went into the second-hand clothes market whose metal doors were all shut for the night. A moped pulled alongside me and the guy nodded behind him. I jumped on and pointed.

We drove past the Dan Tokpa and across the Nouveau Pont. We were heading for the Porto Novo road when the moped turned left and stopped outside a four-storey apartment building. The ride got off. I pulled alongside and transferred. The driver leaned forward so I didn't drip on him.

He remembered the slashed face of Jean-Luc Marnier and he knew where he'd taken him. I offered him 3000 CFA to take me to the same place. He thought about being greedier but I leaned over him and he decided against having me soak into his jacket any more.

We drove back to the Nouveau Pont and turned right just before it. We came off the broken tarmac after a couple of hundred metres and on to beaten track. About a kilometre later we turned off down towards the lagoon. He took me to a corner house with a two-and-a-half-metre-high wall and only slightly shorter gates. No light seemed to be coming from the front of the house. I told the driver to wait.

I walked down the side of the house. There was another wall at the back but lower, only two metres. It went right down to the edge of the lagoon. I clamped my hands on to the top of the wall to haul myself up. Agony. Glass-topped. I unhooked myself and dropped to the floor oozing blood from my palms. I had a short burst of film in my head – the girl blown up in her brown uniform in the bottom of the skiff, the palms of her hands, forearms and knees eaten away. I swallowed hard and leaned against the wall, easing back the nausea.

The sound of groaning metal pulled me back. The gates were opening at the front. Carole's car came out into the road and stopped. She got out and closed the gates. A bolt slid across from the other side. She got back into the car and pulled away, the lights sweeping across the boy astride his moped, shielding his eyes.

I crossed the road and told him to take me home, where I dressed my hands. I found an old piece of matting and went down to the car. I drove back to Marnier's house and parked up five streets away and walked back down with the matting.

A car's headlights flared across the street and I drifted into the shadows. A black official-looking Peugeot pulled up by the gates and gave a single honk on the horn. A man got out and leaned on the roof of his car, impatient. He walked around the front of the car and into the headlights. Then he heard the bolt slide and backtracked. He reversed the car into the gateway.

The man in the headlights was Commandant Bondougou.

Chapter 24

I laid the matting across the broken glass on the top of the wall, got up there and lowered myself into a courtyard. There was a boat on a two-wheeled metal trailer, a launch with a small cabin at the front and two sizeable Mercury outboards. Light filtered into the courtyard from rooms at the back of the house which had reed blinds over the windows. Figures moved in one of the rooms, shadows crossed the stern of the boat. A concrete stairway at the back of the house went up to a verandah with a thatched awning which ran the length of the house. There was a fly screen door to the kitchen which gave on to the verandah.

From the verandah I could see Bondougou sitting on his own on a sofa resting a drink on the top of his gut. There were cooking smells coming from the left and Marnier appeared in the kitchen doorway, also holding a drink, and wearing an apron which bore the design of a pair of breasts cupped in a teasy-weasy bra, a navel and a triangle of pubic hair framed by suspenders and stockings. Bondougou looked at him with no concern, as if this was the most normal attire he could expect from a white man entertaining a senior policeman. They were speaking in French and an electric fan on the sideboard looked from one to the other.

'Why so urgent all of a sudden?' said Marnier.

'Urgent?' said Bondougou, the sound seeming to come from down the back of his trousers. 'You don't think this business has been urgent all the time? My God . . .'

'Which one's that you're asking after?' said Marnier.

Bondougou grinned, which was not reassuring. His teeth were widely spaced and the tongue that came out from between them was twice the size of a whole pork fillet.

'As you know,' he said, 'we have many ancestors who we can appeal to.'

'Which one are you appealing to now?'

Bondougou rubbed his face with his spare hand, picked his nose, squeezed his eyes shut and looked through the galaxy of his cranium and came up with nothing, no God nor ancestors.

'How much time do you need?' he asked.

'Wait,' said Marnier, who went into the kitchen, surprising me that he wasn't wearing the reverse side of the apron on his back.

Bondougou shifted in his seat. The sofa gulped him up a bit more.

'I've already been waiting a long time,' he said. 'As you know, my position is very delicate. The questions are –'

'I mean wait for the meal,' shouted Marnier. 'I'll be back in a moment.'

Behind the sofa was a table laid for two with an open bottle of red wine. Marnier, out of his apron now, added a steaming pot and a bowl of rice. Bondougou fought his way out of the sofa, socked back the remains of his whisky and pulled his shirt back down over his stomach.

They sat down to eat. They didn't talk, but concentrated on the food which they finished in a matter of minutes. Marnier cleared the bowls, came back with some salad and a board of cheese. They motored through that, finished the wine and sat back with more whisky. Bondougou chewed his way through a number of toothpicks – anxious, frustrated, he wanted to get on with things. Marnier smoked and played him like a big daddy salmon.

'When do you think you can make the transfer?' asked Bondougou, annoyed at having to ask the question, hating to chase that fly.

'I haven't found a good enough place on the lagoon yet,' said Marnier, flicking his ash as if he had all the time in the world.

He was lying and letting Bondougou know it. It infuriated the big African, who realized he was going to have to touch on the one thing he didn't want to.

'The contract is very complicated, Jean-Luc,' he said, picking up a Guinness coaster. 'It's a very large project. There's more than two hundred pages of paperwork, fifty drawings. You don't build a barracks, a hospital and a school with a contract written on the back of a beer mat.'

The Guinness coaster flipped out of Bondougou's hand and span over Marnier's shoulder, who laughed.

'Anything's possible if you're a minister,' said Marnier. 'Anything's possible if you're a senior officer in the military and a friend of the son of the President of the Republic of Nigeria. And let's not forget that, M. Le Commandant. We are talking about Nigeria. We don't have to discuss two-hundred-page contracts. We don't have to leaf through fifty drawings. They just have to say yes and make the first payment. There's no commitment on this continent without money and a contract from a Nigerian . . . well . . .'

Marnier scoffed and flourished his claw, dispatching the nonexistent contract into the ether.

'That's completely impossible,' said Bondougou, throwing up his hands, scowling across the table, the two of them entering into the vaudeville with spirit. 'These are government funds.'

'They're selling oil. Look at the oil price. It's not fifteen dollars a barrel any more.'

Marnier turned his chair to one side and stretched his legs out. Bondougou leaned across the table at him.

'We have to show them something. We have to encourage them.'

'This is a very dirty business,' said Marnier. 'I don't like this business at all. I'm only doing this business because of our long-standing friendship, all the work we've done together over the years. You're feeling very exposed at the moment. Delicate, I think you said. My position isn't easy either. It's time for them to suffer with us to get what they want.'

Bondougou rubbed his face again, trying to buff some sense in there, shake this white man up, get him to do what he wanted him to do. Marnier relished his smoke and tapped the table with his claw hand.

'I understand you took in Bruce Medway last night.'

'Oh yes?'

'Carole was there when your men turned up. Have you charged him?'

'No. We've released him. Insufficient evidence.'

'What did he do?'

'Killed a man.'

'No,' said Marnier, shaking his head. 'That man couldn't kill anyone.'

'How do you know?' asked Bondougou, interested for a moment.

'He hasn't got the power. Believe me, I know.'

Marnier the bloody expert.

A horn sounded from the street.

'That's Carole,' said Marnier.

Bondougou stood and came round to Marnier's side of the table. He leaned down and spoke very quietly to his good ear.

'They're safe?'

'Of course.'

'Are they still here in Cotonou?'

'No, no, no. They're out on the lagoon now.'

'No more accidents,' he said, and the horn sounded again.

'No,' said Marnier, standing up. 'Let's go down.'

'I think we should show them something,' said Bondougou, blocking his way, last-ditch attempt.

'It's their turn,' said Marnier, putting a hand on Bondougou's shoulder, turning him in a friendly way to the door.

They left the room. I straightened up, found that I'd been crouching with the tension. I wiped the sweat off my face with my shoulders. The pressure was up, the air heavy and close.

Carole came into the room, kicked off her pumps and sat down on the sofa with her legs tucked up

261

underneath her, the sheath dress just managing to hang on in there around her buttocks.

'He said he released him,' said Marnier, closing the door.

'He wasn't there.'

'A pity. I was looking forward to that. Where did you go?'

'The Sheraton,' she said. 'I'll have a whisky.'

'Did you meet anybody?' asked Marnier, his voice thickening, the curiosity not idle.

'Yes,' she said. 'Did you get anything from Bondougou?'

'Tell me.'

'You didn't get anything from Bondougou.'

'It takes time in Africa. You can't push. You have to nudge. Now tell me about . . .'

'The whisky first.'

Marnier handed her a drink and dropped himself in the armchair in front of her.

'Tell me,' he said again.

'I'm fed up with waiting.'

'Then you shouldn't be in Africa. Waiting here is a way of life. Now tell me what happened at the Sheraton.'

'Well, he didn't look much in the bar.'

'He? Who? What nationality?'

'American. They always go for me. They like to see a girl who keeps her body in shape.'

'How old?'

'Oh, this one was quite young. I shouldn't think he was long out of college. He was with an older guy who left and went to bed.'

'You said he didn't look much in the bar. What does that mean?'

'He looked inexperienced.'

'But when you got him upstairs . . .' Marnier beckoned her with his hand.

Carole rolled her eyes and twisted in her seat. She hooked a leg over one arm of her chair and ran her nails down the inside of her thigh to the black lace panties pulled tight over her crotch. She slipped a finger in under the material. Marnier nodded, sat back and closed his eyes.

'What happened when you got him upstairs?'

'It wasn't what happened, it's what he had.'

'Yes?' said Marnier, placing his hands on his knees.

'He had the biggest balls I've ever seen on a man.'

'Really?'

'Yes, really. But the extraordinary thing . . . was the quantity he produced every time he came.'

'You mean he could produce the same amount each time?'

'It went all over . . . in my hair too which . . .'

'You're lying,' said Marnier, his eyes snapping open.

The glass stilled at Carole's swollen little lips, her finger came out from behind the rim of her panties.

'You're lying,' said Marnier again.

She crossed her legs and took a gulp of whisky.

'I might be.'

Marnier pounded the arm of his chair with his fist.

I left them in their lonely, frustrated little room and drove back home, seeing the geometry of the relationships a little more clearly. Marnier and Bondougou had had a mutually satisfying business relationship over the

263

years. Marnier was an expert on the movement of human cargo. Bondougou had persuaded him to do this nasty little trick but Marnier wanted a reward. The Nigerian construction contract. Big money. If Madame Sokode was the buyer of the schoolgirls then Bondougou must 'do' for her and her people in Benin. Daniel was killed because he couldn't supply a believable reason for the partly stolen money. Bondougou covered for the organization – he saw there was strong evidence pointing to me in the Daniel killing, saw that he could solve a murder and remove a potential troublemaker. But Franconelli was important to him too. He had to let me go to find Marnier but Marnier was vital to him on the schoolgirl deal with Madame Sokode. Only Marnier knew where the schoolgirls were. Bondougou didn't want Marnier found too quickly, so he sent Daniel's boss and minder round to slow me up. Daniel must have told them about me but if I'd been him I'd have omitted the fact that I'd told the white man about Madame Sokode. That would be a definite bullet in the head. He must have just concentrated on the money. So the two small advantages I had at the moment were that Bondougou didn't know that I'd found out that Marnier was the schoolgirl kidnapper, nor did he know that I had my foot in Madame Sokode's door . . . but was it the right door?

Chapter 25

I bought a bottle of Red Label from a stall on Sekou Touré and went back home. I registered that there was a call for me on the answering machine and steadied myself because I was entertaining the wild hope that it was Heike. I prowled the house looking for a sign from her. The place was absurdly neat and tidy. Everything had been cleared away after the police tossed it. Everything apart from a small collection on a forgotten and empty set of shelves at the end of the dining room table. Your heart doesn't get broken by these sort of things, it gets squeezed tight so that each beat is a dim tremble in the fist of unbearable emotions.

Everything I'd ever given Heike was in a small pile on the lowest shelf. The hairpin from Abomey, a ring from Ghana, some bangles I'd bought in Burkina, an amber necklace from God knows where . . . It wasn't going to be Heike on the answering machine.

I cracked the Red Label, poured myself a glass and hit the 'play' button. Dic told me to call him. I dialled his Lagos number and added another finger to my glass.

'It's me,' I said.

'OK,' he said, and roared something in Armenian over his shoulder. The silence was stunned. A door closed. 'I have it.'

'On Madame Sokode?'

'She runs prostitution rings in Nigeria and Benin. She took the business over from her mother when she died. Her mother used it to get favours from men with influence to expand her drinks distribution business. Madame Sokode sold the drinks business and went into construction, like I told you. She still needs those favours from the big men . . . even more so.'

'Why even more so?'

'She wants to get into government work. Very big money.'

'How do you know about the brothels, Dic?'

Silence.

'I've heard she's got white girls,' he said. 'Eastern Bloc girls from the Ukraine, Czechoslovakia, Rumania . . .'

'I know what the Eastern Bloc is, Dic. But is your information reliable?'

'Believe me, it's reliable.'

'Do you know any of these white girls?'

'What? Me? No, no, no,' he said.

Dic's delicate problem. He whores around. I drank the bottom two fingers of my Red Label, hoping it would speed up my understanding of such delicate matters.

'Do you know somebody who knows any of these girls. Preferably one that speaks English . . . my Ukrainian's not been aired for a while.'

'I don't think so,' he said. 'It's not easy to talk to people about this kind of thing. And these girls, they're . . . you know . . . they're looked after.'

There's only so much of Dic's choirboy act I was going to swallow.

'How many children did you say you've got?'

'I told you. Eight.'

'You love them?'

'Of course I do.'

'How old are they?'

'The boys are eighteen, sixteen, twelve and seven. The girls are fourteen, nine, eight and seven. The seven-year-olds are twins.'

'I wouldn't have guessed that, Dic.'

'How could you?'

'Now listen to me. My information is that one of Madame Sokode's brothels is going to take delivery of seven schoolgirls between the ages of nine and six. There were eight of them but one was killed. She tried to escape and they killed her. These girls are all virgins who've been kidnapped off the streets of Cotonou and are going to be sold into prostitution. You understand what I'm saying, Dic?'

Silence. Something ticked on the line. My phone bill racking up.

'I understand,' he said finally.

'Now, do you think you could get me a talk with one of these white girls that a friend of a friend of yours knows?'

More silence while Dic contemplated the ravine.

'I think I can,' he jumped.

'You're a good man, Dic. Call me.'

'I think I might be a stupid man,' he said, and hung up.

I paced the house, picked up Heike's hairpin, sniffed it, caught her smell from it, put it down and breathed back that full, rich past, looked into that dry endless plain of the future. More Red Label. You never get gout from drinking whisky. Who said that? It'd better be somebody reliable. I had to see Madame Sokode again. No more social calls though. No more talking about people she hated, drinking Black Label on Lake Parquet. I had to go with something and I had to see her in the office. It was safer there. I called Marnier on his mobile.

'You're still here,' I said, the words coming out in a single drunken blurt.

'Where should I go?'

'How about as far away from Franconelli as you can get?'

'I have nothing to fear from Franconelli,' he said. 'I heard you saw him.'

'I'm sure Carole filled you in.'

'I'm sorry about that, but . . . you're alive.'

'Maybe it's not much of a life any more.'

'Like I said to Michel . . .'

'. . . you make your choices . . .' I said, in a bored-shitless voice.

'. . . and then you must be man enough to live with them,' he said, and then as an afterthought, 'He smokes too much grass.'

'And I hear that's only good for knocking out your short-term memory.'

Marnier laughed.

'It means you have no new ones and the old ones are very distant,' he said.

'I'm reassured. Now, Jean-Luc, I'd like my bonus if that's OK with you. I think I deserve it.'

'You do, you do,' he said. 'I have it for you.'

'Can we meet?'

'I'll send Carole for you tomorrow. Eleven o'clock.'

'Come to the house. There's a bit of a siege on at my office.'

We hung up. I stripped and lay down on the bed which didn't smell of Heike because the sheets were clean. I got up, walked around the house in the dark, naked, drank more Red Label, half the bottle down, gnawed at the plan developing in my head and got close to doing some praying until I asked myself the same question Marnier had asked Bondougou. Which one? The thunder or the light? By four in the morning I'd exhausted myself and knew I'd be facing real pain in the morning. There was barely an inch in the Red Label bottle.

Saturday 27th July, Cotonou.

I woke having had the full mercury transfusion. My limbs were unliftable. I opened a gummed eye which shrank from the light like a live oyster to a squeeze of lemon. I levered myself up, held my hands out. Pure Parkinson's. The bird fluttered in my chest again. I felt very white, and sick enough to vomit my heels up. I picked up the Red Label bottle with the inch, no top on it. The neck rattled on my teeth until I bit it quiet. I drank. My leg muscles twitched and my guts chupped like a cauldron of curry. Tears streamed down my face with no emotion behind them. I lurched into the dining room and slammed the bottle on the table. My hair fell over my face and my body trembled with an embryonic sob. I turned to the bathroom. Helen stood by the

269

kitchen door looking at me with those heavy-lidded, sad eyes of hers.

'I'm prayin' to the Lord for you, Mr Bruce.'

'Thanks, Helen, I need all the help I can get.'

'I brought dis for you fom my church,' she said, handing me a leaflet. 'It tellin' you 'bout de evil of strong dring, how you can deliver yoursel' fom de dark to de light.'

'I see,' I said. 'Do you mind if I take a shower first?'

She sidestepped me deftly, like an experienced girl who'd seen the leer before the lunge. I got under the shower and hung on to the walls.

The whisky did its work. I smoothed out, popped a couple of Tylenol 500 and managed some wry smiles at myself in the shaving mirror. By eleven I was as bright as a bush baby and the horn from Carole's car didn't feel anything like a cold cleaver down the spine. I took a bottle of cold Possotomé mineral water, the only thing Bagado had put in the fridge, and went down.

The heat outside was crushing. Carole was wearing a cobalt-blue boob tube and a miniskirt. We set off without a word and drove deep into the Dan Tokpa market where we parked. I followed the spinal rift in her muscled back as she weaved through the crowded wooden stalls. We arrived at a wooden shed, a booze shop. Marnier was sitting at the back, fanning himself with a triangle of raffia on a stick. He nodded to Carole, who passed a hand over the small of my back, down the crack of my arse and up to my crotch while the other hand worked my flanks. She gave my balls a measured squeeze and released me.

'He's clean,' she said.

Marnier barked something at her in French – argot, which I didn't understand. She shrugged and sat outside the front on a low wooden stool. Marnier was pouring with sweat in the airless shed.

'You don't trust me, Jean-Luc?' I asked, sipping the Possotomé, giving it to Marnier to swig.

'Not when you're fresh from Franconelli. He's a very persuasive man.'

'He's got plenty of people to do his killing for him and a lot better . . .'

'But no one who can get close,' he cut in, showing me his edge early on.

I took a seat on a crate of Cutty Sark, my shirt patching dark already.

'It worked well,' said Marnier. 'Couldn't have been better.'

'The lie?'

'With Heike there. Perfect.'

'Let's not talk about it.'

'Was she very hurt?'

'What do you think, Jean-Luc?'

'And Franconelli. Did he tell you?'

'He told me something.'

'You see. He can't tell you. What did he say?'

'He said half that gold of yours is his.'

Marnier shook his head.

'Did he tell you he wanted it back . . . his gold?'

'As a matter of fact, he didn't.'

'You see.'

'It was a bad lie. He was tired. He wanted me out of the room.'

'Is he sick?'

'Not so you'd notice. His temper doesn't do his heart much good.'

'Dying in agony from inoperable cancer would be too kind for him.'

'Shall we talk about the gold?'

'Your bonus.'

'Not just yet,' I said. 'I've got a buyer for you. For the whole lot. That's if you're interested in selling.'

Marnier shrugged the merchant's professional shrug. I waited.

'I was going to courier it to Zurich,' he said, 'but if you can get me a good price . . . Where would it have to be delivered? Here?'

'Nigeria.'

'I'm not going to Nigeria with it.'

'Under no circumstances?'

'The price would have to be the very top of the market.'

'Of course it would.'

Jean-Luc checked me for sarcasm and turned back to his one and only fan.

'It would take me some time, too. I don't know anybody to help me across the border on that side.'

'What can you get for it in Zurich?'

'Three-sixty dollars an ounce.'

'How many ounces?'

'Two thousand two hundred and thirty-six. Close on eight hundred and five thousand dollars.'

'I thought you said it was nearly a million.'

'It is . . . nearly.'

'How much do you want to take it to Nigeria?'

'Forget it. It's too dangerous. I could lose everything.'

'Don't they ask a few more questions these days in Zurich? About gold, about money that passes through their hands.'

Marnier looked at me out of the corner of his head.

'I heard gold was a sensitive issue over there at the moment. You know, with the hoo-haa about the Nazi stuff and the American government report due out. Maybe it's not so easy to fly it in . . . no receipts and all that. They're very touchy about handling hot stuff, drug stuff, any stuff . . .'

'This isn't drug stuff.'

'*You* know that.'

The shed creaked in the heat. The market noises seemed distant, muffled by the booze crates. I stared into the earless side of Marnier's head, willing him on.

'Who's your buyer?' he asked, opening up a little, his head hung over his knees, the sweat dripping and soaking into the wooden floorboards of the shed.

'Prominent Nigerian business persons.'

'With names?'

'You don't need to know that yet.'

Marnier winced and scratched his neck savagely.

'If these prominent business persons come to Benin,' he said, 'they can have it for three-sixty an ounce. If I have to go over there . . . they'll have to come up with four hundred.'

'You want nearly ninety grand to go over there?'

'It's a big risk,' he said. 'How much do you want?'

'I'd be happy with two-and-a-half per cent.'

'Take two.'

'All right,' I said. 'I'll show them my lump as a sample. You did bring that with you?'

He took it off the top of a box above his head and handed it to me.

'I assume this is representative of the quality?'

He nodded.

'I'll be back,' I said. 'Start thinking about how we're going to do this.'

'Can't you see?' he said, slowly. 'I'm thinking.'

Chapter 26

Helen made me a salad, cooked me a piece of fish. She served it and her church leaflet, which she put where the wine glass should have been. I pored over it without taking in a word. I nodded. She watched me from the kitchen door. The phone rang. It was Dic.

'She'll do it,' he said.

'She speaks English?'

'Yes.'

'Where's she from?'

'Ukraine.'

'Does she have a pronounceable name?'

'She calls herself Sophia.'

'When can she get away?'

'Between five and six this afternoon.'

'Where?'

'I'm not taking her to my home.'

'You mean I've got to get to Lagos Island in four hours?'

'It's Saturday,' he said, as if that made any difference. 'Take the ferry.'

I took the ferry, caught it at Mile Two just south of the Expressway from Badagri to Lagos. It took me on a stinking trip via the Apapa docks and dropped me on Marina, about a ten-minute walk from Dic's office, a little after five o'clock.

Dic was the only man in his office at this hour. His door was open and he was sitting amongst his palm trees talking to someone out of sight but who was wearing a brown, strappy, low-heeled sandal on their left foot. He beckoned me in and introduced Sophia, who was a blonde who'd made herself blonder from a bottle. She hid behind a large pair of sunglasses which covered most of her cheeks. Her skin was very white which made her red, full-lipped but sharp-edged mouth stand off her face as if it wasn't hers, she was just working it. She wore a simple blue cotton dress with a hemline down to her shins. Put her next to Carole and you'd pick the whore with no hesitation. She smoked Marlboros one after another, keeping pace with Dic.

I sat down. Dic poured me a cup of tea, offered me a smoke, forgot himself for a moment. He was nervous, didn't know what he was getting into, and there was no doubt in my mind that he'd slept with this girl and that she did something for him . . . a hell of a lot more than his wife could do for him from her hospital bed in Beirut.

Sophia? I didn't know what was going on behind those sunglasses. She seemed to like Dic. Dic was easy to like. But he was a punter too and I wouldn't know how that would sit with a woman.

I asked her about where she worked. The brothel was in a private house on Victoria Island. It catered for businessmen, ones with heavy money, but some nights were given over to civil servants, customs men, military people. These were not the paying kind and she didn't like them. They treated the girls badly, made them do

276

things that they didn't want to do, especially the white girls, who they liked to humiliate. She shuddered, sucked hard on her Marlboro heavies and sat back with her tea.

I asked her about the Benin operation but she knew nothing. It was a separate business. She also said that although she knew Madame Sokode was the ultimate owner of the brothel nobody ever saw her. She never came to the house and had nothing to do with any day-to-day running of the house.

'Did Dic tell you what I want to talk to you about?' I asked.

She nodded.

'Have you or any of the other women heard anything about this business?'

'We hear everything,' she said. 'Nobody keep a secret from a whore.'

'I wouldn't have thought men would talk so much in bed.'

'They not with their wifes,' she said, and neither of us looked at Dic.

'Is there anything stronger than tea in your desk, Dic?' I asked. 'I think we're all going to need a drink for this.'

He produced the office Black Label and three glasses. He even had ice in the fridge. We drank. Dic and Sophia lit up again.

'These people, they sick,' she said, and I thought she meant in the head, but she continued, 'seven of the men. Two military, four from the Ministry of Public Works and the father of Madame Sokode. They all HIV positive. They don' wear condoms. Now they scared.

One go to his village and see a big medicine man. The medicine man tell him if he haff sex with a virgin it cure the sickness. He don' get the AIDS.'

Dic looked frozen solid, not believing what his ears were telling him. Sophia took off her sunglasses and rubbed her eyes with the tips of her fingers. She looked across at me with big, clear blue eyes that were both vulnerable and promising.

'The virgins they come soon. A military man tell the Rumanian girl last night. The medicine man comin' down for the thing.'

'Are they paying money for this?'

She shook her head. I knew what was coming.

'Madame Sokode get the big contract from Public Work. They buildin' a barrack for the military, a hospital and . . . other things. I don' remember but millions of dollar.'

She looked at her watch, ran her hand through her hair, put the sunglasses back on.

'Dic say these very young girl.'

'Nine down to six.'

'You know, if they come to the house it's finish. They don' come out the house.'

'How did you get out?'

'No problem for me,' she said, 'but the young girl . . . You haff to find the girl before they come to the house. If they come to the house I can do nothing.'

She took a final drag on her cigarette and stubbed it out, looked at her watch again. She stood up.

'Is time now.'

Dic followed her out of the room. I leaned forward to check their goodbye routine. They kissed each other

278

on the lips. She squeezed his shoulder. It was touching to watch. I leaned back. Dic got himself back behind his desk.

'So ... now you know,' he said, taking a sip of whisky, lighting up, scratching himself behind the ear with his thumbnail. 'It's hopeless, of course.'

'Are you in love with her?'

'No, no, no, no, no,' he said, and jerked his head up. 'Forget about it.'

'She's not in any danger ... coming to talk to us, I mean?'

'I don't know. She didn't say. I saw her last night, explained your problem, she didn't hesitate.'

I nodded to him and asked to make a call. There was no reply from Madame Sokode's office. I tried her home number and she insisted I came to the house. More social horror.

I left Dic in a pensive state about his situation. An Armenian with a sick wife and eight children in love with a Ukrainian prostitute in Lagos. A lot of knots in that situation and most of them pulled very tight.

I picked up the ferry along with a lot of other people anxious to get off the island after work. My car wasn't up on blocks at Mile Two and I joined the crawl on the Apapa–Orowonsoki Expressway up to Ikeja. The gateman let me into the grounds of Madame Sokode's house just after nine o'clock. I joined her Mercedes parked on the slant in front of the steps up to the veran-dah and spent a few moments gathering myself, hoping I wasn't taking a short walk into the snake pit.

Madame Sokode ... Elizabeth, please, let me in. She

was wearing a purple shift which dropped from two thin straps at her shoulders and ended an inch above the floor. She was barefoot and had some elaborate hair extensions on which modernized her look but not for the better. Like last time it was hot and humid in the house. Her feet squeaked on the parquet as she led me to the three-piece island where there was a tray of Black Label and glasses. She sat down and extended an arm to the sofa and drinks. I poured, gave her a glass, laid my bonus lump on the table in front of her and backed off. Excitement flared in her face, her blinking rate went up to humming-bird level and her hand shot out towards the lump before the deportment queen remembered it was rude to snatch. The lump had been rubbed a bit cleaner by now and was looking more seductively yellow.

'Such a weight,' she said.

'If we can agree some basic terms you can keep that . . . get your quality control people to look it over. It's representative of the lot.'

'What are these basic terms?' She snapped into the business brain.

'Price and delivery.'

'What does your principal want?'

'He'd prefer delivery in Benin. If you can accept that you'll get a better price. If you can't he'll come to Nigeria . . . but it'll cost you.'

'I'm not going to pay more than three-fifty an ounce delivered here in Lagos.'

'Then you can give me my lump back and I'll be on my way.'

'What's the rush? I've cooked you some food.'

280

'Not snails.'

'Not fish-head soup either,' she said, turning my lump over in her fingers, getting attached. How that stuff worked.

'All right,' I said. 'Now that we're not in business I can relax. Do you mind if I pour myself another?'

I sat back and let the lump do all the work.

'You don't have any olives?' I asked.

She left the room, taking her new friend with her. She came back with a bowl of fat green olives.

'From Seville,' she said, and sat down.

We started talking at the same time. I let her through.

'No, no, please,' she said.

'I was just going to ask if you were getting into all this football fever with your boys in the Olympic final and all.'

'I don't like football.'

'You don't have to like it to get caught up in the spirit. It's all out there on the streets . . . those miserable, filthy, crime-laden Lagos streets.'

'Mmmm,' she murmured, not listening.

'Spirit's very important,' I said, looking around the empty room. 'Maybe you should have a house-warming.'

She looked up slowly. The sweat was creeping through my hair.

'Who would I invite?'

'Forget it. A stupid idea. It was just talk. I've had a long day talking, talking, talking. Can't stop the mouth when I've had a day like today.'

'What's all the talk been about?'

'Making a living.'

'Loading ships?' she asked. 'Running around the port . . . chasing after work gangs?'

That chilled me. She'd done some sniffing around in Cotonou.

'Who've *you* been talking to?'

She named a shipping agent.

'So now you know I'm not a multimillionaire.'

'I knew that anyway.'

I felt the pressure of her shrewdness. Her eyes drilled, letting me know that she knew I needed this deal as much as she wanted to make it work. It encouraged me that she thought my motives were purely financial, that her Benin people hadn't reported back. Unless she was playing the long game.

'My principal's got two thousand, two hundred and thirty-six ounces. If you're prepared to come to Benin he can let you have it at three-seventy an ounce. If you insist on delivery here then you're going to have to pay four-ten.'

'Do you know what the market was today?'

'I didn't hear.'

'Three-sixty-eight. Why should I pay anything over the market rate? What's my advantage?'

'I don't know. You might have to ask yourself that question.'

'I'm asking it.'

'And it doesn't sound like a positive response.'

'No,' she said. 'I'm not going to pay the market rate and it's going to be delivered in Lagos and that is it. Three-fifty-five on my doorstep.'

Nobody said it was going to be easy, but the toughness of her negotiating made it sound like genuine business, made it sound as if this wasn't any sort of a game, long or short.

'How do you like your steak?' she asked.

'*Saignant*, if it's good.'

'It's good.'

Chapter 27

I woke up still bored from the dinner conversation with Madame Sokode. Yards and yards of stuff about people I didn't know, places I'd never been to, films I'd never see, books I'd never read. Books with titles like *The Hearthunters*, eight hundred and fifty pages about love and flower-arranging.

I called Bondougou's home number and arranged to meet him in his office before lunch. I sat around and let my paranoia off the leash, let it run down dark holes and worry over who knew what about me. I decided Madame Sokode only knew what her shipping agent had told her. If she did know more it was too dangerous for her to mention the uninteresting information she had gleaned and risk frightening me off. But the nature of paranoia is that you never quite believe anything.

Then there was Bondougou. He knew I was circling. Daniel would have talked that much. My Franconelli card was keeping me out on the street but I had to pull Bondougou in tighter to me and take his eye off the ball. The easiest thing in the world if you knew Bondougou.

I arrived at the empty Sûreté just before midday. Bondougou's office was a corner room on the first floor. He was sitting behind his desk with his tunic open, a white vest stretched taut across his belly. He had a very serious look on his face that said he couldn't think of any reason why I should be coming to see him in his office . . . except one.

'Have you found him?' he asked.

'Not yet,' I said, which ironed out a few creases in his forehead.

'What can I do for you?'

'I was hoping I could do something for you,' I said. 'Solve the problem you have with Marnier before I do Franconelli's work.'

He was suddenly concerned and fascinated. His slit eyes bulged at what might be coming.

'What's that?' he asked.

'Franconelli's work?' I said, teasing him along. 'I think you know.'

'Yes,' he said, resting his fingers on the edge of his desk, trying to find the right chord.

'Marnier has close to a million dollars' worth of gold he wants to sell.'

Bondougou's eyebrows hopped over the stile. He didn't know about that and it was very interesting to him.

'What are you proposing?' he asked.

'I have a buyer for the gold.'

'Here?'

'In Nigeria,' I said. 'What I'm proposing is to bring my buyer and Marnier together to do the deal. The buyer pays and leaves with the gold. I satisfy Mr Franconelli's requirements and we, you and I, split the money.'

Bondougou began playing with his nose, trying to

remodel it into something more nose-like. He plugged his nostrils, should any of the large thoughts he was thinking want to escape down that route. He had one big knotty problem now. He'd said Marnier owed him money and I was appearing to solve that problem, but he still had to do that schoolgirl deal. If his greed won out, which I knew it would, he'd have to do the school-girl deal before the gold deal. He was already having trouble moving Marnier along but now there was this other huge incentive. It was good to see the extra press-ure on the man, the weight of his greed pressing down on his chest.

'How are you going to make contact with him?'

'I'll call him on his mobile,' I said. 'I talk to him every day. I just don't know where he is.'

'Don't talk to him about this yet. I have to think about this. I'll call you.'

I knew we were on our way because Bondougou stood and offered me his hand to shake. I took it and he grinned at me, pleased to have found the rich seam of my corruption.

I bought more Red Label on the way back home. The heat was dreadful, the town dead on its feet. Distant clouds boiled and towered, preparing for rain. I shot back a couple of drinks as soon as I got in to take the edge off my brain. I slept until the rain crashing on the roof woke me. I lay in bed and watched the rain pouring down the windows, watched the late afternoon turn to night. The rain moved off. The streetlights snapped on. I got up and sat amongst the floor cushions in the dark with the Red Label in my lap. A car stopped outside. A door slammed. The gate creaked open. Footsteps on the stairs. I knew them. Only high heels could make that noise. She knocked. I didn't say anything. She tried the door. It was open. She came in, shut the door behind her and got used to the streetlit darkness.

'What are you doing sitting in the dark?'

'What are you doing breaking into my house?'

'The door was open. I thought you might be in. You look as if you need company.'

'If you want soda with your whisky, there isn't any . . . just Possotomé.'

She wiggled into the kitchen. The black sheath getting another outing.

'What was it like in that African jail? You didn't say.'

I didn't answer. She came back in with a glass and the water. She poured her drink and sat on the corner of the sofa nearest to me with her knees pressed together. She leaned over and clinked glasses with me, made eye contact.

'You don't have to . . .'

'What do you want, Carole?'

'To see you.'

'I'm not interested in becoming a part of Jean-Luc's fantasy world.'

'I don't tell him everything. And of course . . . I lie too.'

'Then you can lie about me.'

'I wouldn't want to do that.'

We contemplated our drinks for a moment. Carole put some shine on her plum-coloured lips.

'What do you get out of your relationship with Jean-Luc?' I asked.

'I don't have such a bad life.'

'But not a very complete life.'

'He doesn't exercise that much control.'

'You're not answering the question,' I said. 'Does that mean you don't know?'

'I know why,' she said.

'It's not the sex. Not any more,' I said. 'Don't tell me it's money. That would be a big disappointment.'

She shook her head.

'I've run out of guesses.'

'I like bad guys,' she said.

'Somebody's got to.'

'That's very true.'

'What does that say about you? Are you a bad girl?'

She shrugged and looked around the room as if she had a sudden need of a blunt instrument.

'Talking about bad guys ... what's this business between Jean-Luc and Franconelli? What's Jean-Luc done that Franconelli has to cut him up and have him killed?'

'I don't know,' she said, looking up into her head, giving me Marnier's marker for her fibbing.

'I heard it wasn't anything as simple as business.'

'What did you hear?'

'That it was something personal.'

'And what do you conclude from that?' she asked, putting her drink down, running her nails through her hair.

'I haven't bothered to think that far.'

She looked around the room again, bored this time, irritated by the line of questioning. She ran her hands down her legs to her ankles and rested her chin on her knees.

'It's about a woman,' she said. 'If it's not business, that's what bad guys fight about.'

'You should know,' I said, 'which makes me wonder what you're doing here unless you think I've got potential.'

She dropped her eyes, licked her lips, pressed them together and let them spring into the split-plum pout. She raised her eyes and gave me a long steady look that said I could move in if I liked.

'You can kiss me if you want,' she said.

'I've not been in the kissing mood recently,' I said. 'Lost my appetite for it.'

I put my glass down and got to my feet ready to shoo her out. She stood with me, got very close, close enough for her hardish breasts to nudge my stomach. She took my hand, put it round the small of my back and pressed herself into me. I had a sudden dislike for this woman and a rush of nastiness shuddered through me. I pulled her up and gave her an ugly, lascivious kiss, pushing my tongue into the back of her throat. You want kissing, I thought, here's kissing. She tensed with the shock of it. I felt her repulsion. Then her teeth clamped down on my tongue. I let her go. She bit down harder. I looked into her eyes. They had a chill dead look in them. She released my tongue and staggered back from me.

'Don't do that,' she said, wiping her mouth with the side of her hand.

My throat was so full of self-disgust I couldn't swallow. I could feel the dent of her teeth marks, the taste of her lipstick. She backed off to the door, wary, as if I was the date who'd become the rapist. I picked up the drink to swill my mouth out but got hers by mistake and more taste of her lipstick on the rim. She opened the door still looking at me, hate in her face.

'I'm not a whore,' she said. 'Jean-Luc knows that.'

And she left.

I slammed the glass down on the table, picked up my own. These people. They've infected me. I threw back a jag of whisky which travelled down my oesophagus like a chunk of coral. The phone rang. More nasty people wanted to talk to the nasty man. I yanked it to my ear.

'I'm interested,' said Bondougou. 'I'm interested in your idea.'

'That's good.'

'But look,' he said, 'there's a piece of business that Marnier has to finish for me before you do your deal.'

'What's that?'

'He has to deliver something for me.'

'In Cotonou?'

'No, it's in Nigeria as well.'

'That's interesting,' I said. 'Are you supposed to be present at this delivery?'

'Of course.'

'Do you think there's a chance we could do the two deals back to back? You and Marnier make your delivery and half an hour later I bring my buyer along and we finish it.'

'Perfect.'

'Let me talk to him,' I said. 'Don't make any suggestions to him. I'll get him to put the idea to you.'

'Very good,' he said, pleased to have teased that knot straight.

We hung up and I looked at the phone for some time. Bondougou's satisfaction made me think he'd already decided that neither Marnier nor I were going to come out of this business alive. Would he tell Madame Sokode about the gold business she wasn't supposed to know anything about? Get her in on the act, help him solve some of his problems? No. Bondougou would want it all to himself. As far as he was concerned, all he had to worry about was me. I could see the scene playing in Bondougou's head – with the schoolgirl business completed the anonymous buyer would pay for the gold and leave, I'd kill Marnier for Franconelli, Bondougou would take care of me and disappear into the night with the cash.

Then it occurred to me – even if Bondougou and Madame Sokode did compare notes and deduce my role it wouldn't matter. They'd still want me out there on the lagoon where they could get rid of me easily. Whatever happened I was going to be present so all I had to do was make sure my back was protected.

Now that the bees had started to hum in the hive, it was time to ram the stick in and wiggle it about. I went downstairs to Moses's flat, checked the Browning .380, and got in the car. I laid the gun on the passenger seat where it gleamed dully in the occasional streetlighting.

Chapter 28

It started raining as I came across the lagoon, hard, tropical African rain, so that I had to slow to a crawl under the drilling. It was no better when I pulled up alongside the wall to Marnier's back yard. I could barely make out the edge of the lagoon beyond the rods of rain. Thunder boomed and tumbled across the invisible night sky.

I put the gun down the back of my trousers, stepped up on to the roof of the car, slung a mat across the broken glass and climbed over the wall. I was instantly drenched. The lights from the back of the house were a blur in the darkness. I splashed across the yard and up the steps. From under the leaking thatch I took a look in at the Marnier family.

Jean-Luc was sitting at one end of the dining table, which was set for two. He had a newspaper laid out and he was smoking over it as if he was studying form. There was a bottle of Red Label and a glass at his elbow. Water plinked into a bucket set on a dining room chair at the other end of the table where a mobile phone lay on its back. Carole sat on the sofa, out of her sheath now, and into some tight jeans, a T-shirt and cardy. She was reading a book whose cover had a raven-haired girl running away from something I couldn't see, but had to be a big bad man.

Dinner was cooking in the kitchen. The door was open behind the fly screen. I flipped the latch on the screen door with my car key. I squeezed and shook as much water out of my clothes as I could. I raised the Browning, stepped into the kitchen and waited. The rain hardened.

Carole said something to Marnier over the back of the sofa. Marnier nodded in the direction of the kitchen. Carole sighed and got to her feet. I held the gun out at throat height and Carole turned straight into it, her eyes widened and her mouth popped to the usual 'o'. Not a squeak from her though, and even if there had been Marnier wouldn't have heard it over the roar of the rain on the *ondulé*.

I turned her and walked her back into the living room. Marnier glanced up as if expecting her to give him something. His head stilled and his eyes went this way and that. I pushed her to the table and told her to pull out a chair. I sat down and pulled her on to my lap, resting the gun muzzle on her neck where it made red pressure circles. I jammed her left arm under mine and grabbed hold of her right wrist. I pointed the gun across at Marnier and looked down the barrel into his good eye.

'You know what this is?' I asked.

'If you're asking me what make the gun is, it's a Browning, a .380 I'd say. But if you're asking me to explain this situation . . . I can't. Maybe you should.'

'You know a lot about guns.'

'I was trained. Since then they've become a part of my profession.'

'You know what's special about this gun?'

'I'd like you to tell me it isn't loaded.'

'It's loaded,' I said, 'and it's the gun Franconelli gave me to kill you with.' The rain filled in the silence, the leak into the bucket quickened.

'And?' said Marnier.

I dropped the gun to my side, let go of Carole and gave her a little shove in the back towards Marnier. She stood behind his chair and rubbed her neck where the cold wet metal had made its marks.

'As you've probably guessed from your deep well of understanding about these things . . . I'm not in the killing business.'

'What business are you in?' asked Marnier, still careful.

'The selling your gold business.'

'Selling?' asked Marnier, nodding at the gun resting on my leg. 'You only need guns if you're stealing.'

The mobile at the end of the table let out a trill that pierced the thunder of the rain on the roof and jerked our heads round. I nodded at Carole. She picked it up, listened and handed it to Marnier.

'Monsieur Le Commandant . . .' he said, and listened intently. A smile spread across his face which, confused by the scars, turned into a leer. He nodded, staring into the newsprint spread out on the table. He made affirmative and delighted grunts. He finished by saying how pleased he was by the development and that they should meet in the morning to discuss the fine-tuning of the transfer. He switched the phone off, stabbed the aerial into the palm of his hand.

'Gold,' he said. 'You were saying . . .'

'Was that Bondougou calling you to say he had your

contract for you now? Telling you the Nigerians are in a position to make the first down payment on the barracks, the hospital . . . whatever's coming first?'

Jean-Luc Marnier was not in the habit of looking astonished. Astonishment was for girls. Marnier was the one who always knew. He was the one who controlled situations, he was the one who astonished others with his cunning and sophistication, his genius and brutality. Now, twice in one evening I'd thrown him and he gave me a nod of about three microns of respect.

'How do you know about that, Bruce?'

'He told me.'

'He *told* you?'

'When I told him I had to kill you for Franconelli. You see, Jean-Luc, something you might not know about Bondougou . . . he's a Franconelli man. And, as you know, Franconelli is not someone you take lightly. How do you think I got out of jail . . . insufficient evidence . . . run along, Brucey? It's not how that kind of thing works.'

'I see,' he said, leaning back in his chair, rolling his head on his neck to ease the tension.

'Who do you think's more important . . . long term . . . to Bondougou?' I asked. 'Jean-Luc Marnier or Roberto Franconelli?'

Carole started to rub his neck. He shook her off.

'It's not something Le Commandant is going to have to flip a coin over, is it, Jean-Luc?'

'Why are you telling me this?'

'He's also very interested in your gold,' I said. 'I'm sorry about that but I had to give him a carrot. He's got a very suspicious nature when it comes to me.'

'You told him about my *gold*,' said Marnier, the anger building.

'I had to.'

'It doesn't sound to me as if you *are* in the business of selling gold. Maybe you should clarify what business you are in.'

'To tell the truth, Jean-Luc, and I'll know you'll know I'm not lying, I'm in the schoolgirl business.'

That didn't exactly knock him back in his chair but it made him raise his head and give me a long, electric look from his good eye. Carole hit the wall behind him as if she'd taken a crossbow bolt in the chest. It didn't seem possible, but the rain intensified its roar so that she looked up, hoping the roof could take it. The plinking in the bucket evened to a steady trickle. Marnier's forgotten cigarette was now down to his fingers. He felt its sharp sting, tossed it into the ashtray and lit another.

'Yes,' I said, 'that's the business I'm in and, like any business, the better your information the easier it is to proceed. Bondougou and I are the only ones who know all three elements of the deal. The buyer, the seller and the intermediary. We're also the only ones who know the real terms of the deal. Who's going to get what for doing which work. This is a dirty business, Jean-Luc, maybe even dirtier than the drugs business, which has that built-in nastiness to make sure people don't get too many ideas of their own and start using them. I don't think *this* business is *that* different. Some people aren't going to get out of this alive. I've decided I want to and I've decided that you and the schoolgirls are going to survive with me, but we're going to have to work together and there's only one way this deal is going to happen and that's my way.'

'I'm listening,' said Marnier.

'It'll take a glass of something to get this out,' I said.

Carole slid a glass across. Marnier filled it and his own. The rain eased for a moment and came back louder. Thunder crumpled the air and thudded overhead loud enough to judder the window panes.

'Bondougou hasn't got a contract. There's never going to be a contract with the name Jean-Luc Marnier or Côte Oueste Sarl on it. The buyer of the schoolgirls is not primarily in prostitution but in the construction business. The buyer has been guaranteed those Public Works contracts you're so interested in. You are never going to get anything from it and as far as Bondougou is concerned you'll get nothing for your gold either. As far as he's concerned you'll get a bullet from me . . . from Franconelli. And I'll probably get a bullet from him too . . . maybe, even that will have come from Franconelli as well. And Bondougou will walk with your gold money and his share of the construction contract.'

'He just told me he's been sent a signed contract and a four-million-dollar downpayment.'

'In cash, in a Samsonite suitcase delivered to your door? You've been holding those girls a long time, Jean-Luc. It must have been a big worry.'

Marnier drew on his cigarette. It didn't ease the tension that the last week had knotted into his neck. His need for the deal to work had weakened him. Marnier's ego wasn't used to this kind of pressure, the pressure of the unknown.

'What do you want out of this?' he asked.

'I just want the schoolgirls.'

'I told Bondougou that was a big mistake.'

'What?'

'Taking your friend's daughter. I knew that was trouble, mixing the personal with business.'

'That's why I want Bondougou killed as part of the deal.'

'What do I get for doing all this . . . ? Apart from your word that you're not going to shoot me with that.'

'You know I'm not going to shoot you,' I said. 'What you get is your gold and the money for it too . . . and your freedom.'

'How?'

'You're going to have to kill the person who's going to buy your gold.'

'That could have some nasty repercussions, depending on the buyer you've got lined up.'

'The buyer's the same one who's supposed to take the schoolgirls off your hands.'

He took a long pensive drag and let the smoke seep out of him.

'Who's that?' he asked.

'I thought Bondougou would still be holding that card.'

'We all have our cards.'

'Only you know where the schoolgirls are.'

'Exactly,' he said, and drank some more, the strength flowing back into him as he remembered his ace.

'There are a number of problems.'

'Does Bondougou know you're interested in the schoolgirls?'

'Yes, but he doesn't know how warm I am. He doesn't even know that I've found you.'

'What happens if your name comes up in conversation between him and the buyer. The whole deal's blown then.'

'That's the reason I told him about the gold; I'm hoping it'll take his eye off the ball. He'll want to keep that for himself. But even if I do come up in conversation, even if the buyer has found out about my real interest, I'm sure the buyer will still want to do the gold deal and I'll be there when it all happens.'

'Unless the buyer decides to kill you beforehand.'

'That would only happen if Bondougou told the buyer about the gold deal and that you were the seller. I don't think he'll do that.'

'OK, so what are the problems?'

'Bondougou wants to do the schoolgirl deal *before* the gold deal. He wants to get his cut from the construction projects *and* the money from the gold.'

'If Bondougou doesn't know that the buyer for the girls and the gold are the same then we can do the two deals back to back.'

'You're going to have to tell him that. Give him a good reason.'

'I'll tell him I have something else to sell in Nigeria and I don't want to make two trips. I'll assure him that we're going to do the girls first and then it'll be a matter of waiting around for half an hour to do the second deal.'

'I've got another problem at my end. The buyer's going to be very suspicious if both deals happen on the same night in the same location.'

'Ah,' said Marnier. 'Psychology. Your buyer will tell *you* the deals are going be done this way.'

'Go on.'

'Your buyer wants delivery in Nigeria. I only want to deliver in Benin. *Une impasse.* You can talk about the difficulties and danger of moving gold across land borders, how we don't have the right contacts on either side, how for . . . what did you say he was going to pay?'

'I didn't.'

'Well?'

'Three-fifty-five dollars an ounce delivered Lagos.'

'You know what the market is?' he said, fast and angry.

'Thirteen dollars above that.'

'*Putain merde.* You'll have to push for more. You can't give in too easily. And when the buyer won't come up any more you say that I'm not prepared to make the necessary contacts for that kind of money. Three-fifty-five an ounce . . . my God. Then maybe you throw in the possibility of doing something on the lagoon. It's quieter out there. I think your buyer will see the beauty of it. Maybe if you're clever you can get your buyer to propose it even.'

'Where are the deals going to take place?'

'Why do you need to know?'

'Because,' I said, holding up the Browning, 'I'd like to deliver this there in advance. I should think Bondougou's knowledge of your character might make him cautious.'

Marnier pointed to a drawer in the dining table. Carole opened it and laid out a detailed map of the lagoon system up to and including the Nigerian border.

'Where'd you get this from?'

'You'd be surprised what you can dig out in Paris. *L'Institut Géographique National* still has a lot of maps of our ex-colonies . . . all out of date but better than nothing.'

He smoothed the map out with his damaged hand and traced a line from Cotonou up the Lagune, into Lac Nokoué, on to Porto Novo and the Nigerian border. On the other side of the border was a village in the middle of the lake.

'Is that an island?' I asked.

'No, it's built on stilts and completely abandoned. There are only two houses standing and only one of them is safe, the bigger one, which used to be the town hall. There are remains of other houses but they are just stilts sticking out of the water.'

'What's the town hall consist of?'

'A large wooden platform about ten metres by eight. The house is built so that there is a walkway all around it. It's made of canes and dried mud. Inside there are four rooms. The dividing walls are made out of some kind of matting, the doors are wooden and in good condition. The roof is thatch resting on wooden beams. Originally the same matting on the walls was used on the ceiling but it's mostly fallen down. There's only one access point. There used to be four, one on each side, but the steps have rotted. The south end is the only way in.'

'So I'll have the guns taped up underneath the platform next to the steps at the south end.'

'And not too far underneath. The reason the house

is still standing is that it's built on lots of pillars, all close together. You can't get underneath it in a large boat . . . only in a pirogue . . . I don't know what sort of boat you'll be in. The idea is that we exchange boats rather than shift the girls around, and swap them back later. I would think you'd be in some kind of launch. If you're going to do the job you should hire a pirogue to yourself. There's a station outside Porto Novo. You can get anything you like there for the right money. Are you going to do it yourself? Because we can't. We've got our hands full here and it's a day trip out there and back.'

'I can't either, but I've got somebody who could.'

'Somebody you can trust. Not an African, they'll fuck it up, believe me.'

'Bagado will do it.'

'No.'

'I said Bagado will do it.'

'First of all he is a policeman . . .'

'He'll do it.'

'I don't like it.'

'He's the only man I can rely on, and anyway I said at the beginning of this we were going to do it my way so that's the way it's going to be done. I'll need a copy of the map.'

'Take this one. I have the original,' said Marnier, sullen.

'Concentrate on what you're going to say to Bondougou when you find he hasn't got the four million absolutely on him and he hasn't quite got the contract ready. You know what I mean? Don't cave in too easily.'

'I don't cave in,' said Marnier, severe, testy.

I felt Carole's eyes on me, deliberate and cold.

'Where's Carole in all this?'

'She's with me,' he said. 'And what about you? Where are you? You've still got a job to do.'

'For Franconelli, you mean?'

'It's not something I'm likely to forget about.'

'I told you I'm not a killer. You know it.'

Marnier nodded. He knew that. And he also knew that Franconelli didn't take any man's word for anything, especially when it came to the maximum penalty. The Italian would want to see something. I decided to let Marnier think about that. Think about what Franconelli could possibly find acceptable other than his head on a plate.

303

Chapter 29

Monday 29th July, Cotonou.

The streets were flooded and it was still raining hard when I got back home. I left a message for Heike on Gerhard's answering machine and went to bed without drinking any more Red Label. The rain eased off at midnight. I was awake to hear it, couldn't shut down the ticking in my head. I cracked and brought a half glass of whisky into bed with me. It dulled life to a haze beyond the mosquito net and, with the rain gone, I drifted into sleep and a series of long dark dreams that all took place on large expanses of flat, black water and were peopled by faceless beings, some making me kill and others forcing me into sexual liaisons I didn't want to have.

I got up early feeling sour and chill but with a slick of sweat on my forehead that told me I might be getting sick. I cooked bacon and eggs and drank too much coffee without thinking about it. The clouds were still turbulent in the low grey sky. Helen came in and worked around me like a cat looking for attention. I waited until office opening hours and put a call in to Bagado, told him to meet me at the house in an hour.

I drove down Sekou Touré and took a left into the

friperie zone. Amongst the second-hand clothes warehouses and the Lebanese and Indian cloth shops was a small 1950s type place called Trois As which sold medical supplies. I bought the basics for a first-aid kit and a bottle of iodine, along with two scalpel handles, six blades and a litre bottle of formaldehyde. I went back on to Sekou Touré and down to the Caravelle where I bought two croissants and drove home. I got the guns, the Browning and Daniel's revolver, and a half million CFA from Moses's flat and went upstairs. I had Helen make more coffee and sent her out. Marnier called.

'It's done,' he said.

'You got your contract and the four million?'

'I've allowed myself to be fooled. I've just signed the original contract with my name and my company name on it and I've seen a copy of the transfer document from a Nigerian bank for four million dollars. Of course, Bondougou says they need the originals to send the money so I have nothing in my hand but I played nervous and I've agreed to transfer the girls.'

'When?'

'I tried to get you some more time but there was no good reason to delay. It's tonight. He's already confirmed that from his buyer. We're doing it tonight.'

'And the deals are going to be back to back like we said?'

'Back to back and I've managed to push it to midnight. That should be enough time for you.'

'What if it isn't?'

'Then you'll never see those girls again.'

I hung up.

I took the phone, guns and money to the dining table and sat down with the coffee. I put the guns and money on a chair beside me and tore a horn off a croissant. I dialled Madame Sokode's office number.

'The quality's very good,' said Madame Sokode.

'That's a pity,' I said.

'Why?'

'I'll come past your house tonight and pick it up.'

'What do you mean?'

'The deal's off. He's not going to do it, not for three-fifty-five an ounce.'

'I don't understand.'

'It's too cheap. My guy doesn't want to drive over a land border with something like seventy kilos of gold in his boot. He doesn't have the contacts to do that kind of thing and the money doesn't help him pay to make those contacts. It's all off and I'm sick of it.'

'I see.'

'Where are you going to be tonight? I can't get to Lagos until late. If I meet you at your house between ten and eleven will that be OK?'

'Wait.'

She put the phone down on her desk. I heard her pace the room. The door into the living room opened and Bagado walked in. I fingered my lips and pointed him into a chair. He poured coffee and wolfed his croissant. Madame Sokode came back on line.

'Can he get hold of a boat?'

'A boat? What sort of a boat? He's not going out into the open sea.'

'I was thinking of the lagoon.'

'Anybody can get hold of a boat for money, I suppose. What's the idea?'

'There's a village on the lagoon right on the border, abandoned. I'll meet him there.'

'Is there any more money in it?'

'No, the same money.'

'I don't know about that, Elizabeth.'

'Ask him.'

'When would it be for?'

'It has to be tonight, and, this is important, it has to be at twelve thirty in the morning, not before and not after.'

'What's this window of opportunity?'

'It's exactly that.'

'Like I told you, Elizabeth, he's a very shaky guy, out on the lagoon, middle of the night, same money, that's a hard sell.'

'He can't be that shaky,' she said, her shrewdness echoing down the phone line. 'Maybe you should ask him how he acquired the gold in the first place. That might give you an idea how much nerve he has. And on the money. It's the best deal he's going to get on this coast. If he doesn't like it tell him to take it to Switzerland.'

'Have you got a map of this place? This village?'

'I'll fax you.'

I gave her the fax number of the Lebanese stationer's round the corner and hung up. Bagado started on the remains of my croissant.

'Got your appetite back?'

'What have you found?'

'I know who's holding José-Marie and the other

307

schoolgirls. I just don't know where now, but I do know where they'll be at midnight tonight.'

I unfolded Marnier's map and talked him through the abandoned village as Marnier had described it.

'And what do you want me to do?' he asked, as if he already knew.

I took the two guns and the money off the chair and laid them on the table in front of him. He clasped his hands and looked at them very seriously.

'I want you to hire a pirogue, take it out to this village and tape the guns up underneath the platform of the southern access point of the town hall.'

'What's going to happen?'

I shook my head.

'She's my daughter, you know, Bruce.'

I shook my head again.

'You're not thinking of me as a policeman. If you were you wouldn't ask me to do this work. So tell me what's going to happen.'

'You'll just worry about it.'

'I will, but I still want to know.'

I told him the whole deal from start to finish. He nodded his way through it, sat back and thought about it all. I went down to pick up the fax. When I returned he was still in the same position, his eyes glazed with thought.

'One thing,' he said, 'how are *you* going to get there? You can't go with Marnier and Bondougou. They don't want you there until twelve thirty.'

'I'll go with Madame Sokode.'

'You better hope she invites you.'

'That's a good point.'

'I think she'd naturally expect you to turn up with the seller.'

'Very good point, Bagado.'

'Just something that occurred to me.'

'You're back on form, aren't you? The treatment's working.'

'It's working very well. I'm converted.'

'What does that mean?'

He stood without answering.

'Also,' he said, 'your plan relies on Bondougou not talking about your interest in schoolgirls to Madame Sokode, and Madame Sokode not mentioning her gold deal to Bondougou.'

'Why should she?'

'Something you said about her mentality,' he said, pacing the length of the dining table. 'You say she's Nigerian but thinks like a white person. That means endless questions, plenty of talk. Anything could come up.'

'I don't think she'll speak to him. They've already organized their schoolgirl deal between themselves. Do you think she'd call Bondougou specifically to mention the gold deal which has nothing to do with him? She'd probably have to pay him a commission. These people are as tight as a beggar's fist with money *and* information.'

'It feels risky. Maybe her people in Benin have spoken to her about you.'

'If they had I think I'd be dead. They're down that money I took from Daniel, they probably don't want to go talking to her just yet and getting her annoyed. I also understand she keeps her distance from the prostitution operations and that they're run separately. Besides, I imagine Bondougou's thought of a way of solving their little financial difficulty.'

'OK,' he said, 'I was just trying to think about things you might not see when you're close to it.'

'There's a risk, I know. I'm not absolutely certain how much Bondougou knows and there's a subtlety and shrewdness about Madame Sokode that scares me, but the main thing is that those guns have to be there. They can solve *any* risk element, those things.'

'If you can get to them,' he said.

A truck crashing through the puddles outside filled in the silence.

'But don't worry,' he said, 'they'll be there. I'll put on my fisherman's outfit, hire a pirogue this afternoon and be back here by evening. You don't have to worry about the guns.'

'Let me confirm it all before you go.'

I called Madame Sokode.

'You've taken your time,' she said, and I realized I'd been more than an hour with Bagado.

'He's nervous. I had to be persuasive.'

'Will he do it?'

'He won't go out there alone.'

'You can hold his hand.'

'I can't. I told you, I have to be in Lagos tonight and it'll be a late finish.'

'Where will you be?'

'In the Apapa docks.'

'I'll pick you up.'

'And I go with you?'

'Why not?'

'It doesn't solve his problem. He said he doesn't want to go alone. If I can't be with him he has to pay somebody else. Give him an extra dollar an ounce on top, for God's sake.'

'No.'

'OK, Madame Sokode, it's a deal. I'll go with you to the village and back to Cotonou with him. Can you meet me at Mile Two? There's a ferry comes in there from Apapa.'

'Be there at ten.'

We hung up. I called Marnier and confirmed.

Bagado sat back down.

'I think that's it,' I said.

'I spoke to Heike,' he said.

'And you're still talking to me?'

'It didn't sound good, not from her side.'

'You might find it difficult to believe this, but I was lying.'

'What a thing to lie about,' said Bagado.

'If I hadn't lied I'd have been a dead man.'

'And there was nothing else for you to lie about?'

'Marnier invented the lie for me. He thought it was convincing. He thought it would be the only thing I would desperately want to be dishonest about. But I didn't expect to have to tell the lie in front of Heike. She being there was not in the plan. On the other hand, with her there it became the perfect lie. It saved my life and destroyed it in one.'

'You could have lied about anything else except . . .'

'And I'd have been a floater in Lagos harbour,' I said. 'Marnier was right. Sex was the only thing.'

'Maybe that's something you should think about.'

311

'When this is over.'

'I'd like to help.'

'You can help by believing me.'

'That might not be good enough.'

'I know, I hurt her very badly that night.'

'I saw it,' he said. 'What about Marnier? Would he . . . ?'

'I can't see myself bringing those two together.'

'What about with me?'

'After tonight . . . ?'

'Yes. I take your point. He'll disappear . . . if he has any sense.'

'And signed confessions are a bit old-fashioned.'

'I'll help you,' he said, getting up to leave. 'Don't worry.'

He waved from the door, more positive than I'd seen him in months. I went down and rooted about in the garage and came up with an empty bottle of Ballantines. I transferred the formaldehyde into it. I packed the bottle and some clothes into a small holdall, put all the first-aid things, the iodine and the scalpels in a wash bag with the usual stuff and laid more clothes on top.

I put a call through to Heike in her office. They wouldn't connect me, said she'd gone out and they weren't sure when she'd be back. I pushed to find out where she'd gone. The girl said she'd gone out of town, and she didn't have to, but she added, with Gerhard.

I went down to the *autogare* in the Jonquet and caught a taxi to Lagos.

Chapter 30

It was past ten o'clock and I was waiting under the corrugated-iron overhang of a small shack drinking bottled Guinness and looking at the rain, trying to see Madame Sokode's Mercedes through the rain. The shack was barely twenty yards from the quay for the ferry at Mile Two, which was invisible through the downpour. The weather forecast was not good. It was definitely not a good time for trips out on the lagoon, with storms predicted most of the night. It meant one thing. We were unlikely to get any trouble from the authorities out there.

Madame Sokode's Mercedes glided past, stopped and reversed. The driver got out, opened an umbrella and came to fetch me. I got into the back seat next to Madame Sokode, who started the night off strongly by handing me a glass of Black Label from the bar. We cruised up on to the Badagri Expressway and headed west, away from the city.

Madame Sokode sat in a corner far away from me and looked out of the window. She was wearing black jeans, black trainers, a black poloneck and she'd removed the hair extensions leaving herself with a close crop, unplaited. Reduced to this simplicity she looked completely beautiful.

The rain pounded on the roof leaving no room for

talk. Elizabeth had her elbow up on the window ledge, a hand to her face, a finger tapping her cheek. The rain suddenly stopped. The wipers squeaked on the windscreen, wincing through her.

'I hope you've got a cabin on this boat,' I said, treasuring the Black Label. 'They say it's not the last of the rain.'

'There is a cabin, but it's stuffy in there and stinks of fuel. We'll sit under a canopy at the back. It's more comfortable.'

For a woman who didn't like the cold that didn't sound right and my seed paranoia shot up the length of me, thick and prickly as a desert cactus.

'You told your seller not to get there before twelve thirty?' she asked.

'I told him.'

'He's not African, is he?'

'He'll be there twelve thirty exactly unless he capsizes the boat.'

'Does he have a name?'

'He does,' I said, but I couldn't think of it. I couldn't think of anything about him. All I could hear was Jean-Luc Marnier's name and see his leery face.

'Are you going to tell me?'

'If you like. If you think it's important.'

'You don't have to protect your principal now.'

'Bo,' I said, surprising myself. 'His name's Bo.'

'Bo?'

'An odd name. It's Danish,' I said, remembering the real Bo, who was a half-mad kleptomaniac I'd met in the Sahara.

'Does that mean he's not?'

314

'No, no. He's Danish too. As Danish as his name . . . Danish as bacon . . . Danish as . . . what other things are Danish? Pastry?'

'You didn't tell me where Bo got all this gold from,' she said, and I noticed that she was playing with my bonus lump on the seat in between us.

'He nicked it,' I said, widening my eyes, unnerved at how that one had slipped out.

Her head turned slowly towards me.

'Only joking, Elizabeth,' I said. 'He bought it in Togo. You know that stuff that comes across the border there. He buys that.'

'Pity,' she said, 'it would have been more interesting if he'd stolen it.'

'Have you got some scales to weigh this gold with? I wouldn't want you to take his word for it.'

'There're scales on the boat. I had them taken out there this afternoon but I hope we're not going to get down to haggling over three sixteenths of an ounce out there tonight.'

'I don't think so.'

'You said he's shaky. Maybe he's fussy too.'

'I'm sure he'll want to take his money and run along home as fast as he can.'

The Mercedes ploughed through a small lake across the Expressway, sending out two huge curtains of spray into the night, water thumped on the undersill. On the other side of the road a taxi up to its doors in water was being pushed by its passengers through the flood. A four-wheel drive overtook it at speed, horn going solid, and our combined bow waves shifted the taxi to the edge of the road.

315

We passed through Badagri and went out north on a mud road to a southern shore of the lagoon. We parked up on some higher ground. The driver went to the boot and took out a briefcase and a coat and opened Madame Sokode's door. She turned into the coat. I joined them and we walked through the still dripping vegetation to the water's edge. There was a small jetty which was half submerged after the endless rains, and a man of some width was standing on it with his hands, on the ends of very long arms, folded over his crotch. The driver gave him the umbrella and the briefcase and went back to the car.

The boat was large, more of a launch. There was a windowed cabin in the hull and a shielded area behind that for the helmsman. The back was open, apart from a fibreglass canopy with plastic windows. Whatever the motors were, they were inboard. It was an expensive and fast-looking piece of work.

The big man got into the boat and helped Elizabeth down. He took my small holdall off me and dropped it at his feet. He helped me down too and ran a hand over the small of my back which went through me like a thousand volts.

'I'll put the bag in the cabin,' I said.

'Sam will bring it back here for you,' snapped Elizabeth. 'Come.'

I joined her under the canopy. I heard Sam squeezing the bag behind me before he slid it, along with the briefcase, under our seat. He went back up to the front and started the engine, which sounded as if it had some wrist, and cast off.

I could have used that Black Label from the back of

the Merc to keep down the case of body shingles I had. The boat slid out into the channel, the engine thumping, the exhaust bubbling quietly behind. The fibreglass canopy throbbed. We weren't in the main body of the lagoon, but a narrow inlet no more than thirty yards across, and Sam was being careful to steer a course down the middle.

The wind freshened as we got beyond the point but still he didn't open up and the searchlight he had above his head remained switched off. It was black out there, not a glimmer of light on the water, not a spark on the banks of the lagoon, just a faint glow from Badagri and Lagos further east.

We eased across to the left and islands of reeds passed nearby, brushing the side of the boat. This wider channel we were in was still shallow. We moved no faster than jogging pace for twenty minutes. Time clipped past the 11.30 mark. When he'd manoeuvred us out into the middle of the lake he cut the engine and let us drift in the wind which chopped the water with gentle cuffs. Sam got up on his seat and looked out across the lake. Stubby waves slapped the side of the boat. A storm lit the sky over Lagos about thirty or forty miles off.

'Does he know where he's going?' I asked.

'Sam's lived out here all his life,' she said.

Thunder, distant and to the north, crumped like artillery fire. Then a light came on out in the darkness, once, twice, three times. Sam dropped into his seat and restarted the engine. He flashed the light once but didn't open the throttle full. We moved at a steady speed in the direction of the blinking light.

As we covered the water the light out on the lagoon

317

continued to reel us in. I had plenty of big questions lined up for Elizabeth – why, for instance, in her HIV-positive state was she still hungry for this kind of business, yet cancelled the furniture? Why, after her own childhood but with her privileged education, was she prepared to sell children off for what she knew was a hopeless cure? – but I couldn't ask them. And even if I did and she gave me an honest answer what would it be? I'm weird and evil? Thanks for that. I was better off trying to see myself three hours from now, calm and serene in a tub of Red Label, but I couldn't wring the pictures out of my imagination. The here and now, even if it was a boat chugging dully across the darkness, was too demanding.

Elizabeth uncrossed and recrossed her legs. I couldn't see her face or hands. There was nothing coming off her. No tension. No anticipation. If anything there was boredom. In half an hour one of us could be dead. Would it be any different than slipping through the cool blackness as we were now?

I pulled myself back from the brink and concentrated on the task. In a few minutes I had to produce guns and control a situation. I hadn't thought about the driver, Sam. Somebody else who wouldn't be going home tonight, somebody else for Marnier to deal with, a third body to add to the two under the concrete in Grand-Popo, and however many others there were that didn't trouble Jean-Luc's conscience.

A chill shivered through me. The same chill with the same slick of sweat as this morning. I was getting sick, cold from standing out in the rain last night.

As we closed in on the blinking light it stopped, and

Sam took out a torch which he used to check the location of the other abandoned buildings. We drifted past the bare stilts, the caved-in platforms. He cut the engine. The sky lit up again. The storm, closer, moved up on Badagri, the flash strong enough for us to see the main house and the boat from Marnier's yard already moored to the southern corner of the platform.

Our boat was hardly moving as it knocked into the wooden supports under the house, the tyre buffer squeaked and groaned. Sam tied a line to one of the supports and swung the boat round using some impressive upper body strength so that we could get out easily on to the steps. He secured the launch.

There was a faint glimmer of yellow light, hurricane-lamp light coming from behind the windows of the house which were covered with torn raffia matting. People moved inside on uneven planking. Madame Sokode reached underneath her for the briefcase, stood and ducked out of the canopy. I reached down for my bag without thinking, ready to follow her, and found the torchlight on me.

Something solid filled the beam, something that moved slowly towards my head until it connected firmly with my eyebrow. The cold of the metal ran through me. I slitted my eyes to the light, winced at the hardness of the gun barrel that slipped to the corner of my eye socket.

'You're not a stupid man,' said Madame Sokode. 'You're just an unlucky one.'

'Bondougou?' I asked.

'Not Bondougou,' said Madame Sokode, mildly puzzled, and the driver grabbed a handful of hair and hauled me across the boat. I slipped on the wet decking. He brought me up to my knees, the gun resting on the back of my neck.

'Look in the cabin,' she said.

I opened the door. Sam shone the torch in and lit a white naked body, the thighs and buttocks of a naked woman torn by welts and dotted black. The body turned, sensing movement. There was no pubic triangle, a slit and a shaved pubis. The abdomen was smeared with dark blood that had flowed from her ripped nipples. Her head was wound with gaffer tape round the eyes and mouth. Where the skin showed through it wasn't white but blue, bloody, black. The body jerked and trembled. It was a very white body and I didn't need the tape removed to know that it was the Ukrainian girl, Sophia.

I was panting and the sweat was coursing, the girl's terror communicating itself through her uncontrollable trembling. Sam shut the door, pulled me to my feet. Madame Sokode stepped over the side of the launch and on to the wooden stairs. I tried to stop my head shaking on the stump of my neck to see if the guns were there, to see if I had a chance of stumbling up the steps, reaching out . . .

Sam held my shirt collar and pulled me over the side. He kicked my ankles up the steps, my legs not wanting to operate. I fell at the top and rammed my arm through the gap in the steps and felt around crazily for the weapons. They weren't there. Sam cuffed me on the back of the head with the gun barrel, hard enough to move me on. I staggered into the room where two hurricane lamps burned wavering shadows up the wall.

Bondougou, eyes bulging, stood with his back to the window, Carole was in a corner and Marnier sat with his back to the far wall, his head below another window.

'What the fuck is he doing here?' he said, seeing the gun connected to my head, struggling to his feet. It was an inspired moment.

The driver took me to the middle of the room and pressed me down on to the uneven, wide-spaced planks of the floor.

'Have you checked the other rooms?' said Madame Sokode in perfect French, laying her briefcase on a table.

'There's nobody here,' said Marnier.

'Have you checked the other rooms?' she asked again.

Bondougou picked up a hurricane lamp and went to check the other rooms. I could only see Carole now, dressed in a black lycra body suit, night wear for night work. She wasn't looking that scared, a little rigid, her face tauter over her bones, but her eyes, if they weren't smiling, they were satisfied and there was nothing else to be read in them.

'There's nobody here,' said Bondougou, coming back into the room.

'Have you checked under the platform?' she asked.

'I'll go,' said Marnier, which was when I knew we were in big trouble because it meant he didn't have the guns either.

'You stay here,' snapped Madame Sokode. 'Give him the torch.'

Bondougou went out and down the steps, came back up again. Thunder rolled out long and rough as a wooden-wheeled, ox-drawn tumbrel.

'Nothing,' said Bondougou, getting emphatic now

that he'd done what he was supposed to have done before we'd got here.

'What's he doing here?' asked Madame Sokode, giving me a kick in the leg.

No answers, not even from Marnier who had answers for most things. Bondougou shifted uneasily.

'He told me there was going to be someone here to sell me two thousand ounces of gold. Is there?'

Bondougou jutted his head but fell short of letting his mouth go slack. Mean but not stupid.

'*You're* buying *his* gold?' said Bondougou, turning his head on Marnier.

'And who's he?' asked Madame Sokode, following Bondougou's look to Marnier. 'Don't tell me. He's the one who's supplying the girls as well.'

Bondougou looked at me as if I might have some suggestions, then changed the look to half a beat off murderous. Marnier knew it was his turn, he could hear the brains ticking even over the distant thunder, could see the way the combinations were falling, the assumptions beginning to be made. He came into Madame Sokode's idea a bit further down the line than she expected.

'Why?' he asked.

'Is he armed?' she spat at Bondougou, cocking her head at Marnier.

Sam's gun went in Marnier's direction.

'I can see she isn't,' she said, glancing at Carole, who crossed her thighs as if she might pee herself, the lycra so tight you could see the outline of her spleen.

'But what about him?'

'He's clean,' said Bondougou.

Marnier held his arms up, parted his legs.

'Take a look,' he said.

Sam frisked him.

'Why?' said Marnier again.

'I don't understand why *he*,' she said, toeing me in the ribs, 'should come out here on his own. There's a whore from Lagos on the boat out there who says he's interested in what we're doing here tonight with these schoolgirls. So why should he come out here on his own with no weapon?'

Marnier stepped forward, trying to assert himself on the situation.

'You get back over there,' she said. 'You don't need to be in the middle of the room to answer that question.'

'Why should I be working with him?'

'He came into this on *your* gold.'

'But he didn't tell me who you were and even if he had it wouldn't have meant anything to me because Le Commandant hasn't told me your name. I still don't know who you are,' said Marnier.

Madame Sokode glared at Bondougou, who nodded.

'I don't know,' she said. 'I think . . .'

A sudden wind rushed through the house. Thunder boomed closer. The rain approached, hissing loud over the lagoon. It hit the thatched roof of the house with a dull roar, raising the pitch in the room which was already crackling with high-voltage paranoia.

'I don't know what he's doing here,' said Marnier. 'We've come here unarmed. We've brought the girls. I was expecting him to come later on with –'

'Have you checked the girls?' she asked Bondougou.

'They're in the boat,' he said.

'All of them?'

'Yes,' he said, and even I heard the uncertainty.

'You haven't counted them.'

'Why should he . . . ?'

'I don't know,' said Madame Sokode. 'Go and count them.'

'At least wait until the rain stops,' said Marnier.

'Where's the gold?' she snapped at him.

'In the boat . . . with the girls.'

'So it exists,' she said and another flicker of uncertainty twitched at the corners of Bondougou's eyes.

I didn't hear anything but I felt something. Underneath me the plank shifted. Sam felt it too and the gun moved off Marnier. The rain stopped. Everyone in the room was on animal sense. The hiss of the rain moved away. Silence, now, apart from the lapping of the water against the stilts. Then a noise, unmistakable this time, in the next room. Madame Sokode slapped Sam's arm. He left the room. The door closed behind him. A shot roared out immediately. A body hit the planking. I rolled on to my back. Madame Sokode snapped open her briefcase and produced a chrome-plated revolver. She knelt and pointed it at the door. She shook the gun at the door.

'Sam?' she said.

Not a word. A grunt squeezed out from a crumpled mouth but no word. The water rippled underneath us. The door opened in the partition wall, framed a vacant black oblong, revealed Sam face down in the next room, but nobody came through it.

Another roar and Madame Sokode's jaw and cheek parted from her face, her head kicked back, her knees

324

lifted up from the floor, the gun fell from her hand, clattered on the wood and slipped through the planking into the water below. She fell back with a cracking sound as if her knees had popped. Her legs and arms twitched. A gargling noise came from her throat. Her sharp pointed upper teeth were visible through the hole torn in her face. Her black eyes blinked at the roof. She coughed a spray of black blood.

The boats knocked against the stilts. Bondougou was pressed against the wall now, he seemed to be more aware than any of us that there was some terrible avenging presence in the room. I rolled and stood, moving away from him, Marnier retreated two steps, Carole shrank further into her corner, none of us knowing why or what was making us back off.

Bondougou's legs shook in his trousers. His eyes rolled in fear and his hands fluttered about him as if he was trying to protect himself from a bat loose in the room. He dropped to his knees and shouted something out, an appeal, in his own language, to some greater ancestral power. He fell forward on all fours and stared into the floor and was transfixed by it. He grimaced, his head reared back, jiggling on its neck. And only then did I see the barrel of the Browning appear through the planking.

The gun roared three times.

Bondougou's pumpkin head split and sprayed.

The force of the shots knocked him back against the cane wall which cracked and splintered. He fell sideways, landing inches from Carole who was crammed into the corner and looking out of the side of her face.

The water lapped underneath us. Blood, from

Bondougou's appalling head wounds, leaked through the planking. A boat knocked into the stilts of the house.

Bagado, stripped to the waist, shining wet, stepped into the room. He had two weapons, the Browning .380 hung at his side in his left hand, the other, Daniel's revolver, was held at waist height. His face was set as hard as the gunmetal he was carrying.

Madame Sokode was still making grotesque noises. Her life, hard, gritty and stubborn, hung on. Bagado stood beside her and looked at Bondougou's lifeless form. His left hand jumped at the sixth roar of the night and Madame Sokode's stomach arched off the floor and thumped back into it.

Bagado took a step towards Marnier and levelled the Browning. Marnier looked straight down the out-stretched arm and said:

'If you're looking for your daughter, I didn't bring her with me.'

Chapter 31

Tuesday 30th July, on the lagoon near the Nigerian border.

'Count the girls, Bruce,' said Bagado.

'You'll need these,' said Marnier, throwing me the keys.

I picked up the torch and went down into Marnier's boat. I unlocked the cabin. The girls were all asleep, drugged, with their hands and feet cuffed, mouths taped and arranged like the cargo diagram for a slave ship. There were six and José-Marie wasn't one of them.

I crossed over on to Madame Sokode's boat and tore open the cabin door. Sophia was squealing a rat-like noise in her throat, a pure terror noise, convinced that she was next. I stroked her back down, tore the gaffer tape off her face, wrists and ankles. I found my holdall, gave her some clothes and told her to get on to Marnier's boat. She hadn't got a hold of herself yet and I had to carry her across with my bag. I went back into the house.

Two pairs of eyes were fixed on Bagado, whose face was still as hard and as stubborn as pig iron. The gun was still levelled at Marnier. Carole had slid to the floor and was looking at Bondougou's ruined head with fascination. There'd been no chat while I'd been gone.

'José-Marie's not there,' I said.

Bagado, who hadn't seemed to be breathing, suddenly sucked in a deep involuntary breath and sighed it out. Marnier looked away from the gun barrel and shrugged.

'Security,' he said, 'or is it insurance?'

Bagado shivered and adjusted the gun in his hand.

'There's a plastic bag in the pirogue underneath the house. Throw it in the boat for me. See if there's a spare tank of gasoline in the other launch and spray it over this place. We'd better set fire to it and get moving before someone comes out here. What's in the briefcase?'

I kicked it open. It was packed with old copies of the Lagos *Daily Times*.

I threw the plastic bag from the pirogue into Marnier's boat and found the spare jerry can of petrol in the cabin of the other launch. Bagado moved Marnier and Carole into the boat. I sprayed the petrol over the launch and then through the four rooms and over the bodies in the house. I picked up the two hurricane lamps and hurled one into the far room, heard the thump of the gas as it caught, and ran. I threw the second lamp into Madame Sokode's launch and jumped into Marnier's boat, which was already moving away.

Marnier opened the throttle full and the two outboards dug in, the nose came up and we spanked across the black and flame-lit waters of the lagoon, heading for Benin. In a matter of moments the canes, thatch and raffia of the house were cracking thirty-foot licks of flame and belching burnt detritus high into the night sky. After a few minutes, only a roaring skeleton remained until the main tank of Madame Sokode's launch went up and the explosion blew the supports out from under one end of the house. The platform dipped violently, the house broke in half and part of it slid into the orange flickering water.

Carole and Sophia sat at the back, not talking, Sophia still shaking. Bagado, in his mac now, was up front with the gun nosed into Marnier's left kidney. I was sweating hugely as if I'd done twelve rounds in a hot town hall. My guts trembled and I felt the first rush of fever.

'Where are we going?' I asked.

'Another house on the lagoon, on the Benin side,' said Marnier. 'You can tell your friend he doesn't have to point the gun any more. This is a rough ride and I don't want it going off by accident.'

Bagado rested the gun on his knees but kept his eyes on Marnier. I leaned in between them, thought we could get one little thing out of the way before we started on the bigger stuff.

'Tell Bagado what happened that night in Grand-Popo,' I said to Marnier.

'What night?'

'Don't be difficult, Jean-Luc,' I said. 'Your Italian night, remember?'

'The night of your infidelities, you mean?'

'I can see this is going to take some time.'

'But I think we're getting somewhere,' said Marnier. 'I don't think your friend is going to shoot me like he shot those other two.'

'They had to be killed,' said Bagado. 'They were too powerful to let live. You're not.'

'I can tell you I'm not going to an African jail for the rest of my life.'

'That depends if you murdered the girl we found in the lagoon.'

'That was an accident,' he said. 'Very regrettable.'

'The girl was strangled,' I said, hardening up on him. 'That doesn't sound very accidental.'

'Don't you start getting angry,' he said, 'you need me too.'

We rounded a point on the north shore of the lagoon and the flaming house behind us disappeared. Marnier shut down the searchlight and throttled back. The engine ticked over and we drifted in the dark. Marnier folded his arms.

'Let's negotiate,' he said.

'You know what I want,' said Bagado.

'And you're not going to get it, not all of it,' said Marnier. 'I'll take you to your daughter. She's in a house a few miles away but then I'm going to leave you there . . . with the other girls. I want some time to get back to Cotonou and across the border to Togo. And that's *all* I want. Free passage. But if you want revenge, well . . . you won't see your daughter again.'

'I don't think I can accept that,' said Bagado.

'Nor can I,' I said.

'Ah, yes,' he said, turning to me. 'There's the question of your debt to Mr Franconelli. What does he want?'

'You know what he wants.'

'I know he wants you to kill me and I know you won't do it; your friend here might but you won't. But what does Franconelli want . . . my scalp this time? He's already had my dick . . .'

'He wants that tattoo off your back. The one of the joker.'

Marnier roared.

'And you?' he said to Bagado. 'What's your problem?'

'Tell the girl to come up here.'

Carole joined us. Bagado clicked the torch on to their faces.

'Which of you killed the girl we found in the lagoon?'

Carole looked up into her head.

'She did,' said Marnier, and she shot a look at him that should have left him pinned and wriggling on the deck.

'You can go,' said Bagado, 'but she stays with us.'

The French that came out of Carole was not the sort you'd pick up at the Alliance Française, it was the sort you found under whores' shoes on the Pigalle. Marnier smacked her brutally across the face with the back of his hand and she shut up. He pounded her with some thick dialect that could have come from Mount Igman and then lapsed back into French again, telling her she shouldn't have killed the fucking girl. She shrieked at him, a sound so terrible and piercing that he had to hit her again harder with a half-closed fist that dropped her to the floor. She curled up, foetal, and Marnier looked down at her with nothing in his face.

He opened the throttle and we moved off. He turned the searchlight on as the nose of the boat came out of the water.

Twenty minutes later we coasted up to a broken-down jetty which had a house at the end of it which the locals had probably used for drying or smoking fish. Marnier nudged Carole with his feet, pulled her up.

'She'll take you down there and unlock the door,' he said.

Bagado told Marnier to point the light down the jetty and asked him if it would work on batteries alone, then didn't wait for an answer and tore the keys out. The light stayed on. He gave me Daniel's revolver and got out of the boat with Carole in front of him while I tied up to the jetty. Carole set off down the warped wooden planking. Bagado let her get ahead. She reached the door of the house which was padlocked. She asked if she could get the keys. Bagado told her to move slowly.

He adjusted the gun in his hand. Carole's hand went up under the eaves of the house at the right-hand corner of the door frame. Bagado moved forward a pace, shrugged his shoulders in his mac. Carole's hand came back out from under the eaves, but quick, and she span on her heel, her hand coming up in front of her, her body in a crouch, something black and solid in her fingers. Bagado was the perfect silhouette, back lit by the searchlight from the boat. His gun arm was still down by his side when he saw her turning and realized his mistake. He was too square on but he got his gun up and the two guns cracked together in the cone of light.

The force of the bullet from the Browning slammed Carole backwards against the door frame and a noise came out of her throat like the sound of fresh offal hitting a butcher's tiled floor. The door jamb didn't give and seemed to kick her forward so she fell on her face. Bagado twisted and fell. The gun flew out of his hand and into the water. He was still close to the boat and I saw his eyes wide with surprise and the kind of pain El Greco could find in his saints. His mouth was open but no sound came out. He hit the jetty hard, his face bouncing on the wood, one hand reaching out to grab a rung of the nothing night. I wheeled round on Marnier and cracked him on the side of the head with the revolver and he dropped to the deck. Then I was out of the boat and on the jetty and over Bagado who was not moving, one hand down by his side, the other still stretched out. I was panting, sobbing, sweat-drenched as I rolled him. His eyes were closed but his tongue was moving over his lips as if he was desperate to wet them. I reached for the lapels of his mac, felt the stab of horror and a strange compression of thought. Everything I loved about this man came to me then and a black chasm opened up should I lose him, should he be lost to these worthless bloody people. I wrenched open the mac and ran my hands over his chest, his abdomen, his flanks. Clean.

'My shoulder,' he said.

I could have kissed him.

I eased the mac off his shoulder. There was a black hole through the muscle and out the other side.

'Your mac's ruined,' I said. 'The bullet's gone clean through.'

'Stupid,' he said, screwing his face, 'bloody stupid. I knew it was wrong. I was thinking about José-Marie. Took my eye off her.'

I got him up on his feet. His legs had gone and I humped him to the boat and set Sophia to work with the iodine and first-aid kit. Marnier was coming to on the floor. I picked up a baling bucket and sluiced him with lagoon water. Blood trickled over his missing ear. His eyes banged open and he sunk his teeth back into life and held on with jackal jaws. I knelt over him.

'Are you with me?'

'I'm with you.'

'If you'd killed him, Jean-Luc . . .'

'Yeah?' he jeered.

'That would have been enough.'

'Even you could see he wasn't going to let me go. It was in his face. He's not the forgiving type. I had to get that gun out of his hand.'

'Where's the girl?'

'Look . . . you can have the tattoo. Cut the damn thing off my back. It's no bigger than a cigarette pack. I can handle it. But I can't go to prison. Not here.'

'We'll talk about that . . . where's the girl?'

'Back at my house, the one on the lagoon.'

I cast off, took the keys out of Bagado's mac, stuck them in the ignition and hauled Marnier to his feet.

'Now drive.'

Marnier looked back at the body lying face down in front of the house. The light swung slowly away from it and pointed out over the lagoon.

'Is she dead?' he asked.

'I'm surprised you care.'

He answered by opening the throttle and we pulled away.

Within an hour the glow of Cotonou appeared and we came off Lac Nokoué and into the Lagune. Marnier pointed the nose of the boat towards the house, I lifted the outboards and we coasted in up to the gate to the yard at the back of Marnier's house.

I left Sophia and Bagado in the boat, took the hold-all and pointed Marnier up to the house with the revolver. I was quaking inside again and the heat coming off me

334

was not the sort you get from a chill. I was sweating crazily and my vision spasmed.

We walked up to the balcony and into the house. Marnier took me through to the bedroom where José-Marie was cuffed to the bed, her mouth taped, sleeping. I stripped the tape off, uncuffed her and she balled up in the middle of the bed.

'What are they drugged with?'

'I don't know. Carole bought the stuff. Some kind of barbiturate. They'll come out of it. Ten to twelve hours.'

I backed him out of the room.

'You don't look too good,' he said.

'You knew you'd be all right with me, didn't you?'

'I knew you wouldn't shoot me. I thought you were more likely to let me run. We've been through things . . . it joins you.'

'Take your shirt off, lie face down on the table.'

I went into the bathroom and found towels and flannels. Marnier stripped and got on the table. The harlequin tattoo was clear of the weals left by Gio's machete job. It was a rough piece of work, like Franconelli said – prison artisan, nail and ink. The harlequin's face, rather than a trickster's smile, sported a sinister leer, the eyes slit, the mouth a blue-green upward gash in a round face, the tattooist not up to the delicate task of facial features. The diamond-coloured suit was what made it a harlequin and the colours, green, blue, red and flesh, gave it the right effect. Like Marnier had said, it was the size of a pack of cigarettes and was positioned just below the left scapula.

'Where's the whisky?'

'There's a half case in the cabinet.'

I took a full bottle from the case and a half-empty one off the sideboard. I took a few pulls and gave Marnier the rest. I soaked a flannel with whisky and rubbed down the harlequin then rolled it into a cigar and handed it to him.

'You might want to bite on that,' I said.

I took the scalpels out and the bottle of formaldehyde and laid them on the table.

'You came prepared,' said Marnier.

'You wouldn't want me to do this with a fish filleter.'

I washed my hands in the kitchen, wrapped a towel around my head to keep the sweat out of my eyes and put on Marnier's ridiculous lingeried girly apron. I caught sight of myself in a mirror in the living room and it nearly stopped me from going through with this madness. How could it have come to this?

I chose a pointed blade and connected it to the scalpel handle. I recleaned the harlequin with more whisky and a flannel which I left in the small of Marnier's back. I poured a few fingers into a glass and took a gulp. I looked down at Marnier.

'This woman you and Franconelli were arguing about . . .'

'How do you know it was about a woman?'

'Carole told me.'

'She liked you, you know.'

'I don't think so.'

'Not in the end, but before . . .'

'She seemed to have one thing on her mind and I wasn't interested in it.'

'She's French. That's what she thinks men want. She

336

made a mistake with you. You're English. Who knows what you want? Takeaway curry, probably.'

'Tell me about this woman,' I said, axeing through it.

'You know her.'

'I do?'

'Gale Strudwick. Remember your old friend Gale?'

'That's how you knew I worked in shipping.'

'C'est ça.'

'And what happened?'

'She was another one like Carole.'

'She liked bad guys?'

'They gave her a kick. Take a look at her husbands. They went from bad to worse.'

'The one before Graydon was a banker.'

'A banker who's doing time.'

'Graydon used to be a lawyer,' I said. 'Did she like turning these guys?'

'She thought it improved their performance.'

'Then she met the real thing. You and Franconelli.'

'We were both fucking her after her husband died.'

'I didn't think Franconelli was her type and vice versa.'

'As a matter of fact, she and Franconelli had been fucking for over a year,' he said, and I had a flash of Gale dancing in front of Franconelli at a party and trying to get him to join her – 'Come on, Roberto,' she'd said, and there was some intimacy in that, in the way she'd said it.

'And you?' I asked. 'How long had you been sleeping with her?'

'Since a few weeks after Graydon went down. His death shook her up. She resented Franconelli pretty

337

badly for letting him die like that. Not letting him have his drugs . . . Graydon's system collapsed . . . it wasn't a nice way to go.'

'Which is why she took up with you, and Franconelli had her killed.'

'It didn't quite happen like that.'

'I missed out on Gio's machete fest.'

'Yes, Gale made a bad mistake. You know she liked her drink. She was hitting it hard after Graydon died and she went a bit crazy. She had the knife out for Roberto and one day she stuck it in.'

'And she used you to do it?'

'Franconelli and I are the same kind of people.'

'Not macho, by any chance?'

'First of all she told him about me, which was bad enough, and then she laid it on. Said I was better in bed, had a bigger dick . . . all those things you shouldn't say to a guy like Franconelli.'

'So he sent Gio out to punish you.'

'And to punish her,' he said. 'I would not be acceptable in this condition.'

'So why did he kill her if he'd already punished her?'

'He didn't kill her,' said Marnier. 'I did.'

Silence – silence of the postmortem-fridge-drawer variety.

'And why did you do a thing like that?' I said.

'She ruined my life because she liked to get drunk and talk too much.'

'She must have had a shock when you turned up.'

'Franconelli didn't tell her what he'd had done to me. He didn't want to cut himself off from the best fucking he'd ever had in his life. She thought I'd moved on. I tell you, if she hadn't been drunk the day I came back just the sight of me would have killed her. As it was I talked her through a few things. She wept, Bruce, like you've never seen a woman like that weep. Tears, snot, her soul, everything. Not because of me . . . but because she knew why I'd come back. I was nice. I drowned her. I could have done a lot worse. The only thing I'm not proud of, the only thing I regret was afterwards – I realized I'd killed her to get back at Franconelli. I didn't like that. I should have been braver . . . but that fucking guy never comes out of his house. Yes, I regret that a lot.'

'There must be a lot of stuff you regret in your life, Jean-Luc,' I said, and I stuck the scalpel blade into his back and made four fast cuts in a diamond shape around the tattoo. Marnier gasped and jammed the flannel between his teeth. He waggled his feet as if he was swimming.

I removed the pointed blade and replaced it with the round-edged one. I wiped the four cuts I'd made with the whisky-soaked flannel and concentrated on one of the corners. I parted the cut with a thumb and forefinger and slid the blade into the gap and eased it horizontally under the epidermis, taking no more than a millimetre off the top. I sliced from one corner of the diamond to the other, creating a flap of skin about a centimetre wide. I swabbed again with whisky. Marnier bit hard and straightened his legs.

'Keep still or I'll cut you deeper.'

The air hissed into his mouth around the flannel bit. I'd forgotten he couldn't breathe through his destroyed nose. I held the flap of skin back with my thumb and worked the blade underneath another centimetre of skin and slid the blade along the width of the tattoo once more. It was like skinning a tough piece of raw fish, except with the scalpel blades it was a lot easier. It took about fifteen minutes. In the end Marnier had a shape like a seamstress's dart on his back. I asked him if he wanted iodine on it and he spat the flannel out and screamed no.

I opened the Ballantines bottle, rolled the diamond of skin and fed it down the neck of the bottle into the formaldehyde. I asked Marnier if he had any bandages and lint and he nodded me to the bathroom. I got him sitting with a glass of whisky in his hand and strapped him up around the ribs.

'Very regrettable,' I said.

'What?'

'That you've had to lose a piece of your hide to Franconelli.'

'He was always going to have his pound of flesh.'

'You got off lightly then.'

'I'll be going now, if that's all right with you,' he said, easing a buttock off the table.

I pulled the towel off my head, stripped the apron off. I tried to think my vision straight but it wouldn't hold. The sweat came out of me, not like before in streams, but in fat ripe figs. The blood seemed to drain out of me and Marnier's voice arrived in my head from a long way off. I staggered back from the table and grabbed the back of the sofa and tried to get the revolver out of the back of my trousers. The room tipped. I fell back into one of the chairs.

I had the gun out but my palm was so slippery with

sweat and the revolver so heavy I could barely keep a hold of it. I sensed Marnier advancing on me. Then my vision clicked and the fever rush backed off. I wiped my hand on the chair and fixed the gun on Marnier.

'You're sick,' he said.

'I'll be OK,' I said. 'We're going to empty the boat now. You and I.'

'If you're up to it.'

'I'm OK now.'

'You don't want a fever like that to get out of control, believe me. You want some quinine?'

'I'm OK now.'

I got to my feet. The room held. Marnier was looking at me so intently I could feel his brain roaming around the back of my eyeballs.

'You're not going to let me go, are you?' he said.

'Let's get this done, Jean-Luc.'

We went back out through the kitchen and on to the balcony. Marnier eased himself down the steps, shaky, shock creeping in or maybe just some more acting.

'You didn't tell me one thing, Jean-Luc,' I said to the back of his head. 'You didn't tell me what you owed Bondougou that you had to get involved in a shitty piece of business like this.'

'What makes you think I owed him anything?' he said, facing me at the bottom of the steps, backing off across the yard.

'I can see you in the stowaway business, Jean-Luc, but little girls, sending little girls to get infected with AIDS . . . to cure some fat cats who think having sex with a virgin is going to get rid of a virus like that. It doesn't sound like your kind of work. T. S. Eliot,

341

remember, your greatest poet of the twentieth century
... or was that just your one and only redeeming
quality?'

Marnier stopped. He looked down and thought for a
moment, then up at me in vague surprise, running his
claw hand through his thick, dyed hair.

'They're only blacks, Bruce,' he said.

Those words spiked me like a white-hot needle and
found pure anger burning inside me with a blue-coned
flame. I raised the revolver on him and that was the
first time I saw it in Marnier. It leaked into his ruined
face and eyes as if he'd suddenly felt the hemlock growing up his body. It was fear. I knew then that the power
wasn't in the gun and I was feared because of it.

I shot him twice in the chest, watched the shots throw
him into a large, muddy puddle in the yard, saw his
legs trying to pedal him backwards through it, saw his
hands clawing at his life escaping through the red
blooming holes in his shirt. Then his hands dropped
away and he was quiet, the water rippling away from
him.

I knelt down. I suddenly had to get down.

I had to get down on to the floor and put my face on
the ground.

Put my face on the cool African ground.

Chapter 32

Thursday 1st August, Cotonou.

The rats were running the tunnels. Hundreds of thousands, perhaps millions of rats were running the tunnels, scrabbling, seething through the black-blood sewer arteries, the blue-blood storm drains, the red-blood runnels, running, running. Hot little bodies running, running. Squealy throats running, running. Scratchy claws running, running from the rains, from the huge rains that broke open the purple-black sky, that filled the city to the rooftops and flushed the half-billion rats into the ocean where they choked on sea water, rushed into the thumping propellers, drowned into a thick, cold, rat-fur sludge, twelve tails deep.

And the city was clean, scrubbed through, washed and the air was sweet under the blue-white dome. Music was trickling like cool water behind ears and stiff table nappery snapped in the bright breeze.

'Jesus,' I said, 'what is that?'

'Bruce,' said a voice.

'What is it?'

'We don't know what it is.'

'Is it spring?'

Something popped in my head like a decent idea. My eyes opened as slowly as the metal shutters on a Lebanese emporium. Vague shapes shimmered as if I'd been snorkelling without goggles. Edges hardened into yellow bottle glass, a clear yellow tube into my arm. Were they filling me with urine? Were they taking the piss?

'What is this?'

'You're in the Polyclinique, Bruce.'

Heike firmed up in my vision.

'Where did you think you were?' she asked.

'Somewhere postmodern,' I said. 'What's this?'

'Quinine.'

'How long have I been out.'

'A couple of days.'

'You're here.'

'Are you surprised?'

'I think I probably am,' I said. 'Things weren't going so well, were they?'

'They weren't.'

'Did something happen?' I asked and reached out to her belly, her small round belly.

'It's all fine.'

'And you?'

'I'm fine.'

'With me?'

'Even with you.'

'That sounds like an historical turnaround.'

'I went to Grand-Popo. Gerhard took me.'

'Did you speak to the girl? Adèle?'

'She'd gone travelling.'

'Has Bagado explained something?'

'They told me everything I needed to know at the Auberge. They remembered you, the big tall guy and the other one with the face.'

344

'*Le grand Marnier.*'

'They told me Adèle left with her boyfriend, a guy called Shane, who was the driver of the Australian overland truck. They said they never saw you again after you finished your meal and if you'd tried getting into bed with Adèle there probably wouldn't have been much left of you. Shane, apparently, was a rock ape on testosterone.'

'And Bagado explained the lie.'

'He didn't have to. I was there. I saw Franconelli for myself and I don't want to see him again.'

'Oh, Christ,' I said. 'Franconelli.'

'My mother's not coming any more,' said Heike, digging in her handbag, switching away from the nastiness.

'You put her off after all that?'

'Do you know what these are?'

'They look like airline tickets.'

'These tickets are going to take us from Cotonou to Accra, Accra to Frankfurt, Frankfurt to Berlin.'

'And you booked the registry office?'

She smiled, leaned over and kissed me and slid her mouth round to my ear.

'Go on,' she said. 'Say it.'

I said it.

Monday 5th August, Cotonou.

The rainy season had ended. Nobody could remember a rainy season ending so late.

Moses, back to full strength, drove me down to my office. His T-cell count had stabilized. They'd decided at the agency's AIDS clinic that he had HIV 2, a strain peculiar to West Africa which didn't seem to develop into full-blown AIDS.

Bagado was sitting in my office, the bottle of Ballantines on the desk in front of him filled with its grotesquerie. His arm was in a sling but he was still wearing the mac, the holes lovingly repaired. José-Marie was out on the balcony shouting at the boys in the tailor's shack, Bagado not letting her out of his sight.

I ordered coffees and croissants and picked up the phone and dialled the Lagos number that always got me in a sweat.

'Mr Franconelli, please.'

'Who's that?'

'Bruce Medway.'

'Hold the line.'

'Hello.'

'Mr Franconelli?'

'No.'

'Is he there? I'd like to talk to him.'

'What you want to say?'

'It's between me and him, a personal thing.'

A hand went over the receiver. Things were discussed in Italian. The voice came back on.

'Mr Franconelli died two days ago.'

'He died?'

'A heart attack.'

'Please accept my condolences. I had no idea.'

'*Grazie.*'

I hung up and looked across at Bagado, who was studying me carefully.

'He died,' I said.

346

'I heard you.'

'Heart attack.'

'Lucky.'

'It's about time I had some of that,' I said. 'Maybe you'll get lucky. Doesn't it come in threes?'

'I thought that was death.'

'How does luck come?'

'In small timely squirts.'

'Maybe you'll get to be Commandant after all this. You're a hero now.'

'I don't think so,' he said. 'This hero can't front enough money to hold a job like that down.'

'Go and see your medicine man again. He did all right by you the last time.'

'I thought he was a little too strong on the black stuff. If I get him on to something like this, I'll end up the Prince of Darkness.'

'That's only two ranks above Commandant, isn't it?'

He laughed. The coffees arrived.

'The problem with voodoo is that it's a double-edged sword,' he said. 'My medicine man gave me the power to destroy monsters like Bondougou and Madame Sokode but there was another one in Nigeria who was creating monsters by offering AIDS cures through having sex with virgins.'

'The Nigerian football team won the Olympic gold medal too,' I said. 'Have you thought about that?'

'That's just because they're good at football, Bruce.'

He picked up the whisky bottle.

'What are you going to do with this?' he asked.

'Chuck it,' I said. 'I don't want to stagger in here one night and drink it by mistake.'

347

Bagado handed me the bottle. The few times I'd looked at this macabre souvenir I'd replayed those last moments of Marnier's life in the yard, tried to relive it to see if Jean-Luc was lying or, as always, he knew exactly what he was doing. This time I thought nothing and held it up to the window and watched the flap of Marnier's skin swirl behind the brown glass and the leery harlequin slipped into the light, and twisted and scrolled in the slow liquid.

Blood is Dirt

Robert Wilson

Bruce Medway, fixer and debt collector in Benin, West
Africa, has heard a few stories in his time. The one that
Napier Briggs tells him is patchy but it doesn't exclude the
vital fact that two million dollars have gone missing. Bruce
is used to imperfect information from clients embarrassed
at their own stupidity. But this time it leads to a gruesome
death.

It would all have ended there but for Napier's daughter,
the sexy, sassy and sussed Selina Aguia, a commodities
broker. She launches Bruce into the savage world that her
apparently innocuous father had chosen to inhabit – a
world of oil and toxic waste scams, of mafia money laun-
dering, of death and violence fuelled by drink, drugs and
sex. Worse for Bruce, Selina wants revenge, and with the
scam she invents it looks as though she'll get it. But this is
a world where blood is dirt – nobody really cares. Not even
if they love you.

'A vivid and steamy stumble on the wild side'

VAL McDERMID

ISBN: 0 00 713041 4

The Company of Strangers

Robert Wilson

Lisbon 1944. In the torrid summer heat, as the streets of the capital seethe with spies and informers, the endgame of the Intelligence war is being silently fought.

Andrea Aspinall, mathematician and spy, enters this sophisticated world through a wealthy household in Estoril. Karl Voss, military attaché to the German Legation, has arrived embittered by his implication in the murder of a Reichsminister and traumatized by Stalingrad, on a mission to rescue Germany from annihilation. In the lethal tranquillity of this corrupted paradise they meet and attempt to find love in a world where no-one can be believed.

After a night of extreme violence, Andrea is left with a life-long addiction to the clandestine world that leads her from the brutal Portuguese fascist régime to the paranoia of Cold War Germany, where she is forced to make the final and the hardest choice.

'Displaying once again Wilson's gifts for atmospheric depiction of place, this ambitious experiment is streets ahead of most other thrillers'

JOHN DUGDALE, Sunday Times

'A big, meaty novel of love and deceit . . . with this novel Wilson vaults to the front-rank of thriller writers'

PETER GUTTRIDGE, Observer

ISBN: 0 00 651203 8

A Small Death in Lisbon

Robert Wilson

A Portuguese bank is founded on the back of Nazi wartime deals. Over half a century later a young girl is murdered in Lisbon.

1941. Klaus Felsen, SS officer, arrives in Lisbon and the strangest party in history, where Nazis and Allies, refugees and entrepreneurs, dance to the strains of opportunism and despair. Felsen's war takes him to the mountains of the north where a brutal battle is being fought for an element vital to Hitler's blitzkrieg. There he meets the man who makes the first turn of the wheel of greed and revenge which rolls through to the century's end.

Late 1990s, Lisbon. Inspector Zé Coelho is investigating the murder of a young girl. As he digs deeper, Zé overturns the dark soil of history and unearths old bones. The 1974 revolution has left injustices of the old fascist regime unresolved. But there's an older, greater injustice, for which this small death in Lisbon is horrific compensation, and in his final push for the truth, Zé must face the most chilling opposition.

'Compulsively readable, with the cop's quest burning its way through a narrative rich in history and intrigue, love and death'   *Literary Review*

ISBN: 0 00 651202 X

The Big Killing

Robert Wilson

Bruce Medway, go-between and fixer for traders in West Africa, smells trouble when a porn merchant asks him to deliver a video at a secret location. Things look up, though, when he's hired to act as minder to Ron Collins, a spoilt playboy looking for diamonds. Medway thinks this could be the answer to his cashflow crisis, but when the video delivery leads to a shootout and the discovery of a mutilated body, the prospect of retreating to his bolthole in Benin becomes increasingly attractive – especially as the manner of the victim's death is too similar to a current notorious political murder for comfort.

His obligations, though, keep him fixed in the Ivory Coast and he is soon caught up in a terrifying cycle of violence. But does it stem from the political upheavals in nearby Liberia, or from the cutthroat business of diamonds? Unless Medway can get to the bottom of the mystery, he knows that for the savage killer out there in the African night, he is the next target . . .

'A narrative distilled from pure protein: potent, fiercely imagined and not a little frightening'   *Literary Review*

ISBN 0 00 647986 3

Instruments of Darkness

Robert Wilson

Benin, West Africa. Englishman Bruce Medway operates as a 'fixer' for traders on that part of the coast they used to call the White Man's Grave. It's a tough existence, but Medway can handle it . . . until he comes across the formidable Madame Severnou. Warned off further involvement by his client, Jack Obuasi, his energies are redirected into the search for missing expat, Steven Kershaw.

Kershaw, though, is a man of mystery: trader, artist, womanizer . . . and sado-masochist. Against background rumblings of political disturbance and endemic official corruption, Medway pursues his elusive quarry with a doggedness even he cannot explain. But as he soon learns, nothing in Africa is what it seems, and those who seek the truth find out more than they wish to know . . .

'A witty, fast-moving and picaresque tale'

NELSON DEMILLE

ISBN 0 00 647985 5